DISCOVERY IN THE DESERT

It Will Shake the Nations

Tom Thiele

9 Jan 2016

ISBN: 0-615-42501-1 (Paperback)
ISBN-13: 978-0-615-42501-6 (Paperback)

ISBN: 978-0-615-45615-7 (E-Book)

ISBN: 978-0-692-45522-7 (Hardback)

Available from:
Amazon.com (Paperback & Kindle)
barnesandnoble.com (Paperback & Nook)
Apple iBooks

authortomthiele.com

authortomthiele@gmail.com

TO

Juanita Thiele, my loving and tolerant wife,
who allowed me to get lost in this project for several months.
I love you and thank you for being you!

AND ALSO TO

Terry Brinson

Marlene Kelly

Pat Kelly

Kathy Kitch

Carolyn Moore

Laura Popper

Tiffany Ruiz

Scott Smith

Mark Taylor

Darla Valenti

THE DISCOVERY SERIES

BOOK 1
DISCOVERY IN THE DESERT

BOOK 2
DISCOVERY OF ETERNITY

CONTENTS

CHAPTER 1

PROJECT 13-03

During the summertime in Houston, Texas, the humidity can cause many a summer day to seem more like a sauna day than your average Houstonian would care to admit. This is especially true during the dog days of August. So, being the comfort-focused society that we are, the solution to this sauna-like dilemma is easy: you just crank up the a/c and convert your home into an oasis of cool.

David and Angela Hart, a young married couple living in Clear Lake City, knew this summer drill all too well. Both had grown up in the Houston area and knew the proper way to live as natives. Clear Lake City is one of the many suburbs of Houston, the fourth most populated city in the US, and is located on the city's south side.

Home of the National Aeronautics and Space Administration, NASA, Clear Lake City is quite a unique little town. There aren't many places in the world that can boast of citizens that are bona fide astronauts who have actually walked on the surface of the moon or spent months in the International Space Station. David Hart was employed by NASA; however, he didn't have the glitzy occupation of serving as an astronaut. Many of David's fellow employees did consider David to have a glitzy job, it was just different. David was somewhat of a superstar at NASA, joining the organization in 2009, and now just six years later serving on the management team of Project 13-03.

Over the last four years, NASA had undergone quite a shake-up. With large amounts of government money being diverted away from space travel, NASA was forced to redefine itself. This was no easy task.

NASA was synonymous with space travel to most of the thousands of diehard employees and contractors who had devoted their lives putting men and women into outer space for Uncle Sam. A new chief administrator had been named to lead NASA in late 2011, chosen and appointed by President Obama himself. John Stuart had served in the Air Force for thirty years and was a decorated pilot who worked his way through the ranks of the USAF—all the way to the top. Stuart had the look of a military man. He kept his head and face clean-shaven and preferred to wear military fatigues over executive office attire.

After two weeks of being in charge at the NASA facility, Stuart had been labeled General Patton. And a General Patton he was, but with time, his reports grew to respect him because he not only looked like a military man; he walked, talked, and lived the life of a military man.

When Stuart took over, he made it clear that this was no longer an arm of the government focused on space travel. The higher powers in Washington D.C. had decided that NASA's spending for the 2012 budget year would be 70% national defense and 30% space. And furthermore, the defense spending would be focused on new technology. Stuart liked to use the phrase "out of the box thinking" and this is what he wanted his new NASA troops to do: get out of that box and bring him creative ideas. When 2013 rolled around, the agency was spending 90% of the budget on defense.

This is how Project 13-03 came into being. It sounds like some weird code name, but the way that Stuart named the classified military projects that were sanctioned was really quite simple. The names reflect the budget year and the order of sanctioning. So this project was sanctioned in September 2013 and was the third classified project sanctioned that year.

The Project Leader had immediately chosen David Hart as his Chief Technical Director. The leader, Jesse Black, had worked with David shortly after David came on board in 2009. Jesse was a NASA veteran with twenty-eight years of service and had a stellar reputation. Jesse was single and joked that he was married to NASA. Jesse was approaching fifty years old, but had the personality of someone much younger. He was short and pudgy, and seemed to wear a permanent smile. When fully engaged in a project, Jesse brought a child-like exuberance to the table.

Jesse knew that David was one of the brightest assets NASA had brought on board in the last decade, even though David was an "Aggie." Jesse had graduated from "The" University of Texas in 1985 and was a devoted Longhorn. The Aggie and Longhorn rivalry has been a Texas tradition for years. Regardless, once Jesse saw David perform on projects, especially when it came to knocking out technical obstacles, his opinion of this Aggie was one of respect.

Once Jesse had assembled his team, he brought the team up-to-speed on Project 13-03. This indeed was a classified project and all aspects of their work were to remain confidential. No sharing with co-workers outside of the team, family members, or friends. The classified nature of the project didn't bother David one bit; he just wanted to confront and solve the technical challenges and build something. He had no idea how challenging this assignment would become—it ranked right up there with impossible. You see, Jesse informed the team that their mission was to build a time machine.

This project was Jesse's baby, he had been pushing for time travel funding for years, and finally his dream had some backing. Time travel was something that Stuart labeled as not necessarily "out of the box thinking," but more like "out of your mind." Stuart liked it though, it was cutting-edge, but he would only continue to support additional funding if real progress was made during the first year.

From a military and national defense perspective, Stuart truly believed that time travel would provide substantial value to the country. Imagine traveling into the future and bringing back technologically-advanced designs for superior weapons yet to be invented. Or better yet, travel back in time and steal the enemy's plans for an upcoming confrontation or surprise attack. Could something as horrific as the terrorist attacks that occurred on September 11, 2001 have been prevented? There was also excitement growing regarding advances in medicine, bio-medical engineering, computer technology, and environmental protection. Stuart preferred to ignore the bigger moral questions related to the project. For instance, would the tool allow man to change history or steer the future in a different direction?

David poured himself into the project, which meant spending a significant amount of time reading, since Texas A&M had yet to offer a degree in Time Travel. David graduated *summa cum laude* with a degree in Physics and a minor in Aerospace Engineering. Much to his surprise, however, David discovered that various branches of the US military had actually made some tangible progress in time travel research. The general public was completely unaware of this since all the findings and the research was classified.

David had met Angela at a local pub shortly after he had landed the job at NASA; she had quickly labeled him nerd. And a nerd he was. David was quite the Aggie Engineer, sporting out-of-date clothes and a hairstyle that would have made an 80's tennis star proud. Angela, however, thought that he was kind of cute underneath that nerd exterior. David, on the other hand, knew that Angela was a beauty. She had an athletic build, but she was still petite and feminine. David would sometimes get lost as he stared into her beautiful blue eyes. The two ran with the same group of friends and they were always bumping into each other.

Angela reluctantly began to date David, and more importantly, she began to change him. Not his core being, not the person of David, just the external shell. In a few short months, David was sporting trendy duds and a short, corporate haircut; and Angela was not only proud of the changes in her man but was falling in love with this NASA brainiac. This updated version of David was quite handsome. Shortly thereafter, wedding bells rang in Clear Lake City.

Angela was a young professional as well. After graduating from the University of Houston in 2011, she went to work for Pfizer pharmaceuticals as a Marketing Representative. She had built up a significant clientele of doctors and hospitals in the Houston Medical Center during her short four-year tenure with the company. Both David and Angela were borderline workaholics. Their jobs and personal success were very important to both of them.

As David educated himself on time travel, Angela noticed how her bookworm was spending even more time with his nose in the technical journals than normal. This was the first classified project that David had worked on, and Angela was fully aware of the rules. So she exercised self-control and only asked a few occasional questions which David successfully deflected with non-substantive answers. She did, however, glean from the titles of the work that he reviewed, that the project related to the study of time, the fourth dimension of this three-dimensional world we live in.

As the team became fully engaged with their new project, Jesse was tickled. His dream of taking an agency recognized as the leader in space travel and transforming it into the only entity capable of time travel was becoming a reality. The personalities of the handpicked team members were quite similar, so to no one's surprise, they began to live their project. It was not uncommon for a team member to put in seventy hours a week.

The prior military research on time travel had determined that objects could be launched into time by achieving a specific velocity combined with a specific outer body temperature. The specific temperature required was based on the mass of the object while the speed would determine how far through time the object would travel. The team believed that when an object achieved the perfect formula of temperature and speed for its mass, a wormhole would be instantaneously attracted to it. The mouth of the wormhole would seek it out and immediately absorb it. The big unknown left unanswered by the prior research was "how do you bring the object back to the present?"

After fifteen months of painstaking effort, the construction of the prototype one-man capsule was complete and the launching mechanism was almost fifty percent complete. The fabrication crew had grown to two hundred sub-contractors and Jesse and the team had blown through $500 million. This was a BIG number, but just a drop in the bucket in Stuart's mind, since his annual budget was a whopping $20 billion. The "machine" utilized a mechanical arm some 100 ft in length. The capsule was placed in a cradle at one end of the arm, with a crane-like contraption, while the other end attached to a central hub. When activated, the central hub began spinning the arm much like a ride at an amusement park.

The team's computer models had indicated that once the rotational speed of the arm exceeded 350 mph at the cradle, the vessel could be launched into time by raising the temperature of the outer shell of the capsule to exactly 612° Fahrenheit. This was accomplished via millions of miniature heating elements placed throughout the capsule's skin immediately underlying the shell. The outer shell was composed of a modified carbon steel alloy that could withstand temperatures in excess of 1,000°F.

The time destination of the capsule would be pre-programmed by simultaneously achieving the 612°F requirement when the angular velocity of the capsule was at a specific speed. The required temperature, 612°F, was based on the mass of the capsule itself. The bulkier the capsule, the more temperature required. Clockwise rotation would launch into the future and counter-clockwise rotation would launch into the past.

Jesse had sought and obtained Stuart's approval to officially name the capsule *Hercules*. Meanwhile, Jesse had charged David with engineering how Hercules would be brought back to the present day from wherever and whenever, it had gone. David had designed a brilliant type of "capacitor" that would store a tremendous amount of the kinetic energy created when the device was launched into travel. This energy was converted from kinetic to potential energy and then stored as electrical capacitance. The capacitor would also provide the capsule's energy needs while on location during a mission.

David's capacitor onboard Hercules would store the bulk of the energy until the traveler was ready to return to the present. At that time the external shell of the capsule would be heated to 612°F, and the massive amount of stored electrical energy would be released in a twinkling of an eye. The capsule would attract and re-enter the same wormhole and trace the exact flight path that was taken to get to the destination for the return trip back to present day. If all the modeling proved to be correct, Hercules would land, or more specifically appear, back in its launching cradle whence it came.

So many obstacles over the last fifteen months had been overcome with meticulous planning and intellectual foresight. Now, an unforeseen problem had surfaced from thin air! A problem so obvious, so elementary, that the team had completely overlooked it. Who, or what, would be the first astronaut, or more specifically—the first chrononaut? The capsule's state-of-the-art instruments and flight computer could only be operated by a trained individual. How could the team progress any further? Not even Stuart with his get-'er-done mentality would place a human being in harm's way without some type of successful pre-flight test.

Early on, the team had envisioned that the first prototype would be much smaller than Hercules. They wanted to initially perform trials with small, relatively inexpensive capsules. They could just launch the capsule alone into time, no cargo aboard, to test if it indeed exited from the here-and-now. Once the team had fully educated itself on all the prior research conducted on time travel, however, it became obvious that the capsule could not be small.

According to the data, in order for the capsule and its contents to remain intact during flight and not disintegrate required a mass of no less than fifteen tons. Hercules weighed in at a modest seventeen tons and came with a price tag of $200 million. Launching a device of this size had never been attempted; the required size to maintain integrity was based on computer modeling.

Previously military scientists had launched BBs, bullets, and other relatively small objects into time. So the team felt comfortable with the correlations generated from the prior experiments, along with the fact that the items did indeed leave the here-and-now. It was all about the temperature, speed, and mass of the object to be launched. The challenge was to have the capsule return from the journey.

Hercules looked like one humongous, bright silver bullet. It was about the size of the main fuselage of a King Air private plane, forty feet in length and sleek. The main pilot's hatch was centered right on the top of the vessel, similar to the location for a submarine. It had necessary supplies of drinking water and military MREs (meal, ready to eat). The pilot's seat was designed not only for time travel but also for sleep. The capacitor, insulation layering, and computer equipment occupied the majority of the capsule's interior volume.

Now back to the big problem: sure, you could launch a lab rat out into time in a $200 million piece of government hardware to ensure that a living thing would launch, but the success of the project hinged on conducting a round trip, not a one-way flight. What good would it serve if eventually your pilot traveled through time but never came back? It appeared that a man, or woman, would be the only acceptable candidate as a time traveler capable of programming the capsule for the return flight. One-way trips would burn through a lot of $200 million capsules in a hurry.

The day that Jesse realized he needed to share the problem with Stuart was indeed an ugly day. After pacing back and forth in his office for hours, Jesse had reluctantly headed to Stuart's office to share the bad news. The rest of the team sat around Jesse's office sulking and staring at the floor. Jesse returned from his meeting with Stuart, and to everyone's surprise he was smiling. Stuart himself had "saved" the project with his very own out-of-the-box idea.

The first flight would be no-frills, it would be very simple. It would, however, not use a person. If this inaugural flight was successful, the team would then receive clearance to launch a human chrononaut. "So...," Jesse exclaimed, "we're gonna train a monkey to fly this baby! Or should I say, to program this baby for the return flight."

Once the team realized that Jesse was serious, they immediately sought to pinpoint the lucky monkey—the monkey, whose success would ultimately determine whether their project was a winner or a waste of $500 million. "Winner" is an understatement—how about "the most ingenious invention in the history of mankind," David would often think to himself.

Oh, and by the way, Stuart had informed Jesse that, "some heads were gonna roll," if the monkey didn't bring back the $200 million craft. So the monkey business (training) began in December 2014. The launching mechanism, now officially named *Catapult,* was projected to be complete in May 2015.

From December 2014 through July 2015, the project had transformed from one of prestige to one of embarrassment. David was beside himself with anger. Catapult had now been completed and tested. The team had designed and built one of the most technologically advanced machines of the modern era. Yet, over the last eight months, working with world-renowned animal trainers, the team was on their third monkey, and he was proving to be just as inept as numbers one and two.

The joke going around NASA was that Project 13-03 had been renamed *Project Monkey Business.* Pretty soon the project would be scrapped and some had quipped that "NASA would have its very own amusement park ride with the largest price tag of any ride in the modern world and maybe NASA could sell tickets for $10,000 and recoup some of the wasted cash spent on the project."

Stuart was getting frustrated and threatening to pull the plug.

Everyone on the team was disgusted, especially Jesse, who had begun taking frequent two-martini lunches and spending many an afternoon with his office door closed. Jesse's childlike exuberance had given way to childish immaturity.

CHAPTER 2
THE DECISION

On a steamy Wednesday night during August of 2015, sitting in the parking lot of Sherlock's Pub, David made a decision that would prove to be one of the most significant decisions of his life. Angela had left town on a business trip that previous Monday and would not return until Friday. So after another useless day at work, David had forced down some greasy Mexican food at a local hole-in-the-wall and had eased over to Sherlock's Pub for a few beers. This was the pub where David and Angela had met back in 2009. Oh, those were the good old days, his life before *Project Monkey Business*.

After polishing off a couple of Pale Ales and acquiring a mild buzz, David left the Pub, climbed into his Jeep, and cranked the engine. He turned up his stereo and while listening to his favorite Rolling Stones' song, "Under My Thumb," David yelled out in bitter frustration, "Something's Gotta Change!" That's when he made the decision.

As David Hart peered at himself in the Jeep's rearview mirror, he realized that he was looking at the first NASA scientist to attempt time travel. Enough of the monkey craziness—it was time to get proactive. The biggest question mark in his mind was the energy required for the return trip and David himself had designed the capacitor, and he had faith in that design. He was ready to board Hercules, travel through time, and return! He was fed-up and ready to take action.

With the decision made to take matters into his own hands, to get the project "under his thumb," David's demeanor had changed dramatically. He was back to his old smiling self when Angela returned from her business trip. She immediately questioned the return of the old David. "Where have you been, stranger?" was her question to her husband that weekend. "And more importantly, why are you back—some big breakthrough on the project?"

David explained that he had decided to remove himself from the work-caused sulking and frustration and focus on other things. He had chosen to focus on things like…the Houston Texans kicking off a new football season, the arrival of autumn, windsurfing in Galveston, among other things. Yes, this new focus had helped him return to a state of happiness. "There was more to life than attempting to train stupid monkeys to perform complicated tasks anyway!" he thought to himself. David was pleased—he felt sure that Angela believed the reasons he had given for the abrupt change in attitude.

David had decided that he would share his decision with no one, not even Angela. He was about to break every rule in the book, pre-empting Stuart's mandated monkey flight, presumably hijacking a government-owned $200 million aircraft (timecraft?), and utilizing a $300 million launcher to accomplish the mission. Needless to say, David was overwhelmed with anxiety, yet at the same time bursting with excitement. David tried to ignore the anxiety—fear, after all, was for the faint of heart.

Oh, but there was plenty to be afraid of! Based on his intended flight, the launcher would be required to achieve a speed of 640 mph (his travel would cross 2,059 years). In pre-flight testing Jesse had only pushed the launcher to a speed of 450 mph; however, data from all the motion sensors mounted on Catapult was fed into the computer simulator. The simulator indicated that the launcher's integrity would easily allow Hercules to creep up to the maximum allowable speed of 765 mph, just 3 mph below the speed of sound (768 mph).

So, let's summarize:

1. David would program the flight himself,
2. Board Hercules, put Catapult into motion,
3. Ramp up to a speed of 640 mph,
4. Heat the outer shell to 612°F

5. And launch!

Over the next several nights, David slept little and woke up frequently during those nights with many a cold sweat. He had decided that the most important event of his young life would take place on Saturday night, August 15, 2015; or more precisely during the wee hours of Sunday morning, August 16th. His confidence was beginning to build as the weekend approached and the fear seemed to be subsiding. David wondered if his growing confidence was authentic or just stupidity in disguise.

David had decided to venture into the past. He wanted to visit ancient Rome on the day of the assassination of Julius Caesar. According to the history books, Brutus and his band of traitors assassinated Caesar on March 15, 44 BC. David was an avid reader and one of his favorite topics was the Roman Empire. He could not imagine any better way to utilize Hercules for the inaugural flight than to be an eyewitness of this, most horrific of events, during the history of the Roman Empire. He would only stay for twelve hours, a day-trip, and then return.

That Saturday, August 15th, Angela dragged David to Galveston for a day of fun in the sun and sand. It was a beautiful but scorching day along the Texas Gulf Coast. Galveston was a short forty-five minute drive south. As soon as the couple had set-up at a spot on Galveston's East Beach, David sank into his lounge chair, closed his eyes, and began to daydream of returning to their home and the a/c—the oasis of cool. That thought only lasted a moment, and the chrononaut-to-be was once again mentally stepping through the sequence of events that would occur later that night. Angela rousted her husband from his daydreaming by tossing a bucket of Galveston Bay's seawater squarely on his midsection. He sprung from his chair, chased her down, gently tackled her, and gave her a big kiss.

After enjoying a splendid seafood meal at Landry's on the Galveston seawall, the couple returned home. They found themselves crawling into bed later that night around 11:00 p.m. After twenty minutes or so, David told Angela that he was restless and he moved to the sofa in the family room to watch TV. He had already packed a small backpack with travel supplies; he laid down on the sofa, and set his iPhone alarm for

1:00 a.m. Try as he might, he didn't sleep a wink. He turned off the alarm at 1:00 a.m. and eased out of the house.

David drove his Jeep onto the NASA premises at 1:20 a.m. where he went through general security at the main gate. He then drove to the military sector on the far backside of the facility and stopped at the classified security gate for additional military clearance. It was not out of the ordinary for the brainiacs assigned to special military projects to work at odd hours, but at this time on a Saturday night was most unusual. David explained to the guard that he had been feeling a little under-the-weather and had slept most of the day. Now he was feeling much better and his wife was fast asleep; so he had decided to put in a few hours on the project. He autographed the mandatory sign-in sheet and was on his way.

As he entered the enormous hangar and approached the massive Catapult, David saw the colossal contraption in a whole new light. He felt hope well-up inside him as he now saw this wonderful masterpiece of science engineered by some of the finest minds in the world towering before him. He shed a tear. For a moment David wondered if it truly was a tear of hope, or possibly one of fear.

David spent forty-five minutes programming all the necessary data into the flight computer. His excitement was really building when David typed in March 15, 44 BC, 7:00 a.m. This entry was eventually followed by Rome, Italy; the Forum.

Jesse had developed a mathematical algorithm that determined the physical destination of the capsule based on trajectory vectors between Catapult's hangar and the destination (in this case Rome, Italy). The vector determined at what point in the 360° revolution path that the launch must take place. One would be a little disappointed if they wanted to visit Rome in 44 BC but ended up in Beijing in 44 BC instead.

The model determined that Hercules would need to exit from the cradle of Catapult at 286.3° along the 360° circular path in order to achieve Rome, and more specifically the Forum in Rome. Since the trip was into the past, the required rotation direction was counter-clockwise.

David wrote a short note to Jesse, not apologizing for his actions but informing him of his intended destination, location and date, and his plan to return quickly. He hoped that the note would be unnecessary, because David intended to leave at 3:30 a.m. and return one minute later at 3:31 a.m. If it all worked out, he would spend twelve hours in Rome, travel back to present day, return to Catapult's cradle, retrieve the note, erase the flight data, and head home. No harm, no foul.

As David exited the control room and walked toward Hercules, he gave himself a pep talk. "What is the worst thing that could happen?" he asked himself. "The worst thing would be…that there is no launch, no time travel, and the modeling is wrong." He would get a little dizzy and then the whole thing would be over. "Now that isn't so bad is it?" Subconsciously though he knew there were many worse things that could happen than this, especially since Catapult had never been pushed to 640 mph.

The time traveler climbed into Hercules, now donned with his protective travel suit, and helmet. He had his backpack with its paltry amount of articles including his iPhone, journal, and hand gun. He placed a photo of Angela in the pilot's console alongside the first-aid kit. David strapped himself into the pilot's seat and initiated the launch sequence. His palms were sweaty and his heart was racing. The thirty-ton arm of Catapult began to rotate as butterflies fluttered in David's stomach.

Hercules' computer began to announce to the pilot 100 mph and 145°F, all systems go. David smiled. Then 200 mph and 290°F…. This continued for several minutes. Then the tension began to well up in David's chest…eventually 600 mph and 580°F, all systems go. He knew the magic numbers were 640 mph and 612°F. These two key points of speed and temperature were programmed to occur simultaneous with Hercules reaching the 286.3° point in its counter-clockwise rotation.

When the computer announced ten seconds to launch, David whispered a prayer. At five seconds to launch, David envisioned the face of his beautiful wife. At one second to launch—David went unconscious.

CHAPTER 3

THE DESTINATION

As the young chrononaut slowly regained his consciousness, his eyes began to flutter. The brightness of the morning sun was blinding as it beamed through the pilot's windshield; the heat caused sweat to ooze from every pore. When David became fully alert, he realized that he was in Hercules, which was no longer in the cradle of Catapult, and it appeared that some form of time travel had actually taken place!

David switched on the electrical supply, cranked up the a/c, and began cooling off as he activated the computer's GPS system. He requested location coordinates from the system, but all he got were error messages. "Absolutely no satellite reception" was the best his computer could do. "There are no satellites," David concluded. He smiled. This was a positive finding, indicating that he truly had traveled well into the past. As he peered through the pilot's windshield of the craft he saw sand—lots and lots of sand.

He released the upper vacuum hatch, crawled onto the top of the capsule, stood and removed his helmet, then jumped to the ground. David planted his feet firmly on the desert floor and shouted, "Success!" at the top of his lungs. It seemed a little unusual, but the capsule was actually lying in a small crater-like feature, only about a third of the capsule was above ground level.

He looked around and deduced that he was probably on the outskirts of Rome and hoped it was March 15, 44 BC. "The computer must have a glitch in determining the launch point for the trajectory vector, thus not nailing Rome exactly," he thought. As he pondered this, he questioned why he was so confident with the flight computer's programming, and then his confidence began to falter. He needed some confirmation…he needed to investigate his surroundings and determine his location.

David climbed back into Hercules, removed his NASA flight suit, boots, and underwear; and dressed himself in more era-appropriate clothing. He had purchased the more appropriate clothes, two sets, at a costume shop back in Houston and hoped they were convincing enough to cause him to blend-in as a local peasant. He chose the clothes after revisiting some of his favorite books on the Roman Empire and confirming the appropriate garb for the occasion. He felt ridiculous, dressed in a dark brown dress, actually known as a tunic, with a dark brown cloth belt. He completed the look with a simple pair of leather sandals.

He was also well aware that he needed to keep his mouth shut, since he did not know the native Latin language of the Romans, nor the widely accepted Greek. Once fully decked out in his new duds, he locked down and secured the vacuum hatch, placed Hercules' light brown NASA tarp over the vessel, synced his iPhone with the capsule's homing device, threw his backpack (with hand gun) over his shoulder, and began the scouting expedition.

David carried a canteen of drinking water, a compass, and two military MREs for meals, just in case. Based on the placement of the sun in the desert sky, he surmised the time to be about 10:00 a.m. He started to set his wrist watch to this approximate time when he realized it was fried, an obvious casualty of the trip. David spent the first day traveling west of the capsule. He walked for eight hours, four hours due west and then four hours back to home base. He had reluctantly accepted the realization that he wasn't near Rome or any major city for that matter.

Furthermore, he had deduced that he was truly in a vast wilderness region and far away from any form of civilization. The terrain that he had either crossed that day or viewed from afar was quite diverse. There were mountains, cliffs, hills, streams, rocks, and lots and lots of sand. It was extremely dry and hot, but it was also beautiful. This desert seemed unlike what David would have labeled desert. In David's mind, he would have envisioned desert to be miles and miles of countless sand dunes, with very little else. This area did have the dunes and lots of sand, but they were only a portion of the whole. David also found the streams and other water sources somewhat of a surprise.

Back at home base, he climbed into Hercules and closed and locked the hatch. He "enjoyed a gourmet" military MRE of what appeared to be pork roast, rice, and some type of Jell-O for dessert. Following dinner as David settled in for the night, the frustration set in. He didn't know where he was and he didn't even know what year, or century, it was for that matter! The trajectory vector calculations were definitely flawed; he had not landed in Rome, Italy. "What else in the flight computer modeling was potentially flawed?" David questioned as he mumbled to himself.

He found his only comfort in knowing that his return flight would take him straight back whence he had come and he could leave whenever he chose to leave. The return flight wasn't as risky since the theory was that the capsule would just trace the exact path taken to this destination, regardless of when or where he actually traveled. The design of the return flight was also David's key contribution to the project and, even though he was somewhat modest, he had lots of faith in his work.

David knew that he really needed to wind down. He was running on pure adrenalin, he had done the mental math and determined that he had gone without sleep for over thirty hours now. He plugged his earbuds into his iPhone and cranked up the Rolling Stones. He and the Stones had a lot in common on this night. He knew that the Stones' music was timeless. And here he was, somewhere in the history of the world in a time unknown—he was *timeless*.

He scrolled through his phone admiring pictures of Angela and his friends back home. He fell asleep after scoring a personal best of 428 aircraft landed on his favorite iPhone game app...*Flight Control*.

On his second day, David set out very early in the morning heading due east. He planned to venture in this direction for four to six hours hoping to find something, or more importantly, someone. He knew that he, once again, needed to return to the capsule before dark for safety reasons. When he first awoke, David had considered returning home to Angela and his NASA team but then asked himself, "Why return home from this first trip with no clue as to where you had gone or when you had gone?"

After walking for an hour or so and working up quite a sweat, David began to notice some faint, distant noises behind him. Within the next several minutes he was able to make out gray silhouettes in the direction of the noise. It was wolves; at least three of them were on his trail. He had the handgun in his backpack but preferred not to think about a potential standoff with a pack of hungry wolves. So far he had only counted three, but there might be more wolves than bullets.

He surmised that the pack had probably been searching for food all night and the wolves now knew they could return to their all-day slumber with their bellies full, courtesy of their new-found prey. David began to walk much faster, but to no avail. He quickly realized that the pack was gaining on its potential meal. As true fear set-in, David began to run.

Running on this wilderness terrain was no easy task. He began sprinting at a full clip, then suddenly the tip of David's left sandal caught a rock and he fell flat on his face. The impact with the hard rocky ground knocked him unconscious. The pack would reach him within minutes…

When David woke up, it was dark and cool. His head was throbbing and he could hear the crackle of a fire. As he sat up, he found himself covered in blankets with a bandage wrapped around his head covering his newly acquired wound. It appeared he had been brought to a small campsite. The camp was tidy and complete with tents, donkeys, supplies, and the fire. David remembered running from the wolves and falling and nailing his forehead. But that was all he remembered. Where was he? Whose camp was this? Where were the wolves? Where were the people from the camp?

Then, a moment occurred in David's life that he would never forget. He saw Him. The man exited from the largest tent in the camp and approached the campfire. He warmed His hands over the fire and smiled in David's direction. The man had a warm smile; He looked physically fit and well groomed. It was almost as if the man had exited his tent after sensing that David had just woken up.

David would place Him at twenty-five to thirty years old. He had an olive complexion, shoulder-length dark hair, and stood about six feet tall. The man was wearing a white garment that looked like a thin house coat. "The proper name for the house coat was tunic," David thought to himself. "Just like the tunic he was wearing." David then muttered under his breath, "That's probably why I fell earlier—I was trying to run in this damn dress!" The man's tunic hung to about mid-calf and was tied in place with a dark brown cloth belt. He had well-worn sandals on His feet.

David was an ardent tennis fan, and the man's appearance reminded him of Rafael Nadal, but the man was slightly thinner with a smaller build. He was dressed very similar to the peasants of Rome that David had studied in choosing his own attire for his day in Rome. David had surely traveled into the past, and based on his observations at this campsite, it might very well be 44 BC. He instantly concluded that he still might be able to visit Rome as he had originally planned, even if he missed the actual day of Caesar's assassination.

David smiled, looked at the man, and said, "Hello."

Much to David's surprise the man smiled back and returned with, "Hello."

David immediately realized how odd of a response that was. Based on the man's dress, the vintage of the tents in the camp, and the use of donkeys for travel; this time pre-dated the existence of the English language. Yet, the man's response was clearly "Hello!" He was definitely speaking David's native tongue and did not show any sense of surprise that David spoke English.

The man turned toward one of the camp's smaller tents and called out, "Nathan." A small, smiling fellow exited from the tent. "We need to prepare dinner for our visitor. He has awakened." Nathan disappeared back into the tent and David immediately heard the rattling of pots and pans.

David slowly stood up and eased his way over to the campfire opposite the stranger. David smiled and then reluctantly asked, "Why are You speaking the English language?"

The reply was quite simple, "Because that is your native tongue, right?" David nodded in total amazement.

The stranger then told David that He and His companions had rescued him just in the nick of time from a pack of hungry wolves earlier that day. "I am ever so thankful," David replied. He also indicated that he needed to head-out early in the morning; he was on a "tight schedule."

David attempted to get a more definitive answer regarding the English thing a second time and asked, "So, how is it possible that You know English?"

The reply, again, was quite simple, "As you get to know Me, the answer to your question will become obvious." The stranger said that they would visit more while David was eating, and He excused Himself and left the camp area.

Nathan resurfaced from his tent, walked up to David, held out his hand, and said, "Hello, my name is Nathan. I am very pleased to meet you."

David shook Nathan's hand while replying, "Very nice to meet you also. My name is David, David Hart."

With that, the little fellow turned to the fire and began warming what appeared to be some type of soup in a small pot.

David laughed and asked, "Is that enough food for the three of us?" Nathan explained that this soup was just for David. David became slightly startled as another little guy crawled out of the other small tent in the camp, his size and demeanor were very much like Nathan's.

"Hello, my name is Marcus," said little fellow number two in a meek and mild voice.

"My name is David, very pleased to meet you," was the American's reply.

David watched as Nathan scurried to and from a small brook that ran behind the tents. It was obvious that they used the brook for their water supply as well as for cleaning. David assumed that the brook also served as the bathtub. "Man do I need a bath," he thought. On the following day, David would begin using this outdoor bathtub himself.

After ensuring that it was nice and hot, Nathan handed David his soup in a small, wooden bowl and the three men sat around the fire on small stools made of wood and cowhide. David chuckled to himself as he thought how these two little characters were the spitting image of *Snow White's* dwarfs. Once each was situated on a stool, neither fellow's feet touched the ground. Nathan was definitely *Happy* while it appeared that Marcus would pass for *Bashful*. These two were actually larger in stature than dwarfs, but not by much. They also appeared to be relatively young—probably in their early thirties.

The mysterious stranger returned to the campfire and sat opposite David. He looked directly into David's eyes and said, "You will find this conversation to be quite overwhelming, so rather than delay, let's talk." The man said this in a very matter of fact delivery, "My name is Jesus, I am from the city of Nazarth; Nathan and Marcus are angels. We were expecting you."

David released an uncomfortable laugh of surprise, then said, "You mean, *the Jesus*, and you mean, God's angels—from heaven, no less?"

"Precisely," Jesus answered with a calming smile. Thoughts were racing through David's mind at a mile a minute. Jesus gave their visitor a few moments to let His previous statements soak in.

As David attempted to deal with his astonishment, Jesus went on to explain that He planned to spend forty days here in the desert and Nathan and Marcus were there to accompany Him. They had arrived the previous day and had just finished setting-up their camp when they rescued David earlier that morning.

Jesus then pointed out that this was a very important and trying time in the wilderness, away from civilization, and in order for Him to remain focused, He was fasting. This meant He wasn't eating; the purpose of fasting was to bring Him closer to God the Father. Jesus explained, "Fasting is an avenue whereby your persistent hunger constantly reminds you to focus on prayer and devotion."

Jesus was right. This conversation had overwhelmed David. How bizarre! David didn't know what to think! Of all the potential places and times in the history of the world for his time travel to take him, he ends up face-to-face with Jesus Christ Himself, accompanied by two angels, no less! This had to be either a dream or a farce. So David jokingly said, as he stood and spread his arms to the sky, "Yeah, and I am Zeus, king of the gods!"

As David laughed loudly at his clever remark, he soon realized his company found no humor whatsoever in his statement.

"So," Jesus said with a gentle but convincing tone, "maybe this will help you to believe Me. For one, I am speaking English, not My native Aramaic, which you have already pointed out as unusual since English has yet to surface as a language. Your name is David Hart, your parents are Jonathan and Nancy Hart, and you were born in Houston, Texas on November 18, 1986." Jesus continued, "Your wife is Angela Banks and you were married on October 23, 2010. You are a physicist, employed by NASA, and you believe that you truly just traveled through time to ancient Rome in a capsule Jesse Black chose to name Hercules! You launched at 3:30 a.m. on August 16, 2015."

David was astonished, and now convinced, that this man must truly be whom He claimed to be. David had known that Jesus was a good man and teacher; he did not know, however, that He could see into the future. (David would eventually grow to understand that Jesus knew all, not just the future, but also the past.) Then the underlying message in Jesus' prior statement hit him!

David blurted out, "What do You mean that 'I believe I have traveled through time?'"

Jesus expanded on his prior statement, "I'm sorry, you did indeed travel through time. It's just that the flight had nothing to do with Catapult, the speed of 640 mph, or the temperature of 612°F. You achieved time travel because God the Father gently removed Hercules, and its precious cargo, from the cradle of Catapult and placed you here in the Judean Desert in the year 27 AD."

At first David wanted to react in disbelief and claim that the time travel had occurred because of the science his team had harnessed with their mighty invention. But after just hearing Jesus recite key events in his life (which would occur two thousand years into the future from 27 AD), he felt confident that Jesus was speaking the truth. So, David's thoughts immediately went to the return trip. How would he get home?

Jesus told David that he was part of God the Father's perfect plan for a special remnant of mankind. That David had been chosen as the one to perform a very important task for God. David must have asked ten times, "How will I return home?"

The young American finally gave Jesus a chance to reply, "You will spend the next thirty-eight days here with the three of us in the desert. At that time, our task here will be complete and we will address your trip home. Rest assured, your future is in My hands and the hands of My Father."

Jesus turned to Nathan and Marcus and asked them to fetch some fruit for David to enjoy as they prepared for bed. David choked on the last of his soup as he watched the two angels spring upward and soar into the night. His eyes were as big as silver dollars when he turned to look at Jesus. The two smiled, then broke out in laughter.

Jesus said good night and disappeared into His tent. Ten minutes later, Nathan and Marcus floated down from the night sky with two shiny red apples, gave them to their visitor, and retired to their tents. David finished off one of the apples and laid down to get some sleep. He smiled as it had just dawned on him that both of the angels had been speaking English the entire time as well.

He had so many questions for Jesus, but they would have to wait until morning. He pulled out his iPhone and plugged in his earbuds. Tonight was a night for some smooth Jazz, no words—just soothing music. He scrolled through his pictures reflecting on home, especially Angela, and then closed his eyes. "Jesus?" he whispered to himself. He rolled over and was convinced that when he woke up he would find all of this to just be one crazy dream.

CHAPTER 4
HOUSTON, WE HAVE A PROBLEM

Angela rolled over in their cozy king-size bed at 8:30 a.m. Sunday morning and laid her arm across *nothing*? She immediately sat up in bed. Where was David? When did he come back to bed? Did he come back to bed? Then she grinned and realized he had probably fallen asleep on the sofa. She tromped into the family room to find the sofa unoccupied—no David. She quickly checked both bathrooms—no David. Where had he gone? This WAS NOT like her husband to leave without informing her!

She looked outside and, with a mild hint of anger, confirmed that David's Jeep was not in the driveway. She called David's cell…no answer—just voice mail. She called his office phone…no answer—just voice mail. Where did he go? What should she do? That hint of anger was transforming into fear, and more than just a hint of fear.

She dug out the main phone number to NASA, called and was greeted by the operator. After a short conversation with the operator, Angela's call was directed to the military's classified security gate. Angela was told, in military speak, that, "one David Hart had signed-in at—oh one hundred and twenty-eight hours (01:28) and had yet to exit the premises." When she hung-up the phone, Angela breathed a deep sigh of relief. She had successfully located her husband, so now it was time to give him an earful of her disappointment with his actions. Apparently her Aggie-Engineer husband had been restless and had snuck off to work, choosing not to disturb her—bad idea!

Throughout the morning she called David's cell and office phones several times, but to no avail. Then finally, an answer! At 11:30 a.m. an answer on his office phone, "Hello."

"Hello!" Angela interrupted, "you have some explaining to do, and then you are going to have to beg for my mercy!" she ordered.

"Is this Angela?" the man asked.

"Of course it is, mister!" she replied.

Jesse laughed, "Angela, this is Jesse; I haven't seen David around this morning, so I picked up his phone. It's been ringing off the hook you know."

Angela explained the happenings of the morning to Jesse. Jesse looked out of the office window and saw David's Jeep sitting in his regular parking spot. He told Angela that he would track the young stray down and have him call home. Jesse was surprised that he had not noticed David's Jeep earlier when he had arrived and parked.

As Jesse was walking to Catapult's hangar, he couldn't think of any pressing item that would cause David to come to work in the middle of the night, especially on a weekend. The project's primary effort that had been going on for months was monkey training, unfortunately. The only reason that Jesse was there on a Sunday was to catch up on e-mails and flirt with the cute blonde working the weekend shift at the military sector security gate.

When Jesse entered the flight control room, he immediately found David's note and his heart began to race. He knew David was daring, but not to the point of endangering his life! For a good five minutes he sat in the control room motionless, staring at the note in disbelief:

Jesse,
Just in case my return trip is delayed, lol, I wanted to drop you a note. I decided to play "monkey" and take Hercules for the inaugural flight. The team is running out of time and we have too much invested in this baby to let it get scrapped. Headed to Rome, 44 B.C.
I'll bring ya back a toga!

– David

Once Jesse stood, he slowly walked over to the main viewing window of the control room in a fearful trance. He was almost too afraid to peer into the main hangar area and see what had potentially transpired with the loose cannon's attempt at the inaugural flight. Catapult was motionless and intact, everything looked to be in order. As he continued to systematically survey the area, Jesse's eyes slowly focused on Catapult's cradle, his heart sank. The government's $200 million piece of hardware, Hercules, was gone!

This also meant that David Hart was gone! David had taken the inaugural flight! Jesse wondered, "Would Hercules ever return? And even more importantly, would David ever return?" He quickly queried the flight computer and determined that the flight had indeed launched at 3:30 a.m. bound for Rome in the year 44 BC. Jesse turned and punched the side wall of the control room so hard that, for a moment, he thought he had broken his hand.

Once he had calmed himself down, Jesse called Angela and asked her to meet him at David's office. He then, after practicing his words very carefully, called Stuart and asked him to do the same. It was an emergency. Jesse knew better than to tell Stuart any of the facts of this dire circumstance over the telephone. Stuart might have brought a gun with him if he had known the entire truth! Jesse contacted the security gates, spoke with the cute blond, and advised her to give Angela Hart, wife of NASA's David Hart, clearance for entry into the military sector of the facility.

After Jesse had brought the two up to speed on his findings, he showed them David's note. Jesse surmised that David felt he would have returned before anyone would actually have found the note. Since David knew that Angela would be frantically looking for him after she woke up on Sunday morning, he must have intended to return before sunrise.

This caused all three of them to panic. Stuart was afraid of the media hell that he was about to experience. Jesse was afraid that his baby had, at least partially, failed since David was tardy on his return and Jesse may have also lost a very close friend.

Angela was beside herself with anger! First of all, what was all this talk of time travel and David taking a flight? A flight where? How do you launch into flight from the inside of a building anyway? Angela's body began to tremble as she cried out to her absent husband, "Mr. David Hart—you had better get your butt back here right now!" She felt silly screaming into thin air, but she was overwhelmed and confused. She did recognize David's handwriting when she looked at the note he had left for Jesse, and he did say he was headed to ancient Rome. Was David joking in his note? Had NASA hired some handwriting expert to fabricate the note to appear as if her husband had written it?

Angela continued talking. It was as though she was speaking thoughts as they passed through her mind, more so, than as if she was actually conversing with Jesse or Stuart. "David is my best friend and he is the love of my life. We are planning to have our first child next year. Not only does David have a genius mind, he has a magnificent heart as well." Jesse looked at Angela with a strong sense of compassion as she slowly came to grips with the severity of the situation. Meanwhile, Stuart was so focused on his game plan for damage-control, knowing that this situation was headed for national, probably international, attention—he never heard a word Angela said.

She then turned to Jesse and Stuart and declared, "I will get to the bottom of this! I will not accept a simple statement that 'David is missing.' Do the two of you realize how incredibly ridiculous that sounds? Missing... you don't just lose a human being!" Angela stormed off the premises and headed home.

John Stuart became a household name that day, but for all the wrong reasons. He was plastered across TV screens all over America, and the world for that matter. He explained that a NASA employee was missing after conducting an unauthorized experiment on the agency's premises in Clear Lake City, Texas. The employee's name was being withheld and all details of the incident were considered classified. America struggled with the term missing. How do you lose somebody while they are conducting an experiment 'on the premises?'

Stuart's hard-nosed response to that obvious question was, "A lot of our military-related classified projects involve cutting-edge technology and missing was indeed the proper word to describe this particular situation."

As Jesse attended and listened to Stuart's press conference, he began to become irritated. He became irritated at himself and Stuart. In the midst of the day's commotion, neither one of the two had given any serious thought to the fact that the NASA team had accomplished the impossible! Sure, David Hart was missing for the moment, but he could very well return in the next day or so. This engineering marvel, created and built by Jesse's team, had actually launched Hercules into time. This scientific feat was a first in the history of mankind! NASA had launched a seventeen-ton, time travel capsule into time itself. All seventeen tons of capsule and its contents, including one human being, had miraculously vanished from the here-and-now.

"Furthermore," Jesse whispered to himself, "NASA, and more specifically, Stuart, owed him proper recognition via a healthy raise, a sizeable bonus, and a bigger office!"

After arriving at home, Angela called her and David's parents informing them of the alarming circumstance. She told them that the government had warned her that the project was classified and that she was allowed to share very little of the details. Not that she felt that she really knew many of the details. For right now, she asked them to stay in touch and hope for the best. She was confident that David would be turning up over the next several hours and this would just turn out to be one giant misunderstanding.

Angela then contacted Jackie Kitch. Angela and Jackie had known each other since they were both eight years old. They initially became friends while attending the third grade at Brookwood Elementary School. They essentially grew up calling each other best friend as they became closer, year by year, as they grew into adulthood. They went on to attend the same middle school and high school together. Now as married, working adults the two were still close friends, just not as close as they were prior to marriages and full-time jobs.

Jackie also had a three-year-old son, Mikey. She had obtained a bachelor's degree from the University of Houston and was now working as an RN at Clear Lake Medical Center. Jackie had yet to lose all her baby fat after having Mikey, so she was slightly plump and continued to walk with the pregnant waddle that she had developed during her last trimester of pregnancy. Jackie kept her dark black hair short and was always wearing a set of hospital scrubs, whether she was at work or not. Angela referred to Jackie as *Miss Cheer-Me-Up*, since Jackie had a knack for boosting Angela's spirits, even from the bleakest of moods.

"I need a big dose of Miss Cheer-Me-Up," Angela thought as she punched Jackie's name in her cell phone's contacts list.

"Hey, girlfriend," Jackie announced as she answered her cell, knowing from the caller-ID that it was Angela.

"Hey…," Angela declared ever so softly, clearly on the verge of tears.

"What's up? David ignoring you today? Let me guess, he's watching the Texans get schooled by the Philadelphia Eagles? My hubby is doing the same—only he's down the street at the sports bar, not sitting here moping on the sofa. Do you think that the Texans will ever make it to the Super Bowl?"

"I wish David was here parked on the sofa and watching the Texans get schooled by the Eagles," Angela moped.

Jackie quickly sensed her friends misery. "Okay. You have my full attention now," responded Jackie. "I'm all ears, what's up?"

"I need you to come over, right away, if you can. This is *major*. I just puked my guts up and now I'm dry heaving. David isn't here, I have experienced the ugliest day of my life, and I need a shoulder to cry on. I don't want to get our parents too worked up until we know more."

"Give me ten minutes!" Jackie said as she hung up the phone.

Within a few minutes Jackie was rapping on Angela's front door. "Where is Mikey?" Angela asked as she opened the door and found Jackie to be unaccompanied.

"Oh, I asked my next door neighbor to watch him for a little while. You have me scared, Angela! This is not like you to be so needy. What is going on? Tell me everything!"

"Well...I don't know where to start. Let's see...David was very restless when we went to bed last night so he moved to the family room, he said to watch TV. Sometime during the night, since he couldn't sleep, he must have decided to head over to NASA and spend some time at the office. I didn't even know that he had left the house until I woke up this morning. And after a few hours of searching and several phone calls, I found out that he was over at NASA. I spoke with his boss over the phone, who was at the office and he promised to track David down."

"And?"

"He called me back after his search. He seemed to be in somewhat of a panic and asked me to drive over to the facility. He said he didn't want to discuss the situation over the phone. So I hopped in my car and charged over there. When I got there, David's boss, Jesse, was there with the NASA director, John Stuart, the head honcho over the whole damned place. That is when I realized that something big had apparently happened. Jesse introduced me to Stuart, who had arrived only about five minutes before me. Stuart was a tough-looking customer and was fully decked out in military fatigues."

"Well..."

"They basically told me that David had been working on a time travel machine."

"Cool!"

"I already knew that David had been working on a classified military project. Once I grasped Jesse's statement regarding time travel, I just could not understand why David or any other sane person would believe that time travel actually warranted so much time and effort. Well, I'm not sure I believe the whole time travel bit—but it helped them in telling me their cockamamie fairy tale."

"I have never seen you this angry!" Jackie interjected.

"Jesse then informed Stuart and me that David snuck up there in the middle of the night and launched the time travel machine without authorization! Jesse claimed that David programmed the flight computer, wrote Jesse a short note, then boarded the machine, and launched."

"So, where did he program the machine to go? Or should I say, to when did he program the machine to go?"

"Jesse indicated that the machine and David were launched two thousand years into the past. Jesse also had the gall to declare that not only had David traveled well into the past, but that he had also intended to land in ancient Rome. Rome—on the other side of the world! Then... then...they said that both David and the machine had not returned yet. They claimed that this caused them extreme concern because David had promised, in his note, that he planned to return very shortly after he left. I saw the note and it did appear to be David's handwriting. And the note did specifically mention Rome." Angela looked into Jackie's eyes for comfort as the tears started pouring relentlessly down her cheeks.

"Well then, if he's running late, when do they expect him to return?" Jackie questioned, sounding somewhat lawyer-like.

"They say that the capsule...that's what they call it...the capsule...has never been launched before and they fear that it may never return. If the capsule never returns, that means that David will never return!" Angela tried to regain control of her emotions as she realized that she had just shouted her last statement. Her hands were noticeably trembling.

"So, why do you think David would have been so daring as to take the first flight. Furthermore, why would he do it in the middle of the night, all by himself?"

"Well, that's the unsettling part of their story. They allege that David had become extremely impatient over the last few months as the progress on the machine slowed to a crawl. So, they believe that he thought he could get the whole project back on the fast track by proving that the technology worked. How better to prove the technology than by taking the first successful trip?"

"Well, do they have a plan?" Jackie inquired.

"They said the FBI will be investigating. They are telling the public that David is 'missing.' They aren't releasing his name at this time. Meanwhile, I am supposed to keep my mouth shut and wait for periodic FBI updates."

"What do they mean by missing?"

"I don't know! I do not believe this whole time travel tale. Frankly, I don't know what to believe. The capsule, they named it Hercules, is apparently gone. David was up there last night, I saw his Jeep parked in his regular spot. David is apparently gone! I'm worried. I am very worried!"

"Angela, he has to turn up. People don't just disappear! That's crazy!" Jackie exclaimed.

Angela slowly walked from the foyer to the kitchen. She eased into a chair at the breakfast table and looked hopelessly at Jackie. The dejected young wife was unquestionably in shock.

"Angela, I am here to help! We will not rest until we know the truth," Jackie asserted. "We will not rest until David is found and NASA will be liable for any harm that has come his way!"

"Jackie, I need you. I do truly need you." Angela said as she stared helplessly at the kitchen wall.

"I'm here girlfriend. I'm here."

"Jackie. I worry…I worry that David was injured while conducting some outrageous, top-secret experiment and this is a cover-up. They are claiming that he is missing to make the cover-up easier to accomplish. That director, Stuart, seems like a devious good-for-nothing. I'm sure that Jesse has been forced to play along with whatever position the government has chosen to take. Or worse yet, why was Jesse up there? Why was Jesse up there on a Sunday? Is Jesse right in the middle of the whole 'David-is-missing' fiasco?"

"If so, we'll find out and those responsible will pay!"

"Jackie, what if…what if…David is dead? What if I never see him again? I feel so small, especially when facing something as big as the US government and NASA. I bet I will never know the whole truth. They probably fabricated that letter that Jesse alleges was written by David. I bet *big brother* gets away with some devious blunder just because they can!"

"David is not dead, that's absurd!" Jackie assured her devastated friend. "Let's call the hospital. My boss is working today and she knows a great Houston-based attorney who has influential connections in Washington DC. We need to start building a powerful team to ensure that we get to the bottom of this. We're not going to take on NASA and the US government alone—we need serious help. So, serious help we'll get!"

When NASA employees returned to work that Monday morning, the facility was swarming with FBI agents who converged on Project 13-03's team members and the Catapult hangar. Jesse had already been ordered to only share details of the project with the FBI, "Tell no one else about time travel," Stuart had huffed.

Over the course of the morning, the FBI had narrowed their focus to this:

- Where was David Hart?
- More importantly, where was the $200 million Hercules capsule?
- Drop the time travel crap and tell us what this machine was really designed to do...

Stuart received a phone call from one J. Mark Wilson. He was Angela Hart's newly hired attorney and he needed to meet with Mr. Stuart and Jesse Black immediately! He would be filing a law suit against NASA and the federal government regarding the disappearance of one Mr. David Hart. He wanted to speak with the two men prior to submitting the suit to the courts later that afternoon.

CHAPTER 5
THE CHAINS OF TIME

David slowly awoke as noise emanated from outside his tent. "My tent?" he questioned as he tried to orient his groggy mind. He had fallen asleep outside, under the stars, not in a tent. Apparently Nathan and Marcus had moved him into one of their tents after he had fallen asleep (a move that David had no recollection of). Since he found himself waking up in the same camp as the night before, our time traveler reluctantly admitted to himself that this was not some crazy dream.

As he painfully crawled out of the tent, David saw Nathan busily preparing breakfast. When David stood up, it seemed as though every single muscle in his body ached. The aching shouldn't have been a surprise, since he had slept on the ground. In addition, the knot on his forehead was throbbing with pain. He needed a handful of aspirin but his first-aid kit was back at the capsule. "Handful of aspirin," he mumbled to himself, "I need something much stronger than that."

"Did you get the license plate of that truck that ran me over?" David joked to Nathan.

"What do you need, David?" was Nathan's response as he looked inquisitively at his new camp mate.

"Oh, nothing. What are we having for breakfast, Nathan?" asked David.

"You mean what are you having?" Nathan corrected. Nathan explained that neither he nor Marcus actually ate food. He further commented that they did not require sleep. Food and sleep are required for human beings, not angels. The human body needs food and sleep to restore energy, but angels receive their life energy in abundance from God the Father. David asked Nathan why they had brought food for the trip if they didn't eat and Jesus planned to fast. Nathan declared, "We brought it for you—we knew you were coming."

David produced a big smile and asked his new little friend, "Do all the angels look like you and Marcus? Small like you? And aren't angels supposed to have wings and wear white robes?"

Nathan let out a big belly laugh. He caught his breath and said, "No, there are different 'sizes and shapes' of angels. First of all, all angels were created to give glory to God, but we also have specific responsibilities. Angels like Marcus and I were created to serve, to help, much like a manservant. Many angels have more significant responsibilities and power than us, and some of those angels are much bigger than us. Marcus and I don't need wings to fly, but some angels do indeed have wings."

Nathan handed David his breakfast, retrieved some supplies from his tent, and began removing the bandage from David's head—it needed to be replaced.

"What about Jesus?" asked David. "Is it the same for Him? Does He need food or sleep? Why did He talk about hunger pains during fasting? Or will He only become like you when He presumably goes to heaven?"

"You mean when He returns to heaven," Nathan corrected him again.

Nathan explained that Jesus, just like God the Father, was not created. The two have always existed and will always exist. God is not a creation, He is the Creator, and likewise for Jesus. God is the very heart of life and the universe.

"So who is God," David inquired, "Jesus or God the Father?"

"They are both God," Nathan declared. "Furthermore, God is actually three persons in one, not just two. The third person in the Trinity is the Holy Spirit of God."

David, knowing that he himself wasn't much of a religious person, felt awkward about this Trinity concept. So he fell back on his fundamental understanding of God and the Bible (which would prove later to be incorrect). David responded, "Everyone knows that God created the Heavens and the Earth, and it is God *singular*. Furthermore, Jesus didn't enter the scene until His birth on Christmas Day in Bethlehem, thousands of years after the creation."

Nathan smiled at David and quipped, "You see what we have here my friend is a 'failure to communicate,' or should I say a failure to translate." Nathan explained, "The book of Genesis, the first book in the Bible, was originally written by Moses in the Hebrew language. In the Hebrew language, the word used for God in the book of Genesis regarding creation is the plural form of the word God, *Elohim*. Much like when a couple gets married and people say the two have become one. This one is a plural meaning two people, but unified as one. So it is with the Trinity."

Nathan also pointed out the verses in the book of Genesis, "'Then God said, Let us make man in our image, in our likeness, and let them rule over the fish of the sea and the birds of the air, over the livestock, over all the Earth, and over all the creatures that move along the ground.' Did you hear the us's and our's?" Nathan inquired with a smile of triumph.

Nathan went further..., "There is only one true God. This one true God is three persons: God the Father, Jesus the Son, and the Holy Spirit. The three are individuals, but One in relationship, One in unity—*Elohim*. The Son submits to the Father, and the Spirit submits to both the Father and the Son.

"God is altogether perfect and is the very essence of life, intelligence, beauty, and righteousness. All three persons of the Trinity are this God. This God created the Heavens and the Earth, created all that is seen and unseen.

"Now, back to your question about Jesus and His 'need or not' for food and sleep," Nathan continued.

As David listened to this little angel he sensed Nathan's wisdom, inner peace, and self confidence. Nathan was like a little piece of this bigger God of life, intelligence, and beauty. "Not to imply in any way that Nathan was beautiful, like attractive beautiful, but beautifully content," David thought.

Nathan went on to explain, "In heaven we have heavenly bodies, no pun intended, bodies that are appropriate for heaven. A human body could not last in heaven for many reasons, but the most obvious being exposure to God the Father."

Nathan lowered his voice and spoke in reverence. "God the Father is almighty and pure, the very essence of life. He emanates glorious light. Anyone who is not pure and perfect cannot survive in His presence; they will be consumed in His glorious light, much like being consumed by fire. This is the case with the human body. All humans are impure and imperfect. Up until now, that is…Jesus Christ is here now to become the one pure and perfect human. This is how Adam and Eve existed in the Garden of Eden before the fall of man; they were perfect and lived in the presence of God.

"Jesus, in His heavenly body, does not require food or sleep." Nathan looked toward the sky, "Jesus not only exists in heaven in that body, but He reigns on high with God the Father and the Holy Spirit there. They are worshiped and glorified by the angels and saints.

"Jesus, however, is now serving here on Earth and has elected to step down from heaven and occupy a human body, to come 'on the scene' as you stated earlier. So, today, Jesus is human. Blood courses through His veins, He requires food and sleep, He needs oxygen to breath and water to drink.

"Jesus, you see, is heaven's champion! The Creator humbled Himself beyond imagination, agreeing to occupy the body of a human creature. The Creator becoming the created! Jesus is also the champion, or should I say, Savior, of the remnant of mankind." Nathan stopped and took a deep breath.

David spoke up, "What do you mean by Jesus is serving here on Earth? Who is He serving?"

Nathan pointed his stubby index finger directly at David's chest and answered, "He is serving you. He is serving all of mankind. Without Him man is nothing, with Him man can achieve the spectacular, the supernatural. He is here to pay a debt to allow you the opportunity to spend eternity in heaven. Man is hopelessly lost in his sin. He is completely separated from the Father and forbidden from heaven. Jesus is here to remedy this huge problem and restore a way for men to reestablish their relationship with the Father. This wonderful act of courage and sacrifice will demonstrate to mankind the loving mercy of God.

"David," Nathan said as he reflected on the previous day, "all this explanation regarding Jesus' involvement with creation wouldn't be necessary if you had been able to witness Jesus interact with those wolves yesterday. As we came upon the scene, the pack had surrounded you. I would say there were six of them. It became apparent that the biggest one, also the one closest to your motionless body, was the leader. The leader was poised and ready to kill you.

"Jesus approached him directly and spoke a command, the wolf immediately sat, and then all the wolves sat. This lead wolf definitely knew who was the Creator and who was the created at that moment. Jesus went straight to the leader of the pack, looked him in the eyes, and patted him on the head. Jesus spoke a second command and the leader trotted off, followed by the rest. It was a miracle."

"So," David summarized, "you are saying that Jesus walked directly into the midst of this hungry pack of wolves, unarmed—He wasn't even carrying a stick. Then, as they sat at attention, Jesus commanded them to leave. And, upon His command, the wolves instantly obeyed!"

"Yes, that is exactly what happened."

The thought of that scene truly amazed David. He slowly finished the last of his breakfast as they concluded this exchange. Nathan suggested that they take a break from all the conversation and venture out beyond the camp. Marcus had gone with Jesus to His "prayer place," leaving just the two of them here at the camp.

"Where should we go?" asked David.

"How about a trip to your ship Hercules," Nathan suggested as he flexed his right bicep in classic Herculean-style. This display of Nathan's coaxed a hearty laugh from his new American friend. David had noticed from the previous night that any talk about the capsule got Nathan excited.

After they arrived at his ship, David removed Hercules' tarp. David looked upon the capsule in utter disappointment, now having realized that the project resulting in the production of Hercules and Catapult was not the cause for his trip through time and space. David turned to Nathan and didn't see any disappointment in Nathan's eyes—he was giddy with excitement.

"It's so big and so beautiful!" uttered Nathan as he stared at the exterior of the ship in complete awe.

Nathan's initial impression of Hercules made David step back and take another glance at his capsule. "Nathan was right," he thought, "this ship is an engineering marvel." As David looked at the name HERCU-LES gleaming in bright blue brilliance painted on the shiny silver shell, he reaffirmed to himself that NASA would eventually get this time travel technology to work. It seemed as though they were so close.

David opened the vacuum hatch and he and Nathan climbed into Hercules. He showed Nathan the brain-center of the capsule as he powered-up the controls utilizing stored energy in the capacitor. Nathan was amazed by all the buttons, lights, and gauges.

David opened up the pilot's console and pulled out his favorite pair of sunglasses, Ray-Bans, of course. He put them on and asked Nathan his opinion of the look. After five minutes of listening to Nathan's "oohs and aahs", David removed the sunglasses, handed them to Nathan, and said, "Happy birthday, my friend." David then showed Nathan a picture of Angela that was also in the console.

Nathan admired Angela's beauty and then turned to David, smiled and said, "Angela is an Angel, just like me." They both laughed as David shook his head indicating an emphatic, NO!

"Angela and Nathan were very different!" David mumbled under his breath.

"This capsule, Nathan," David declared, "will be part of a major upgrade when I return to NASA and we will determine a way for time travel to actually work."

"Time is such an important aspect of life here on Earth, isn't it?" Nathan asked.

"It's huge," answered David, "it's the fourth dimension of this three-dimensional world. You have height, width, and depth all on the move through time." David went on to explain how traveling through time, either into the past or future, would be the biggest scientific feat ever accomplished by mankind up until the year 2015.

"Unfortunately, for all you hard-working, brilliant scientists, it will never happen," Jesus stated as He walked up to the opened hatch and joined in on the conversation.

"Huh?" rolled out of David's mouth. David turned and saw Jesus with His quiet sidekick, Marcus, standing beside Hercules. David saw the sweat on Jesus' brow due to the long walk from His prayer spot to the capsule.

Jesus explained, "David, men are groomed and developed during a lifetime. The experiences of life on Earth, hammer a man into the finished product that he becomes. Just like a blacksmith hammers iron into its final shape. Much of the hammering in a man's life is painful and demanding, but some is joyous and rewarding.

"You see, David, this 'time thing' that you and your NASA team have spent endless hours and significant money attempting to overcome, is actually a key component in My Father's perfect plan for mankind. Man will never free himself from the chains of time on the human side of life. Time is the world's fourth dimension and always will be!" Jesus proclaimed. "Time will produce, through the hammering, the remnant of mankind who will choose the Father through the Son, supplying heaven with devoted saints—saints who *have the knowledge of good and evil* because of Adam's fall.

"David, We knew before the creation of Adam that he would fall," Jesus said.

David asked, "By fall, do you mean when he and Eve ate the fruit from the forbidden tree?"

"Yes," answered Jesus, "We, however, knew that a different kind of saint would be the 'finished product' from the Fall. You see, from mankind will come saints of experience and choice. This was caused by the first man, when he chose to partake of the fruit from the tree of knowledge of good and evil, the forbidden tree, in the Garden of Eden. Because of Adam's choice to defy Our single command, all human beings are born into a world of sin. From the very beginning, humans were empowered to choose. Adam and Eve used this power in choosing to disobey."

"It was more like an abuse of power," David added.

"Everyone's ancestry traces back to Adam and Eve, so everyone is born into their world of sin. This is often referred to as original sin. Because of the Fall, all humans experience the evil: temptation, wickedness, pain, and loss; as well as the good: accomplishment, goodness, joy, and gain; from birth through death."

Jesus continued, "During their lives, each adult makes a choice; they either believe in Me as their only path to heaven, or they don't. The ones that accept Me, bring to heaven a very special soul. That soul has the knowledge of evil as well as good, and in the end that soul chose good—they acknowledged God.

"Now prior to this choice, the soul is lost in sin and completely unacceptable to the Father. Man's sin draws the wrath and anger of the Father in a very fierce way—the Father is perfect in every way. The day of the Fall was a day of catastrophe. We had given man only one command to obey, one command in the midst of providing for him all his needs. And in no time, Adam and Eve had conspired to break that one command. So little time had passed when they committed sin that they had yet to bear their first child."

"Satan was in the Garden of Eden with them, right?" David asked.

"Yes, that is correct," answered Jesus. "Now back to the saints. When a person places their faith in the Trinity, their soul is renewed by Us. Their soul is restored to the state of Adam's soul prior to the Fall. The Holy Spirit, God, then occupies their soul and they are once again in relationship with Us. The men that never believe in Us will never be restored to Us. This decision must be authentic in order for Us to renew the relationship.

"The person that does place their faith in Us is transformed by the very presence of the Holy Spirit within their soul. The Holy Spirit actually lives in them. Because of My personal blood sacrifice on the cross, these saved souls become perfect to the Father and acceptable for entry into heaven. These souls that receive God, these souls that have the knowledge of good and evil bring something to heaven that angels can't bring. By creating man in Our image, We gave him free will. Each individual is given their own unique opportunity to accept the truth or reject it."

Jesus went on, "You see, angels were created, but they were created to dwell in heaven from the start. They don't really face the daily battle of life on Earth that men do. Angels live holy lives in submission to Us, pure from the day of their birth, so to speak. So they don't really possess the knowledge of both good and evil and don't really choose one over the other. That is, of course, except for the fallen angel, Satan, who was thrown out of heaven. We cast him out, along with his band of followers, when he decided he should reign supreme in heaven, even over God the Father. This was a specific time in history when the angels were allowed to choose, and many chose to follow Satan."

Jesus asked David, "Does this difference between angels and saints make sense to you?"

David nodded, "An angel is created to live in heaven from day one, and he really doesn't experience the hardships of life—the hardships each human being experiences on Earth. The saints who will eventually live in heaven, endure the hardship of life, and ultimately place their faith in God."

"That's it," Jesus affirmed, "And these unique saints will glorify God in a most special way, having placed their faith in Him, or I should say Us, of their own free will. The saint turns toward the Trinity at the time of his salvation and asks for forgiveness and mercy knowing that he is a helpless sinner. Our grace redeems him. Our grace gives him value, allowing him entrance into a perfect heaven that he doesn't deserve.

"Now regarding the issue of time on Earth. You see, David," Jesus added, "the Earth is enemy-occupied territory. Satan and his band of fallen angels work diligently day and night against Us. They are bitter for being cast out from heaven, and they know that the power of God the Father is too great for them to ever overcome. So, being relegated to Earth and eventually to the darkness of hell, they want to recruit as many souls as they possibly can. 'Misery does indeed love company.' Maybe, in his own twisted way, Satan believes that if he is able to recruit a large enough army, he has a chance to defeat Me at the world's end. I can assure you, that will never happen!

"Here is a good way to envision a human's time on Earth. The outcome of the war, good versus evil, is already known. In the end, Satan, his demons, and all the unbelievers will be cast into the great lake of fire to spend eternity apart from God. The Trinity wins the war. But on Earth, prior to this final known outcome of the war, evil works diligently to grow the ranks of the unbelievers. So, even though the war has essentially been won, evil still has opportunities to win battles. Lost sinners are hopeless unless they turn to Us, to the Trinity. When they do, We can enter their battle and ensure that their soul is not doomed to eternity in hell. If they don't turn to Us, then Satan claims their soul.

Jesus continued, "I know it may sound odd to you now, but the Devil is alive and well in the year 2015 on planet Earth. There are many unkind and evil souls living twisted lives headed for eternal companionship with Satan. The harder concept to grasp is how Satan has successfully lured so many into lives of *complacency* with respect to God, comfortable places. These lost souls aren't unkind or evil, they are just without God."

Jesus' eyes became fixed and hard, "A walk with God is not a walk of comfort!" He exclaimed. "A walk with God is much more than that. It is a walk for eternity, it is a walk of faith, it is a walk of work, it is a walk of hope, it is a walk of sacrifice, but in the end it is a walk of victory.

"The saints, in heaven, will forever experience spiritual life and the souls cast into darkness will forever experience spiritual death. Since We have created man to live eternally with Us, those who are eternally separated from Us will yearn for heaven, but to no avail! These separated souls will spend eternity with Lucifer, the Devil, in the darkness of hell.

"It is extremely difficult for a human being currently bound by time to fully appreciate the concept of eternity. Maybe a physical example will help you to understand this concept." Jesus knelt to the ground and scooped up some sand grains in His left hand. He then carefully removed a single grain from His left palm with His right thumb and forefinger. He held the grain at eye level between Himself and David as He dumped the remaining sand in His left hand back on the ground.

Jesus spoke, "Look across this vast expanse of desert wilderness, take it all in." As Jesus spoke, David slowly scanned the panorama of desert all around them.

"David," Jesus looked intently at the solitary sand grain as He kept speaking, "imagine this sand grain as representing one's human life on Earth." David strained his eyes to see the solitary grain held in Jesus' right hand. Jesus then dropped the grain to the desert floor and extended His arms full-length to either side and said, "Now envision one's eternal life as represented by the millions upon millions of additional sand grains in this desert."

David reflected on the thought, then said, "Your example makes the time spent here on Earth seem so meaningless."

"Don't let the relative magnitude of a lifetime here on Earth lead you to believe that it is meaningless. I think the more appropriate term is to call it brief, with respect to eternity. But this human life is extremely significant with its meaning to each soul's eternity, even though in the overall scheme of eternity, it is indeed very brief. This illustration demonstrates two important options for mankind."

"And those two options are...?" David questioned.

"Option one—the foolish man will be the one who builds his treasure here, on Earth, investing in this brief existence. His coveted treasures are wealth, fine automobiles, real estate, worldly status, earthly pleasures, and so on. This man has traded an opportunity for eternal life (millions of sand grains) for tangible treasure here on Earth (one solitary sand grain). The fool never turns to his Creator for guidance and wisdom— this guidance and wisdom is all tavailable, it starts with the Holy Bible."

Jesus concluded, "What a miserable predicament. This person will live millions of earthly lifetimes in the darkness of hell, and for what—a failed attempt at happiness on Earth? Happiness here cannot even compare to the happiness of heaven! This soul will not invest the necessary time, during his earthly existence, to understand God's truth and realize that he has sacrificed his eternity in heaven for a very brief pursuit of happiness on Earth."

"Option two—the wise man discovers the truth of the Bible, the special message given to him by his Creator." Jesus continued to explain, "He allows Us to change him into a man that builds his treasure for his eternity, his future in heaven. He places his faith and trust in Me, and the rest of the Trinity. He toils to earn heavenly rewards that will not perish when this world is no more. He understands his human life (one solitary sand grain) is the most significant aspect of securing his eternal life (millions of sand grains).

"The wise man places God in the center of his earthly existence and serves Us. And as he serves Us, We constantly grow and transform him over time, to fulfill his earthly purpose. He spends the necessary time to grow his understanding of the Bible because he knows it's worth it."

"What about," David asked, "all the people that are uninformed? The ones that don't know God's truth?"

"That is where the urgency of communicating the Bible's message comes in. It is the Christian church's number one priority—to share the good news of the Gospel. David, when We create a man, We place the desire of seeking his Creator in his very heart. A human cannot, especially in your day, witness the marvels of creation: the human mind and body, the millions of stars in the heavens, the essence of life itself; without acknowledging an almighty Creator."

Jesus then returned to the topic of the saints in heaven, "You see, David, in heaven the fourth dimension is not time, heaven is not bound by time. In heaven one will live the equivalent of millions of earthly lifetimes. The fourth dimension in heaven is spiritual relationship. My Father and I are glorified when We are able to experience the true love of saints, and express Our love to them."

As David's eyes were fixed on Jesus, he felt a tingling within his chest. It felt like the butterflies he had experienced in his stomach three days ago just before launch, only higher up in his chest, surrounding his heart.

Without batting an eye Jesus looked directly at David and said, "And I see the Spirit is beginning to stir in your soul. He is there to comfort and guide you. Come, let's head back to camp."

CHAPTER 6

DAVID'S PURPOSE

As the crew sat around the campfire that night, a thoughtful grin emerged on Jesus' face as He stood and raised His right arm. He instantly caught David's attention who became perplexed. Jesus was motioning with His right forefinger as if He were writing on an imaginary chalkboard directly in front of Him.

"I hope You plan to share Your thoughts," David announced to Jesus. "I have got to know what You are doing. The 'not knowing' will drive me nuts! I see You smiling and writing on Your imaginary chalkboard... You have certainly aroused my overactive curiosity!"

Jesus shared, "I am mentally walking through the mathematical algorithm that Jesse derived for Hercules' physical trajectory vector. It's brilliant! Jesse is one of the most intelligent and impressive people employed by NASA. He is almost as bright as you, David."

"Whoa, just a minute!" David interrupted. "No offense, but Jesse spent years upon years studying to master the skill of applying complex mathematical equations to the physics of life science applications."

"I know. He attended the University of Texas, he graduated with honors." Jesus was surprised by David's reaction.

"So, Jesus, how is it that You are able to grasp this algorithm?"

No sooner had he asked that last question, than David had wished he could take it back. For that brief moment, he had foolishly looked upon Jesus as nothing more than a mortal man. A mortal man, uneducated, and living in the first century; wearing the clothes of a Roman peasant. A man living in an era before the evolution of the calculator, no—not the calculator, it was hundreds of years before the evolution of the slide rule.

But David knew better, he knew that this was God! "I am so sorry!" David quickly announced before Jesus could respond. "How foolish of me!" David literally sank to his knees in shame.

Jesus smiled, then responded in a serious tone, "For a moment there, I presume that you forgot that the Trinity did not derive equations to apply to science, We *created* science itself. We did not generate equations to determine the vector trajectories of physics, We created physics." David nodded and rose back to a standing position.

There was a long period of silence as David reflected on the very magnitude of Jesus' intelligence. The more he thought…the more in awe he grew. This is the intelligence that created an entire universe, a universe of which man only understood a minute portion. He pondered on the miracle of engineering the atom, the most basic building block of matter. Then he overwhelmed himself with the thought that not only had the Trinity engineered the atom, they had created the composition of the atom itself…the electrons, protons, neutrons, and so on. The same applied to life—humans, plants, and animals; only the basic building block was the cell instead of the atom.

David was thinking aloud as he continued, "The Trinity then took these very building blocks that they created and formed an entire universe: A universe that flows in complete unison, balancing the movement of galaxies, solar systems, and planets. Then, more specifically here on Earth within our specific solar system, God has provided the harmonizing flow of nature on our precious planet. Plant and animal life thriving in balance with human life as the Earth hurtles through space at thousands of miles per hour. We humans are nestled in the comfort of a world that supports us biologically with a climate, atmosphere, and cycle of day and night created just for us.

"And we rush through daily life taking all this for granted as we focus on so many trivial distractions. We are given just the right level of oxygen in the air to support the human body's needs. We have the existence, and abundance, of water—one of our most precious natural resources. We enjoy ample warmth from the sun for wonderful beach vacations, but yet not so much that that the north and south poles melt away and ruin nature's balance."

Finally, David snapped himself out of his self-induced trance. When he regained his conscious composure, he turned to Jesus and timidly asked, "Was Jesse's algorithm correct?"

Jesus looked at David with a very matter of fact demeanor and said, "Yes, it was absolutely correct. His assumption to apply the solutions of a projectile motion vector in conjunction with a kinematic equation in three-dimensional space to time travel was monumental. Unfortunately, the original time travel hypothesis, furnished from previous military scientific work, related to speed and heat is flawed. The particles do not travel through time, as believed, but when they disappear from the here-and-now, they actually disintegrate in the process, regardless of their mass. This leaves the scientist with the appearance that the object traveled through time. The object does not time travel."

The truth of this moment, Jesus' statements, hit David like a ton of bricks! He thought to himself, "Jesus would be the most intelligent man to ever walk the face of the Earth. Jesus, one of the Trinity, did not need mathematical equations to capture relationships in science, Jesus was the Father of Science. He created it! His mind wasn't brilliant, it was more—He created the human mind! Heck, Jesus created the very Earth that He now walked on!"

"Your capacitor, David" interjected Jesus, "was another ingenious invention. The ability to achieve the capture of such a tremendous amount of kinetic energy during launch and then store it as potential energy by way of a capacitor was phenomenal. Then, to engineer the device to occupy less than one-third the space of the original prototype to suit the limited space availability within Hercules—extraordinary!"

"Thank you," David responded. This was a very proud moment for the young physicist. The very Creator of physics was congratulating him on his feat in that highly complicated field.

Jesus suggested that the group get some sleep. It had been quite a day and it was getting late. Jesus then turned to David and suggested,

"We should try and stay away from the technical conversations. The science is mesmerizing and with your level of modern education we could have day-long discussions on a tremendous number of topics, but we have more important work on which to focus."

As David lay in his tent that night—Nathan and Marcus were now sharing one tent—he pondered over all the information that had been shared with him since he arrived in the camp. He couldn't make sense of it all. He had grown up in what his parents referred to as "a good Christian home," but he felt so uninformed regarding things of religion, or as he would later refer to as truths of the Bible.

Sure, he believed that a man named Jesus did truly live during the times of the New Testament. He had been taught that Jesus was a good man and teacher. He knew that Jesus had established the Christian Church and that He was crucified by the Romans.

As an adult, David felt that he and God had eventually come to an acceptable relationship. David believed in God, Creator of the Heavens and Earth. David knew that he himself was a good man. He provided for his wife and knew that he would be a good provider for his children when they entered the equation. David was a responsible husband, employee, and citizen. Additionally, he attended church on occasion and gave to charities. And he was pretty sure he was baptized as an infant. David had been confident that he and God were in a good relationship, and after all, he could acknowledge God without being some type of a holy-roller.

But now, David was questioning this comfortable place he had thought he and God were sharing. This comfortable place was where Jesus had said Satan actually wanted men to be. Apparently, Jesus was a whole lot more than just a good man and teacher. Jesus was not a created being, He was God. He was the Creator, One of the Trinity, the One who chose to step down from Creator into creation.

Jesus was the only One of the Trinity that took on the body of the created. How did Jesus fit into David's relationship with God? Surely Jesus was a very important part of the framework.

"Why? Why did Jesus step down from heaven? What purpose did

He serve in so doing?" David recalled that Jesus had said He was a blood sacrifice. "Really?," David questioned to himself, "the Father requires a blood sacrifice. His own Son!"

He also wondered why his parents never taught him that Jesus was part of the Trinity, that He was God in the flesh. It seems like the most important aspect of Jesus' ministry on Earth. Then he thought, "My parents do not know the full truth." He surmised that millions do not know the full truth.

As his mind drifted, David began to think about home. He decided that when he returned, he would still want to stick with his original game plan and return at 3:31 a.m. on August 16, 2015. He needed to make sure that Jesus was aware of this. Then he thought "Make Jesus aware of it! He is God in the flesh. I am sure He already knows!" David fell asleep with the image of Angela in his mind's eye. His heart was yearning for his best friend—the love of his life. He did not touch his iPhone that night; he fell asleep listening to the music of the desert animals and the whistling of the wind.

David awoke very early the following morning. He crawled out of his tent and into a quiet campsite. It appeared that he was the only one awake. He laughed to himself as he wondered what Nathan and Marcus did each night while he and Jesus slept. Did they pretend-sleep, play possum?

David decided to take a walk and headed east toward the sunrise. It was a beautiful sunrise. The sky was without a cloud and bright orange rays of sun were bursting from the eastern horizon. After walking for about twenty minutes, David noticed Jesus kneeling under a large tree near a wide stream directly ahead of him. It was a beautiful setting. David had noticed since his arrival that this Judean wilderness had these wonderful oases scattered about. This was one of them.

David quietly approached Jesus and noticed that His head was bowed and He was speaking. The language was unrecognizable and David deduced it was probably Jesus' native Aramaic that He had referred to the other night. Jesus was praying to God the Father. Jesus heard David, stood up, smiled, and motioned for David to join Him.

"You sure spend many an hour praying," David announced. "And You seem to want to do it away from the camp," he added.

"Yes, and yes," Jesus answered. "You see, My time here on Earth is coming to a close, and My most difficult work is ahead of Me. Prayer with God the Father supplies Me with spiritual strength as the end approaches, and prayer also allows Me to honor Him. I prefer to be in a quiet place with no distractions when I pray. I also enjoy being outside and experiencing nature—this oasis setting with the trees and the meandering stream is beautiful.

"I am here in the desert to face Lucifer, the Devil, the Prince of this World. It is a faceoff unlike any I have experienced with him in the past and, believe Me, we have an extensive past. In this faceoff, I am bound to this human body. My Father will allow Satan to test My spiritual strength—no, My Father actually requires this Satan-test."

Jesus added, "The future of mankind now rests squarely on My shoulders. Remember when Nathan explained to you that only pure and perfect creatures can exist in heaven? Well, that is true. So, when We decided to create mankind knowing that he would fall, a requirement arose. The remnant of mankind that would eventually choose good over evil—choose God over all else—could not occupy heaven because God the Father could not tolerate their impurity and imperfections. All men sin, commit wrong, during the course of their lives, it is inevitable. By the Father's very nature, He would not—He could not—reward them with heaven.

"This is where My choice comes in. Remember when I said that one of the greatest gifts each man receives from God is eternal life, or more specifically eternal existence, since only the remnant of man will experience eternal life? That some will spend eternity in heaven, but many will spend eternity in darkness, apart from God? My Father mandated that all human beings following Adam's fall would bear the cost of exposing their souls to evil and sin. The cost? Death. 'The wages of sin is death'...this demonstrates just how much the Father hates sin.

"This death," Jesus said as He held up two fingers, "is twofold. First you have the death of the human body, physical death. Additionally, the Fall caused man to be spiritually dead and separated from God. Before Adam sinned, while he was still perfect and living in the Garden of Eden with Us, he was enjoying both physical life and spiritual life. Adam did not deserve either death prior to his fall. When he sinned, he was cast out of the Garden, separated from Us, and he and Eve immediately became spiritually dead. He was cursed to also experience physical death at the end of his life on Earth.

"So," Jesus explained, "only a perfect human being does not deserve death, a perfect human being who is not born into Adam's original sin. You see David, I am that person. My Father is God, My Father is not of Adam's bloodline. I was not born into Adam's original sin. The Holy Spirit came upon My mother, Mary, when she was still a virgin. She became pregnant with Me before she and Joseph married. My birth father is God the Father, not a mortal man. I elected to step down from heaven, to take on the challenge of living a perfect human life."

David interrupted, "Why, Jesus? You came down from heaven and if You live a perfect life, You will not be subjected to death and You will earn the right to return to heaven. What will You have accomplished?"

Jesus explained, "Because, if I am successful, rather than immediately returning to heaven, I have chosen to be killed."

David immediately retorted, "Why? The only human that doesn't deserve death, that doesn't earn death...why will You be killed?"

Jesus replied, "I will be the perfect sacrifice in My Father's eyes for the remnant of mankind. This is the ultimate justice that makes the plan of creation complete; that makes it perfect. The perfect life—the one human not earning death, serving as the blood sacrifice for all the fallen. You see I pay the debt of death for all the saints. This makes the circle complete. We create man to live eternally, man falls in committing sin and is forbidden to live in Our presence. We redeem man through My death, allowing him to return to Us after his physical death by believing in Me. Man glorifies Us and reigns with Us forever in heaven. His eternal life, eternal spiritual life, fulfills its purpose: but only through My sacrifice."

Jesus stopped and thought for a moment, then continued, "After Adam, all men are born into original sin. As I shared with you earlier, men are bound on Earth by the chains of time. Men are also bound by the chains of sin. Sin, over time, destroys the human soul. Unlike time, however, man can be released from the chains of sin on the human side of heaven. Man can break away from the misery and find peace. He finds it with Me: I have the power to break those chains.

"Now, to further explain this time in the desert and the testing of My soul. Satan would love nothing more than to see Me fail in My attempt to rescue mankind. The Father, whose very nature requires justice that is complete, will not allow My death to be considered an authentic sacrifice unless I am genuinely tempted by Satan. I have faced human temptation during My thirty years here on Earth, but now I must face the most challenging of temptation. If I am successful, I will have proven to the Father My perfection as a human being.

"Since I am one of the Trinity, even though I am relegated to a human body, My temptation will be more powerful than the Devil's temptation among other humans. The Father will allow Satan to employ all his supernatural powers in tempting Me. This will occur on My fortieth day here in the desert. I will not have eaten since I arrived, but I will be ready. Each day that goes by, My body grows weaker but through constant prayer, My will grows stronger."

David was dumbfounded. "So," David summarized, "you are the Son of God, and You have elected to come to Earth as a human, God in the flesh, be tempted supernaturally by Satan himself, and then allow Yourself to be killed, experiencing a death that You do not deserve. Essentially sacrificing Yourself for the fallen, all of whom have sinned."

"Precisely," Jesus answered with a look of conviction.

"Then," said David, "all men can be rewarded with an eternal life in heaven because of Your sacrifice."

"Not all men, just a remnant," answered Jesus.

"There is one requirement. One requirement, David; which so many generations have failed to grasp. One requirement that you, David, should know, but you don't!" Jesus spoke sternly. David looked down in embarrassment. "No man can enter the gates of heaven without acknowledging Me as His Savior, recognizing Me as his blood sacrifice to the Father. In the eyes of the Father, the blood of a living creature is the very fundamental sign of life, the life given to that creature by the Trinity.

"You see, the Father can only accept a pure and perfect human being into heaven. No human being is pure and perfect. So, only the men who recognize My sacrifice, My blood, to cover their sins can enter the Kingdom of Heaven. My Father then sees them as perfect, all imperfections cleansed by the blood of the perfect sacrifice. That is why you have heard repeatedly from Me and Nathan that a remnant of mankind will enter heaven, not all of mankind. Most will never choose Me."

As David was taking in all this new knowledge, Jesus could tell that it was a lot. "Let's head back and see what Nathan and Marcus are up to," Jesus suggested.

When they arrived back at camp, David ate a cold breakfast that the angels had prepared much earlier. Nathan and Marcus were now tending to the donkeys. Jesus asked David if he had brought any type of notebook or journal. David told Jesus that he had brought a journal but had struggled with writing in it.

"My problem is this," David explained, "when I return home, no one will believe that I have spent forty days in the desert with Jesus Christ and two angels named Nathan and Marcus. And furthermore, I don't believe many would believe all the overwhelming things that I have learned since I have been here."

"It is a disgrace, isn't it," Jesus stated.

"What is?" asked David.

Jesus resumed, "Do you know the bestselling book of your time David, or more specifically of all time? In that book, available to the entire world, almost all that I have shared with you is explained. It is the Holy Bible and by the year 2015, billions of copies have been printed and they have been printed in thousands of languages. In the Bible is the nature of God the Father, My reason for coming to Earth as a man, My ministry on Earth, the need for a perfect sacrifice, and the importance for men to choose Me as their Savior. It's all there!

"Establishment of the Jewish law and the need for blood sacrifices to atone for sin," Jesus was counting off His points with the fingers of His right hand, "the twelve tribes of Israel, Jerusalem and the Holy Temple, the predictions of the prophets along with the fact that many of those predictions have been fulfilled, and the most important thing for the generations following My physical death."

"The most important thing?" asked David.

"My resurrection!" proclaimed Jesus. "My resurrection—conquering Death! My dead body will be laid in a cave following My crucifixion, then on the third day I will rise from the dead. This is Indisputable Proof to mankind that I indeed am God in the flesh. Thus, knowing that I am God in the flesh demonstrates to man the validity of My teachings and My deity. The Bible clearly indicates that hundreds of people will see Me following My resurrection. Hundreds of eyewitnesses to My victory over death itself!

"Here is the problem, David, only a few dig into this book and learn. Only a few see it as important enough to read and understand. The book is the User's Manual for Life. It is the *Holy Bible*! It is the most import-ant, tangible gift bestowed upon your world from the Trinity, yet it is ignored!"

Jesus paused and collected himself, He had become quite emotional. The emotion was anger and it was obvious.

Jesus continued, "Even though the book is everywhere, most people would probably not believe your account of our time together and the facts that you have just learned, because most haven't read the book! And this, David, is why you are here. You were brought here to write a letter, similar to the writings of the apostle Paul. Paul will, over the next century, write a large portion of the New Testament. This is another fact that you should already know. All of his books in the Bible will be letters written to various Christian communities or individuals—letters to the Corinthians, Thessalonians, Philippians, and so on.

"David, your purpose in fulfilling the will of My Father is to write a letter to the nations of your generation. Alert them about the urgent need for learning the truth of the Bible, share with them the details of your time here with Me, and urge them to respond to the beckoning of the Spirit! Remind them that the Bible was written many centuries ago and that they need to seek to understand it. This requires studying the customs and traditions at the various times throughout history, thus giving the chapters and books their full meaning. They must study in order to understand and then apply this knowledge moment-by-moment in their lives. They will grow through the ever-present power of the Holy Spirit within those who choose to follow Me.

"Now before you begin writing your letter, there is something I need to do." Jesus approached David and placed His hands on top of David's head. He said a very short prayer under His breath during which David felt a pulse of energy travel through his head. "There," Jesus announced, "done."

"With what?" David asked.

"You need the full knowledge of the Holy Bible in order to write your letter. You haven't read it. So I have blessed you with it," Jesus answered. David felt embarrassed. Jesus added, "I have blessed you with knowledge of the complete Bible, including the New Testament which, as of today, has yet to be written." Jesus finished and excused Himself to return to prayer.

"Please wait, Jesus," David called out. "One more thing. Why me? Why did You pick me?"

"Easy," Jesus answered, "We know your heart. We don't just see you as you are today. We see you for what you will become with Us—complete. This will occur as you fulfill the purpose for your life."

Excitement began to slowly well-up within David. Now God's purpose for him was becoming tangible: the trip through time, this awesome experience with Jesus, and now David himself writing this letter to take back and share with his people, the nations of his generation.

David had a wonderful dream that night. He saw himself returning to NASA as he piloted Hercules back to the cradle of Catapult, with God's help of course. Stuart immediately would call a press conference where David would brief the world on his travels through time and across the Earth to Israel. David Hart, the first time traveler in history. He would speak of his personal experience with Jesus Christ and His angels in the Judean Desert.

He would alert his generation to read and learn the Holy Bible, "The User's Manual for Life." He would publish and share his *Letter to the Nations*. He felt sure it would hit the *New York Times'* bestseller list during its first week of release. David saw himself appearing on *The Tonight Show* and conducting an intimate interview with *Oprah*. He envisioned himself giving impassioned sermons in mega-churches where converts would flock down the aisles in droves.

CHAPTER 7

DAVID'S CHOICE

Our new author awoke early the following morning with a beaming smile on his face and a specific purpose in his heart. He was motivated, yet somewhat overwhelmed, with all his new knowledge. He was amazed as he reflected on his Bible learning through Jesus' miracle yesterday. Having experienced the Bible as if he had read it from cover to cover, David felt what many devoted Christian men and women had surely felt over prior centuries.

When you have read the Bible from beginning to end, you know God in a new way. All the loose ends come together and you are better prepared to contribute in a relationship with your Creator. You feel the faith well-up in your soul as you come to know the truth. He sensed that the Trinity specifically blessed each individual who completed the task of reading the complete Bible.

What amazed him the most, were all the references and support in the Bible for Jesus truly being God in the Flesh during His ministry on Earth. He now knew that Jesus was the only reason that creation occurred, because without a solution for the Fall of mankind, there would have been no need to create man. Jesus is that solution.

Another significant truth that he learned with all his new knowledge was how real God was. He had always envisioned God as an older, gentle grandfather-type. This gentle God was the one that David felt he had developed a comfortable relationship with. This was his fabricated vision of God, the God that would let just about everyone enter heaven. Now that he had experienced God, especially in the Old Testament, David knew how his prior vision of God could not have been further from the truth.

God was mighty and powerful, the very force that not only created the universe, but controlled the universe and permeated everything within it. He wasn't powerful, He was All Powerful. God has many personality traits that an older, gentle grandfather does not have. God is a God of wrath. He is a jealous God. In the Old Testament, God handed over many a vicious army to the Israelites in battle. God is a demanding Father with tangible expectations of His children. David realized that God is to be feared and that facing Him on Judgment Day as an unbeliever would be devastating. God should be feared just like a child should fear a strong and responsible parent.

Along with this appreciation for God's nature, David also had a much deeper appreciation for the definition of sin. Up to this time in his life, the word sin was an odd one for David. He couldn't grasp its meaning. He couldn't relate to sin, so when church leaders preached against sin and its evil, it never really 'hit home' with David. Well, the Bible changed all that!

Now that David had the knowledge of the Bible between his ears, he was very aware of the meaning of sin. Sin, in a nutshell, is action against God the Father. He now understood the nature of God, so anything that went against that nature was sin. So since God is all that is good and right in the world, sin is all that is evil and wrong in the world. "Oh, and one other thing," David said to himself, "God hates sin! He cannot tolerate the sight of a sinner."

As he reflected on sin, David realized that one of the greatest sins he had committed as an adult, and probably one of the greatest sins that American adults were committing in the year 2015 was inaction. One of Satan's favorite cards to play is complacency—complacency toward learning the Bible, toward recognizing the urgency of salvation, toward fellow humans living in poverty, toward active church support, and on and on and on...

David felt a strong desire to pray. He eased out of the camp and went to the oasis where he had happened upon Jesus praying the previous day. David knelt down, and for the first time in his life lifted up an authentic, heart-felt prayer to God the Father.

David's prayer time was an emotional experience for him. He was new to the "prayer thing" but was able to assemble a very appropriate prayer based on all the biblical knowledge that Jesus had blessed him with. David had a simple purpose with his prayer. He asked God to forgive him; to please forgive him. He asked for forgiveness for his neglect of the Bible, his inactive church life, and his ridiculous belief that he and God were in a comfortable relationship. As he was closing his prayer, and as tears were streaming down his cheeks, he said, "And dear Father, please forgive me for the greatest oversight in my life up until this day—my ignorance of the debt paid by Your Son, Jesus Christ."

Jesus walked up and knelt next to David. As David was about to close his prayer, Jesus gently laid His hand on David's shoulder. "David," said Jesus, "at this point in a prayer like this, you would ask Me to become your Savior, as you place your life in My hands. So, if that is indeed your wish, you can do that now."

David looked in Jesus' eyes and said, "King Jesus I want You to become my Savior. I want to join the remnant of mankind that enters heaven knowing that You are the blood sacrifice for me, that You are the only way for me to spend eternity in heaven glorifying my God, the Trinity." The two men embraced, both emotional; David's heart full of thankfulness and Jesus' heart full of love.

Jesus placed a hand on each of David's shoulders and proclaimed, "Your salvation is secure forever!" David smiled from ear to ear.

Jesus continued, "You are spiritually alive, you now have eternal spiritual life! From this day forward you will spend eternity with Us. There is but one death in your future, and that is the death of the body."

David asked, "Jesus, if I had died in my attempt at time travel last week, would I have been headed for eternity away from God, to hell?"

"Yes," Jesus affirmed with sadness, "You had allowed yourself to become content without seeking to know the truth. Up until our time together here in the desert, you had never acknowledged My sacrifice for you. David, you must convey in your letter that ignorance of the truth is not an acceptable excuse to the Father."

David already knew the correct answer to his question; he just needed Jesus to confirm it. David knew that he had become *of age* around twelve or thirteen years old, yet he had never had a genuine moment in his life since then, where he chose Jesus to become his Savior. Heck, he didn't even know before his time here in the desert, that Jesus was the only way to gain entry into God's kingdom.

Jesus continued, "There is something else we need to do while we are here by the stream. You need to be baptized. John the Baptist just recently baptized Me. It is an act of symbolic obedience." David understood.

The two men entered the stream and walked to the middle, the stream was about three feet deep at its center. Jesus looked David squarely in the face and said, "David, I baptize you in the name of My Father, Myself, and the Holy Spirit. I lay you below the surface, indicating the death of Adam's David." At that point Jesus completely submerged David beneath the surface of the water.

"And now I raise you up," Jesus said while raising David back to his standing position, "signifying the birth of your new and eternal life through and with Me. Congratulations David, you are the only person of your generation that will ever physically be baptized by Me." The two men walked out of the stream and back onto the bank.

"Jesus," David wondered out loud, "the New Testament teaches that following Your sacrifice on the cross, all Christians will be blessed with the gift of the Holy Spirit living within them at the time of their salvation decision. I realize that Your time on the cross is still three years into the future from now, so will I not receive the Holy Spirit until after I return home at the end of the forty days?"

"Good point," Jesus stated as He smiled with approval at His young protégé. "As you correctly stated, until My sacrifice on the cross, it is the holy priests who serve as the primary intermediaries between God and man. The Old Testament, however, does provide examples of special saints being filled with the Spirit prior to My day on the cross. These special saints were blessed with God's presence in their souls, though it did not happen often."

"I know," David moped as he looked at the ground in disappointment.

"But…," Jesus continued, "David, you are a special saint. You are My disciple and the chosen one to write the *Letter to the Nations*. You need the Spirit's presence in your soul for such a significant task."

David looked up as a smile grew from ear to ear. Jesus looked at David and saw that even David's eyes were smiling with excitement. Jesus turned to David and instructed, "Please kneel to the ground and close your eyes."

David kneeled while Jesus stood directly in front of him, He raised and spread His arms toward the heavens. Jesus spoke loudly and with authority, David assumed that the language was Aramaic. Even though David had no idea what the words meant, he was confident that Jesus was speaking to the Holy Spirit Himself. When David closed his eyes he could sense a small breeze begin to whirl around and around the tiny oasis. Within minutes he was somewhat frightened as he and Jesus became engulfed in the midst of a full-fledged whirlwind. Jesus finished speaking.

David sensed a calming sensation engulf him as the fear vanished— he felt at complete peace as the whirlwind reached its peak. The whirl-wind slowly subsided and Jesus said, "Welcome, David, to a spiritual relationship with Us. You have been blessed with the presence of the Spirit in your soul. Always remember to cherish the fact that your body is now a temple of God. Care for your body and protect this temple."

David slowly returned to his feet. He felt as though he could have floated right off the ground, much like Nathan. He was overcome with a sense of contentment. He would not be able to speak for some time.

Once he came down from his spiritual high, David felt so blessed. He thanked Jesus for the gift and promised to guard his temple. "I'm not sure I completely understand what just happened," David related to the human third of the Trinity.

"David, the Holy Spirit is misunderstood so often. The concept of the Trinity is difficult enough of a concept for humans to appreciate. Then, regarding the three individuals of the Trinity, the Holy Spirit is the one most often misunderstood. Here is a wonderful way to view the Holy Spirit—it was the Holy Spirit that came upon Mary, My mother, and caused her to become pregnant with Me. That Holy Spirit is Who each saved soul is blessed with at the time of their salvation. Here is what just happened…the Holy Spirit, God Himself, stepped down from heaven and occupied your soul. How does it feel?"

"It feels spectacular!"

After some time had passed, David's demeanor began to change as he realized how this was the proper relationship to share with God, not the comfortable place that he had previously fabricated.

David's mind began to drift…he started to feel ill.

David felt like he was going to vomit as he reflected on how clueless, or more specifically how useless, of a life he had led up until now. How he had truly believed, prior to this time in the wilderness, that he was heaven-bound and a good Christian man. His spirituality had been a lie, and he was so uninformed about the truths of the Bible that he had 'no idea!' He laughed an eerie laugh as he realized that he actually kept a copy of the Holy Bible on his nightstand at home, but yet he knew nothing of the contents.

The Bible truly was the user's manual for life, but like any other user's manual, it serves absolutely no purpose if it's not read. He was embarrassed as he thought about his Fantasy Football League back home. David and the other five men in the league could spout off statistics from memory on hundreds of players. They knew the players' years in the league, past injuries, colleges attended, body weight, time in the forty-yard dash, the list was endless; but he felt certain that most of them didn't even know the difference between the Old Testament and the New Testament in the Bible.

He reflected on his years in college and the hours upon hours he spent poring through textbooks, attending class, and conducting labs… the endless studying and all-nighters. Yet there was one book that had not received any attention from him all his life, and he now realized that that book was the most important one of all.

Another concept that David had grappled with for years was hell. This whole 'hell thing' sounded like a fairy tale to David, a place of fire and brimstone, what was that all about? But now David had a very clear picture of hell in his mind. It was a place of eternal torment. He realized that human beings are created to live eternally with their Creator.

Existing eternally in hell, completely apart from God, was against nature. All that a soul thrives on—love, acceptance, happiness, goodness, and much more—is all absent in hell. Hell is home for evil, a home for Satan and his demons. It is no place for weak, lost humans; yet millions of humans will call it home forever. He then reflected on Jesus' illustration with the sand grains. David thought, "I wonder how many people have invested in their solitary earthly sand grain not knowing that with that investment they have chosen to sacrifice the millions of sand grains of eternal life? These people need to be enlightened; they need to know that the truth is right there in their Bible."

"David," Jesus continued, interrupting David's intense thought process, "you must emphasize in your letter to the nations that God the Father, by His very nature is justice. Justice requires My sacrifice to gain entrance into the Kingdom. Without choosing Me, justice will not allow entry. It cannot. It must be a personal choice, made by an individual.

"A person will not be rewarded heaven because of church membership, the prayers of family members, infant baptism, or any baptism for that matter, the blessing of a holy leader, or good works; they must accept Me as their Savior. Now, many of these things may be considered good and proper, but—they do not earn salvation. One cannot earn heaven; it is a gift from Me. But one must ask Me for it, acknowledging the sacrifice I have made for that person.

"Your words must be bold, David. They need to rattle men to the point of causing them to want to change. Gentle words will not do—use words that motivate!" Jesus was emphatic. "Now, anyone who truly devotes their life to Me will ultimately perform good works as they grow in their faith. Authentic faith is always exemplified by good works."

"Jesus," David looked at Him and said, "I now appreciate that You are God. How did You derive the courage to do it, to be killed?"

"It's My nature," Jesus answered. "You see I am completely aligned with the Father. We love man! We made him in Our image. We love man in a manner similar to how a couple loves a child. You see, that couple feels like they 'created' that child. With man, We don't feel like We created him, We did create him…it's an even stronger bond. We want to spend eternity with man as he reigns with Us. So, with the creation of man came My desire to give to him the right of entry into the kingdom. I must die on that cross for My Father and for man.

"My death on the cross will be horrible. Suffering, however, is something that I, the Father, and the Holy Spirit are very familiar with," Jesus explained. "I know it sounds crazy, but We have suffered much. After the initial creation, We were forced to destroy all of mankind, less eight people, because of the rampant evil. This of course was the great flood during Noah's time. That was extremely painful.

"When Our people, the Israelites, served as slaves to the Egyptians for hundreds of years—that was difficult. The frustrations with the Israelites in the desert led by Moses wandering about for forty years caused many a tear in heaven. When the Israelites turned to worshiping false gods on several occasions, Our hearts were broken. The burning of the Holy Temple and destruction of Jerusalem was a tragedy."

Jesus continued with His eyes clearly fixed on visions in His mind, "After My death and resurrection, thousands of Christians, including most of My apostles, will be killed for their faith in Me. But before that, I, the Father's only Son, must be killed.

"Ironically, a great deal of the suffering that We experience is a direct result of things that We either allow or cause to occur. These things must be done to align with Our perfect nature. It's similar to the pain a good parent experiences when they administer proper discipline of their child. As long as mankind is battling the enemy on Earth, it is the

Trinity that is still fully engaged with the happenings in the world."

"Jesus," David assured, "I'll make sure and include the suffering of the Trinity in my letter as well."

David headed back to camp as Jesus stayed for his morning prayer time. David heard some noises just north of the camp as he approached. He recognized the voices; it was Marcus and Nathan. He headed in the direction of their voices, and as he got closer, he heard laughter.

The brook that ran near the camp fed into a larger stream north of the camp, probably the same stream that flowed by the oasis where Jesus chose to pray. This is where the two angels were—they were playing in the larger stream. As they came into view, David was surprised to see the two angels swimming (not necessarily a pretty sight). He ran over, stripped down to his skivvies, and jumped in. As David joined in, Nathan suggested that he and David enter into a little contest. Nathan challenged David to see who could hold their breath under water the longest.

"You are on!" David said. "On the count of three. One, two, three…," and under the water the two contestants went. David was thinking to himself that he was a dead-cinch winner. How long could Little Chunk hold his breath? After what seemed like an eternity, David surfaced first, gasping for fresh air. Nathan slowly surfaced afterward and smiled at David. He was not gasping for air, but grinning like a cat.

"Did I forget to tell you the other day," asked Nathan, "that in addition to not requiring food and sleep, we angels don't require oxygen either? I am the champ!" Nathan quickly waded out of the water and performed an obnoxious victory dance on the bank.

David bid his angel friends farewell for a while, returned to his tent, put on some dry clothes, retrieved his journal, and ventured out from camp. As he walked, he remembered something he had heard so many people say over the course of his life. "Why would a good God let so many bad things happen, especially to good people?" As he reflected on Jesus' recent comments about suffering, he realized the answer.

First, God knew that suffering was a necessary part of life with man, and second, God Himself suffered a great deal. It wasn't like He was allowing men to suffer while He was immune to it. "No," he whispered, "Suffering is actually something that the Trinity and man have in common. It is important."

"We learn and grow from suffering," was David's conclusion. He wondered about the Jewish holocaust, knowing that Israel was God's chosen people, and how God must have suffered immensely during those years. He then contemplated what it would be like to allow Your only Son to suffer a horrible death at the hands of barbarians when You had the power to stop it, yet You knew allowing it was the right thing to do. God is so true to His nature that Jesus' crucifixion had to occur to allow men an opportunity for eternal life.

As he walked, David found a large odd-shaped boulder with a flat top at the foot of a small cliff. At this time of the day, the cliff protected the boulder from the sun. He climbed up on the boulder's flat top, sat down, crossed his legs, and began to write.

"A Letter from David Hart, a disciple of Jesus Christ, to the Nations of the World…" (imitating Paul's writing style from the New Testament). David stopped and reflected on those words in his journal. A strong, peaceful feeling came over him. He realized that for the first time in his life, he was working on something that was strictly for the good of others and not for the next paycheck, or the next atta-boy for a new technological feat on a project.

Over the last several days, his life had dramatically changed and he couldn't have been any happier. Knowing his life's purpose definitely made him a more complete person.

CHAPTER 8

MISSING AND PRESUMED DEAD

David had been missing for over four weeks and Angela was completely exhausted and grief-stricken. The fact that there was no information trail to utilize in tracking down her husband had left the FBI helpless. There was no evidence at the scene of David's disappearance to indicate foul play. Nothing in David's Jeep or office seemed to provide any clues that he had planned to stage his disappearance.

Since that dreadful Sunday, other than Angela's transactions, there was no activity on any of the couple's credit cards, no money had been withdrawn from any of their bank accounts, and not one phone call had been made from David's cell phone. During the first week of the investigation Angela had asked for a temporary leave of absence from work. She was a complete mess. There was no way for her to focus on work.

Jesse's team had been questioned beyond extensively. But try as they might, the FBI could get nothing from a single team member other than "Hercules was a time machine." All the documents retrieved from all of the team members' offices indicated that the project's specific purpose was to build a capsule that would travel through time.

All data on all the PCs used by the team, as well as all data on the sophisticated computers in the control room, supported the time travel position. The FBI was not only helpless, they had become hopeless—hopeless with regard to ever finding David Hart.

The media frenzy had come and gone. The big news this week involved a governor of some southern state whose wife admitted to being in an inappropriate relationship with another woman for the past three years. Any media coverage on the NASA thing was old news. Project 13-03 had been put on ice and the team members had been assigned to other tasks. Stuart had taken it upon himself to fire Jesse Black, citing his oversight regarding lax security measures which allowed a rogue employee to "hijack" a $200 million piece of government property.

Angela's attorney, J. Mark Wilson, had been informed by a posse of government attorneys that if he did indeed choose to file a suit against NASA, he would be disbarred. Additionally, the posse pointed out, that no court in America would allow the wife of a government employee to file suit against the federal government when that employee had breached protocol and stolen government property. J. Mark Wilson couldn't excuse himself from that meeting quickly enough. Mr. Wilson relayed the news of the meeting to Angela and immediately withdrew his services. Angela then contacted Stuart and demanded a meeting—pronto.

Angela met with Stuart soon thereafter. Stuart pointed out that Project 13-03 was a classified military operation. All employees privy to the secret details of that operation, including David Hart, had executed documents under legal oath that released the federal government from any liability associated with loss-of-life while on a mission (other than payment of life insurance benefits, of course). Furthermore, Stuart had filed documents with the military jurisdiction governing NASA, charging David Hart with breach of protocol and theft of government property.

It was evident that Stuart had become one angry man because of this circus and he felt absolutely no compassion for Angela or any of David's family. He then calmly informed Angela, "If you leak one bit of information to the media, family, or friends regarding the technical details of this classified project, you will be arrested by the FBI and prosecuted by the US Judicial Courts as a traitor. The last thing this country needs right now is foreign intelligence agents attempting to steal this coveted time travel technology from us."

It took Angela quite awhile to recover from that horrible meeting with the military-produced, unfeeling, poor excuse of a man. Now, a month after her husband had vanished, she was planning a memorial service for him. The FBI had informed her last week when they withdrew from the case that David was officially 'missing and presumed dead.'

The day they told her, Angela fell apart. It was so easy for the chief FBI agent to look her in the eye and say, "I'm very sorry, Mrs. Hart, but we are closing our investigation and your husband is officially missing and presumed dead. The government will now allow you to claim spousal benefits as a documented widow."

Angela recalled looking at the Chief and responding with, "Why is it so easy for you? You show up here and perform your little investigation. You make sure and check all the proper boxes on each of your dandy little forms, and then you waltz in here and tell me that my husband is presumed dead. You have no more proof that he is dead than you have proof that he is alive!"

Just the word…*dead*. It was so cold, it was so final, and it was so empty. Angela had another strong word in mind. Hate. She hated this predicament. Angela was a kind and caring person but this tragedy was challenging her ability to maintain that demeanor. She felt like she was very close to the point of directing that hatred at individuals like this unfeeling FBI chief or that good-for-nothing John Stuart!

The entire family had been in a state of shock since David's disappearance. David's parents had flown in from their retirement home in Aspen, Colorado and had been staying at the Hart's home with Angela for over two weeks. Early on, when they first arrived, there was lots of anger. Anger primarily focused on Stuart and NASA. The anger eventually gave way to hope. And now, with the grim news from the FBI, the hope was giving way to grief.

Although she didn't share it with David's parents, in addition to grieving for her young husband, Angela was angry with him. Oh, and was there a lot to be angry about! He decides on a whim to sneak off and be *Superman*. He sneaks off without even informing the most important person in his life. It wasn't like he was flying off to Vegas for some crazy, spontaneous evening—he was attempting "time travel" in an unproven capsule with no team support—he was playing the *Lone Ranger*. Well, now she was the *Lone Ranger*, and not by choice. She felt so alone and completely abandoned.

Angela became affectionately known as the wife of the loser NASA employee who had single-handedly destroyed Project 13-03 after two years of painstaking labor and a $500 million investment. "Great," she thought to herself. "If he ever returns, I get to see him receive a military court martial and get sentenced to numerous years in federal prison."

Angela couldn't eat, had absolutely no energy, and had resorted to Ambien to get any type of rest that resembled sleep. Angela was a completely broken person. The thing that she kept asking herself was, "Who can I turn to?" She had made David the center of her universe— her life revolved around him. There was this huge void in her soul, in her life. She was completely alone. Her future? She couldn't envision herself moving forward in life without David. She and Jackie were close, but Jackie had a life. Jackie had a full-time job and a family to care for.

In the complicated craziness of planning David's memorial service, Angela had decided that she needed a break. She called her best friend, Jackie, and asked for a date. "I need to have a drink and I need to talk," Angela confessed to her best friend. "I need some down time."

"You bet," said Jackie. "I've heard the talk floating around NASA that the FBI has been no help whatsoever. Why did I foolishly presume that the FBI was going to get to the bottom of this? I cannot even begin to imagine where you are at emotionally. Let's go on our date tonight."

Jackie picked up Angela early that evening for dinner and drinks. The duo headed to Landry's Seafood Restaurant at the Kemah Boardwalk. Angela loved Jackie's choice of restaurant and the boardwalk at Kemah was the perfect environment. Kemah is located on Galveston Bay and is only a twenty minute drive from Clear Lake City. The setting would allow the two friends to stroll along the boardwalk, experience the atmosphere of the bay, and share conversation after dinner. There were several restaurants and stores along the boardwalk, along with live music and other healthy distractions. And oh, how Angela needed some distraction!

During dinner Angela had brought Jackie completely up to speed on all the latest news. Now, having left the restaurant, the two meandered along the boardwalk trying to enjoy each other's company.

Angela concluded, "Dismal, isn't it?" as she reflected on all the news, "every piece of new information is bad. There is absolutely no good news. It appears that my husband will never surface. It appears that I am officially a widow. I'm not even thirty years old and I have already become a widow! How can that be, Jackie? What's that crappy saying? 'If it wasn't for bad luck, I would have no luck at all.'"

Jackie squeezed Angela's hand and stated in a reassuring tone, "The news will get better. The truth will come out. This dilemma is far from over."

As Jackie replayed her own statements in her mind, she wondered if she even believed them herself. The news was awful, David was missing, and too much time had passed. How could you search for a missing individual with no evidence, no leads, and no witnesses? Angela was right. She was, most likely, a widow. Jackie swallowed hard as she reflected on that last statement.

"I've got a wonderful idea!" exclaimed Jackie as she managed to produce a happy face in hopes of causing her friend to smile. "I want to buy you a margarita at the Cadillac Bar and Grill! They make the most awesome margaritas."

"Now that's the best offer I've had in days!" responded Angela as a smile gradually developed across her beautiful face. Her beauty showed through, despite the faded mascara lines that marked the length of both her cheeks. The Cadillac Bar was right there on the boardwalk. The two women headed in that direction.

Three hours later, Jackie guided Angela to the car after Angela had polished off her third margarita. Jackie had resorted to chips, salsa, and water after her first drink but continued to feed her friend the liquid potion that numbed her mountain of pain. "Even though the numbness is only for a night," Jackie surmised, "this poor soul needs it. Her life is the definition of misery. I know it will eventually get better but only God knows when and by what means."

Jackie had no idea how wise that last statement would turn out to be!

CHAPTER 9
THE MEN

As the days turned into weeks, *The Letter to the Nations* was growing in length and spiritual depth. David had spent a significant amount of his time clarifying some key issues with Jesus. Nathan and Marcus kept relatively quiet during this time as they sensed that both of their human companions were keenly focused on their tasks.

Nathan and Marcus focused on upkeep of the camp, cleaning and cooking (for David), washing clothes, and tending to the donkeys. David was completely immersed in his book while Jesus was fasting, praying, and teaching David. David could tell that Nathan missed spending time with him; Nathan was pouting a lot. David questioned the very concept of an angel pouting—their entire existence was complemented with the constant presence of God. Maybe Nathan was putting on a show to make David feel missed.

One evening as the four of them were visiting around the campfire, winding down another hot day in the desert, David announced, "I have been here in the wilderness for thirty-three days. I have spent thirty-one of those days with the three of you, for which I am forever thankful. I feel that my letter will be completed by the time day number forty rolls around and I hope, Jesus, that the finished product will please both You and God the Father."

Jesus smiled and replied, "I have full faith in you and the content of your letter, David."

David informed Jesus that he still had a few important concepts to clarify and wanted to discuss them on the following day. Jesus immediately agreed. Jesus also told David that He had a few additional items He wanted to share with him for inclusion. As they all disappeared into their tents for the night, David laid reflecting about the last thirty-three days. This had truly been the adventure of a lifetime. What was so odd was the setting.

Here he was in the wilderness in an era with no electricity, no phones of any kind, no means of modern transportation, no air conditioning, no comforts of life as he knew it. He was eating bland food and sleeping on the ground. He spent a large portion of his day alone, writing in a journal in the arid heat. Yet here he was, David Hart, NASA physicist, calling this the adventure of a lifetime.

He was starting to realize that life was all about values. This was something he definitely needed to include in his letter. David began to ponder on this. God created man to give Him glory. God is a God of love, a God of relationship. So He creates man, and the very first man created falls from grace. So God remedies this Himself by sending Jesus the Son.

Jesus steps down from heaven, pays the debt for man's fall with His human life, rises from the dead proving that He indeed is God, and ascends back to heaven. Then God ensures that future generations have the Holy Bible which documents all these things, especially the resurrection. So what are God's values?

God's values? Obviously mankind is something God values immensely. What else? God is love, life, holiness, power, intelligence, truth, righteousness, beauty, and so much more. And oh, don't forget justice! What was now obvious to David is what Jesus had explained earlier. God's personality traits are the very characteristics of a great relationship, this fourth dimension of heaven.

David deduced that the problem with man, especially educated men of David's generation, was how man had grown so far from his Creator. Man was all about money, dominance, immediate gratification, materialism, and self-advancement. How could man glorify his Creator when man had chosen to become all that God wasn't? How could man expect to spend an eternity in heaven with a God he had nothing in common with? God would never allow such a ridiculous calamity.

Men of David's generation wanted to make God in their image. They wanted Him to understand the fundamental importance of the almighty dollar, to understand that their lives had grown so busy that they did not have time for church or Bible study, to understand that if you didn't squash your competition at work, then the competition would squash you. Surely God could understand that after the work week, Saturday was errand day and Sunday was for rest and televised professional sports—not for church. The world had become so complicated; it was nothing like the world during the time that Jesus walked on the face of the Earth. God needed to adjust.

"No!" David rolled this over in his mind. "No! Don't be such fools. Here is what men need to understand! God—*Elohim*, created man in Their image. Men must humble themselves before their Creator and honor God's nature. The nature of the Trinity is the very reason that man was created to begin with. Men must grasp the truth, regardless of how much it goes against their sinful nature, that things of heaven are more important than things of this world."

David spoke to himself as if he were addressing the men of his time, "How are you going to fit that BMW and powerboat into your coffin? Or better yet, how are you going to explain to your children in the darkness of hell, that the reason you didn't have them in church on most Sundays was because you were a devout fan of the Houston Texans, Astros, and Rockets?" These were powerful concepts that David needed to include in the letter.

Jesus says love your neighbor. David didn't know most of his neighbors. Jesus says take care of the poor, the widows, and the orphans. David had never befriended and helped any people like that. Jesus expected man to attend church regularly. David went once or twice a year. God expected a tithe of obedience; David may have placed a twenty dollar bill in the offering plate on the rare occasions when he attended church. David felt ashamed as he realized that he had spent more money on bottled water in his life than he had in giving to Godly causes.

God said have no other Gods before Me. David now realized that his gods were his wife, his job, his home, his toys (cars, flat-screen TVs, computers), and his 401K. Jesus was selfless. David felt selfish, but was ready to change.

"Damn it," David said to himself. "I am a product of my times, but I am also a product of my choices." He now knew that the old David had fabricated this comfortable relationship between himself and God. Why? Because it was a cop-out. Because he wanted to be like most men in the rat race, climbing up that career ladder, padding that savings account, continually upgrading the size and prestige of the house and automobiles, blah, blah, blah…

His life's dreams, his life's goals had nothing in common with heaven. They were in no way aligned with his Creator. Yet he, and millions just like him, believed he was a good guy and heaven-bound after his days on Earth ran out. What a joke! What a sad, sad joke!

Ironically though, Jesus had pointed out a very significant aspect of the whole rat race thing. He explained that a Christian man who has secured his salvation and is a devout follower of Jesus can still be successful while on Earth. A Christian can become wealthy, can rise to the top of a corporation, can own an expensive home…God wants to bless His people with success. The key is to cherish God first—then He has the option to bless a person in many ways, one of those ways is financial success. The financially successful Christian should help to further God's kingdom with this blessing. But success, however, comes in many various forms—wisdom, good health, commendable parenting, and so on. The key is that the true Christian is driven to utilize this success in the furthering of God's kingdom, not just his own.

Look at the Israelites. They went from slavery in Egypt to conquering the Canaanites and claiming the Promised Land. In other words, God brought them from slavery in Egypt to the land that is present-day Israel. Then He blessed their armies and they conquered, with God's constant aid, all the armies from this region and made it their own. David really liked this story. It further supported his position that God was in no way this old grandfather God he had previously pictured. "Old," he repeated to himself in amusement, "God has no age; He is not bound by the chains of time. He is timeless!"

David also realized how blessed he was to be chosen for this mission. Not only had he learned a lot, but in the process he had aligned himself with his Creator. He knew that he was heaven-bound. He also knew that he was now ready to align his priorities with God's priorities.

His mind instantly converged on a startling thought, "What about Angela? Angela needs to know the truth, and she needs to know the truth now!" David didn't even want to consider the possibility of an eternity in heaven for himself unless he could at least share this truth with the one he loved the most on the human side of heaven.

After realizing the urgent need to share with his wife, David began to appreciate just how many people in his life were lost. He started mulling over in his mind the list of those he knew who were lost: his mother, his father, many of his close friends and coworkers, and several other relatives. Ironically though, almost every one of these people, if asked, would honestly proclaim to be heaven-bound. Like David, prior to his newly attained salvation, they were all relatively good and responsible people who felt they were in a comfortable relationship with God. Sometime in the midst of all these thoughts bouncing around in his mind, David fell asleep.

David tossed and turned as his dreams continually disturbed his attempts at achieving some peaceful rest. Periodically, he would speak out in his sleep. Some of the words were recognizable, while many others were just garbled and fragmented.

In the midst of David's restlessness, Jesus entered his tent and gently shook him awake. David immediately sat up and mumbled some unrecognizable sound. "You have been dreaming, my friend," Jesus said as He let out a subtle laugh, "and it sounded like unpleasant nightmares. So I thought it best to wake you. I heard you mention Angela's name several times. You even shouted once or twice."

David nodded as he wiped a small amount of sweat from his forehead.

"They were nightmares alright. With all my new knowledge, I have become concerned about so many of my family and friends. I want them to understand the importance, or should I say the need, of establishing a relationship with You. They need to know that You are the only way to heaven, to eternity as it is meant to be experienced. In my dreams, I keep attempting to return home in Hercules but I always end up somewhere else in time and space."

"I am so pleased to see this predicament stir your soul," Jesus said. "Sharing the good news of salvation is what the first Christian churches will soon call the Great Commission. It is My Great Commission. The message needs to be conveyed with great urgency, especially when you come to appreciate that the population of the Earth in 2015 is in excess of six billion souls."

"I am definitely ready to get back to that world and share Your message, Jesus. There is something else that has been bothering me as well."

"What's that?" Jesus asked.

"The men," David stated.

"The men?"

"Yes. When I reflect on my world, the world of 2015, the men are too busy. Especially the American men. Most of us work forty to sixty hours per week, then we spend our Saturdays on yard work, handyman projects, and kids' sports. When Sunday finally rolls around, we want some downtime. I know because I have lived it! This presents a huge problem, because I now know that our men's priorities are, well, they are so…wrong. Each one of us has been blessed with the gift of life and most of us fail to give any honor to the Creator that made that very life possible."

"I fully agree!" Jesus nodded His head.

"Then to add to the whole convoluted mess, I have another issue with our men! So many of them—I mean us, think that outwardly professing to be a devout Christian is a sign of weakness. In a world of men focused on careers, families, professional sports, individual sports, and toys—cars, boats, guns, golf clubs—there appears to be no place for the modern Christian man." David continued, "I now know that I need to realign all the priorities in my life, thanks to this wonderful experience with You, Nathan, and Marcus. I need to place You in the center of my world. But, somehow, I need to convey this to all the men of my generation."

Jesus grinned and once again said, "I agree."

"I think that the society of my world expects to see rugged men. You know, tough guys. Guys that can make the big play under pressure. In the corporate world, the big play may be acquiring a competitor for one-hundred million dollars. As the head of a household, the big play may be installing a swimming pool, complete with a Jacuzzi and water-fall in the backyard. Within a group of outdoorsmen, the big play may mean climbing to the summit of a mountain in the Rockies. And on and on…. Our world doesn't view Christian-focused men as big play-makers." David explained.

"Yes," Jesus nodded, "I am well aware of these big plays and their supposed importance. David, I think that the men of your generation need to understand that, with God, these big plays that drive them are readily available, but with just one exception."

"One exception?"

"Yes. With God, big plays have the potential to be huge plays."

"I don't understand…how do I express that in my letter?"

"Easy!" Jesus proclaimed. "Explain to the men of your generation that a God who created the Heavens and Earth, a God who created the human body, is a God perfectly capable of orchestrating huge plays in their lives. What better team to play on than God Almighty's? God longs for His children to succeed, to grow."

"I love that concept," David said. "I just don't know how to convey it in my letter."

"Look at King David. He aligned himself with God and progressed from the lowly existence of a shepherd boy to the reigning king of one of the most powerful nations on Earth. He became a mighty warrior and a leader of men. From shepherd boy to powerful King—that must be a huge play."

"I would definitely call that huge!" David agreed as he nodded his head.

Both men were fully awake now. "Joseph," Jesus continued, "was sold into slavery by his older, jealous brothers. He eventually found himself in prison in a foreign country—Egypt. Joseph was very outspoken about his love for God, even in prison. Joseph systematically rose from foreign prisoner to the second most powerful man in Egypt, directly under the Pharaoh. Joseph then used his powerful influence to rescue his family from famine and relocate them to Egypt. I would also call that a huge play."

"Another great example," added David. "I wonder about modern day examples?"

"Rick Warren comes to mind," Jesus said as he pondered the question. "Rick has become so successful that he actually reverse tithes. Rick founded a small Christian church in California in 1980 with a handful of new members. Today he is recognized worldwide as a pastor, author, global strategist, theologian, and philanthropist. Growth of his church and his ministry has been exponential—he has thousands of followers. Rick is able to live quite comfortably off 10% of his income while he gives the remaining 90% to Christian causes. He is a great modern example of Christian success."

"I would have to agree. He sounds like one accomplished guy."

"And over the years, David, We have blessed thousands of Our children with success. One must just keep it all in perspective. In Our eyes, success is so much more all-encompassing than in the eyes of the world. A hard-working single mother in Houston, Texas who organizes the area's meals-on-wheels program is a success to Us. The businessman who left the corporate world in New York City to earn his degree from a seminary and is now leading a small Christian church in upstate New York is a success to Us. The examples are endless.

"Yes, David, men of your generation need to fully comprehend that, with God on their side, they can accomplish so much more. It always helps to have the supernatural on your side as you progress through life. The Trinity wants to help Christians accomplish great success as those individuals fulfill their God-given purposes. Ironically, through history, most devout Christians have failed to achieve all that was attainable."

"Why is that?" David inquired. "With the Trinity on their side, what was holding them back?"

"Themselves!"

"I don't understand," rolled out of David's mouth as he gave Jesus a bewildered look.

"So many followers underestimate the magnitude of Our love. They set their goals too low, too safe, too comfortable. We want the best for Our children, just like most parents do. Tell Christian men, David, in your letter, to rise up. Challenge them to read the Bible and get close to their Creator. Once they have established a close walk with Us, the opportunities are without limit."

Jesus continued, "Christian men need to realize how BIG their God is. David, it is so frustrating for Us when a son We love has the inborn potential to be the CEO but he settles on becoming the district manager. Do you see the irony in this? We want to experience this journey to the top with him, but he sells Us and himself short. I will rise from the dead, I will walk on water; surely I can bring the supernatural to the lives of the natural Christian men and women We love!"

As David was nodding in agreement, he could tell that Jesus wanted to steer the discussion in another direction. "There is something else I wanted to share with you," Jesus said as he changed topics.

"I realize that we have been talking about all the ways for your generation to get in tune with their Bibles. To study and understand, so they can truly grow into the people they were created to be. But I need to emphasize an important fact regarding the Christian believers of your generation as well.

"David, I am so pleased with the devout Christians of your day. There are an abundance of active, giving, loving believers in the world in 2015. The huge church movement in the United States that has been growing over the last two decades is a commendable force. This movement of non-denominational, Bible-focused churches is winning new souls by the thousands. This movement is so very pleasing to the Father.

The men and women behind this movement truly understand the message of the Great Commission."

"That is definitely some good news for me to include in the letter."

Jesus then added, "But there are so many more souls to win! The population of the Earth continues to grow so rapidly. We need to do so much more!"

David nodded. He had been writing notes in his journal during the majority of this discussion.

Jesus yawned, then David yawned.

"Okay, enough! Let's get some sleep," Jesus said as he crawled out of David's tent.

CHAPTER 10

OF MEN, PRIDE, AND WORSHIP

Early the following morning, David awoke to Jesus gently tugging on his foot. Jesus had reentered his tent to wake him up. "Good morning?" eased out of David's mouth as he looked at Jesus inquisitively.

"Good morning. I want us to take a little trip."

"A little trip. Where are we headed?"

"2015."

"You mean the year 2015?" asked the young American.

"None other," quipped Jesus.

Jesus placed His hand around David's ankle and the two men vanished from the tent.

As David acclimated himself to the new surroundings of their instantaneous destination, he realized that they were now attending a professional football game. The Cleveland Browns were facing the Cincinnati Bengals and the stadium was packed. It appeared to be a bright and sunny Sunday afternoon in Cleveland, Ohio. David and Jesus were there in spirit only but David could still feel the electricity of the crowd. Although he followed the NFL, at least close enough to recognize the teams, David was a much bigger tennis fan.

As David glanced at Jesus, he did a double-take. Along the way, Jesus had apparently thought it best to dress appropriately for the occasion, even if no one else could see them. There he was, God in the flesh, sporting an official Cleveland Browns' jersey. David then saw that he too was in a Browns' jersey. "Well," thought David, "man is made in God's image. It is good to know that God also has a sense of humor."

"Today's topic," Jesus announced, "is worship."

"Worship?" asked David.

"Yes. David, the vast majority of men of your generation claim that outward worship makes them uncomfortable. They claim that raising their hands in church makes them feel foolish. Many claim that singing in church is embarrassing. Furthermore, most do not want to pray publically, volunteer to teach children in church, or lead bible studies. All these things make grown men feel unsettled, or so they claim."

As David reflected on Jesus' words he responded, "I would agree with that. I have not attended church regularly, but the things that you have said make sense. I know that I have felt that way when attending church."

"So, I want to ensure that your letter addresses this issue. I can assure you, David, that the issue has nothing to do with being uncomfortable in public with worship. The issue does, however, have everything to do with what the men have chosen to worship. The Trinity created man to worship, and believe Me when I say that the men of your generation, regardless of all their whining, are very good at worshipping!"

"I assume that we are here in Cleveland for that reason…so I can begin to understand how men do truly worship?"

Jesus grinned and affirmed with, "Great assumption!" He then turned and looked directly at a specific section of fans in the stadium. David turned to focus on that same area.

David read the huge banner that hung in front of the proud men of the Dawg Pound. The Dawg Pound is famous for its devoted, somewhat crazy, fans that love their Cleveland Browns. As David took in the full experience of the Pound, he began to understand Jesus' issue with men and worship. There, and at this moment directly before the very God that created them, the men in the Pound were sporting their famous plastic dog noses, bone shaped hats, and some were even wearing full-faced dog masks.

The Browns offense was on the field driving for a touchdown and the men of the Pound were standing at full attention, cheering on their beloved team, and chanting, "Here we go, Brownies, here we go. Woof!

Woof!" They chanted this over and over again. The leader of the group was orchestrating the chant with great conviction as though he were leading the performance of an award-winning symphony orchestra.

After attempting to restrain himself for more than five minutes, David burst out in laughter. These grown men were a riot. They were definitely in full worship mode and doing a great job. David then questioned the word great. Maybe a more fitting description would be ridiculous, yes, they were doing a ridiculous job. One stern glance from Jesus was all it took and David squelched his outward amusement.

Jesus turned to David while pointing in the direction of the Dawg Pound, "Rituals like this, maybe not to this extreme, are occurring all over America today. Men of this generation worshiping their treasured football teams. It appears to Me that these men are experts at worship. I know that professional football is a very popular sport and that fans do support their teams—fine. The point for your letter is this, 'humans are wired to worship and the act of worshiping is alive and well in the year 2015!' You see the guy, wearing the number fourteen Browns jersey, leading the chant in the front row of bleachers?"

"See him, how can I miss him?" replied David. "He looks to be in excess of six feet tall and over three hundred pounds. He takes his job of orchestrating the Pound very seriously."

"His name is Charlie Edelson, he has been a Christian for twenty years. Charlie attends every home game the Browns play. He is also a season-ticket holder for the Cleveland Cavaliers and he tries to catch at least two dozen of the Cleveland Indian's baseball games each season. He has a good heart but I miss him. He hasn't attended church in more than twelve years and he stopped praying six years ago."

"Why do you think he stopped?"

"His excuse is that he doesn't have the time. He has a demanding job, he and his wife are raising four kids, and he helps his sister in caring for their handicapped mother."

"But, based on what You said about his sporting event attendance, he must clock hundreds of hours per year in the stands at professional football, basketball, and baseball games."

"You're right. He does."

"So, he does have the time."

"Right again. Charlie is the perfect example of the American man who has become too busy for Us. In the process of Charlie determining the importance of his time and where to spend it, he left Us, his Creator and God, out of his time budget."

"How sad."

"Yes, and how wrong!" Jesus responded. "And furthermore, back when Charlie did attend church, he was too uncomfortable to openly worship."

"Well," David declared, "based on his behavior in the Dawg Pound right now, the man definitely has the worship skills. One would be hard pressed to find another fan in the stands worshiping the Browns with the vigor and determination of Charlie. His touchdown dance has to be one of the best in the league."

"Do you think Mr. Edelson is uncomfortable as he worships in public? Do you think that joining-in during the singing of a hymn in church would cause him undue amounts of embarrassment?" Jesus inquired of David.

David looked towards the Dawg Pound and took in an eye-full of Charlie. "I would have to say that not only is Mr. Edelson comfortable with his public worship, I would venture to say that he is downright proud of it!"

Jesus placed his hand on David's shoulder and the two men vanished.

David let out a suppressed cough as he and Jesus arrived at their next destination. The cigarette smoke was thick and the lights were bright. The carpet was plush and the smell of money was in the air. The familiar background sounds of slot machines and live bands immediately led David to believe that they were in a glitzy casino in Las Vegas. And he confirmed his hunch as he read *The Mirage, High Rollers Tables* flashing in bright lights before him.

Jesus peered into David's eyes and said, "This will be a short visit. The extreme amount of money that is wasted in this city is appalling and I do not want to stay here long. But the waste is not the topic for the letter. This visit is about the worship. Follow Me." Jesus' anger was obvious as He walked across the room to the craps table. David followed, but chose to walk very slowly. David had been to Vegas twice in his life. During his last visit, two years ago, he not only learned the rules of the game of craps, but he actually had made craps his game of choice. David was feeling very uncomfortable as he followed Jesus to the craps table.

The two companions stopped just a few feet from the table and watched the crowd. Jesus looked on with anger and disgust. A cowboy named Woody was currently the shooter of the dice. Woody was tall and lanky, his cowboy hat pulled down close to his brow, and he was sipping on a Budweiser longneck. Two young women were on either side of the lanky cowboy and each had an arm wrapped around Woody's thin waist. Periodically one of the women would lean over and kiss Woody on the neck. Neither woman appeared to be jealous of the other. Both were dressed provocatively and eyeing other men at the table. It was obvious that they were working girls.

Each time that he prepared to roll, one of the girls was asked to kiss the two dice in Woody's palm before he flung them across the table. As Woody would shake his dice-filled fist prior to hurling another roll, most of the thirty or so men and women gathered around the table would chant, "Woody, Woody, Woody, Woody, roll…" Then, each time he flung the two dice across the table, a loud roar would ensue. Everyone would survey the results of the throw, clang their glasses together in a victory celebration, and chug their drinks.

Then the process would start all over again.

Jesus looked at David, "Get the idea?" He asked.

"Unfortunately, I do. It looks like we have found some more expert worshipers."

"Yes. But the worshiping always seems to end when the luck runs out and the money dries up. It's so predictable and so insane." Jesus turned to David and proclaimed, "Five billion dollars each year."

"Five billion dollars each year?"

"Yes! That is the revenue of the gambling casinos in Vegas each year."

Jesus looked in the direction of the group plastered around the far end of the craps table. "Do you see the bald guy wearing the navy blue sweater?"

"Sure do."

"His name is Gary Benson. He is forty-five years old and lives in Dallas, Texas. Gary has been a Christian since he was fifteen. He is a hard working husband and father, he has two teenage boys. Gary works hard for his money. He built his own commercial construction company from the ground up. Unfortunately, over the years, Gary has grown to love money more than life itself. Gary loves his money more than his wife. Gary loves his money more than his teenage boys. Gary, and this is hard to imagine, seems to love his money more than he loves himself."

"Yes," David affirmed, "money is the root of all evil."

"No," Jesus shook his head, "not money. It is the *love* of money that is the root of all evil!"

Jesus looked directly at Gary and continued, "Gary quit going to church when he turned thirty-five. That year, was the first year, his business came of age. Mr. Benson's income that banner year was slightly in excess of one million dollars."

"Wow! One million dollars!" exclaimed David. "Why would he stop going to church when his business was growing and doing so well?"

"The love of money."

"What do You mean?"

"Gary was a devoted tither, he always gave ten percent of his income to the church. When he reached the million dollar milestone, he realized that his tithe had grown to $100,000 per year. This fact, as it continuously grated on Gary, pulled him down into a depression. He loved his church and he loved contributing to God's work on Earth, but he felt that his success had caused his tithe to get out of hand. He knew that the tithe was utilized to support good causes, but did they need such a sizeable amount from one individual?

"At first, Gary just started reducing his giving. Every time he reduced the amount he gave, he felt better. It seemed like such a relief to him to keep more money for himself. So before long, Gary was giving very little. When he quit going to church, after a year of routinely reducing his weekend gifts, Gary had ratcheted down to fifty dollars per week. I miss Gary's presence in the church. Down underneath that money-loving crust of his is a loving, giving soul. Gary has just lost himself."

"Why did he quit going to church?" asked David.

"He quit going because his soul was ashamed. The human Gary wanted it all, the money, that is. He wanted all the money. He loved the money. So, the flesh drug the soul out of the church. That is when his downward spiral began. He began cutting corners with his business, to save cash. He reduced the salaries of his employees to below industry standards. He delayed payment of invoices to his suppliers to hold onto the cash as long as possible. He hounded his wife about how she spent the family's money and questioned most of her purchases. Gary truly became a monster. He is now a devoted worshiper of money, his precious money.

"We, the Trinity, do indeed create man with a longing in his soul to worship. And believe Me, David, men of all generations worship. When they choose to worship the wrong thing, that's when their souls suffer. The Bible instructs to 'love the Lord your God with all your heart and with all your soul and with all your strength, and with all your mind.' This is where man needs to direct his worship in order to satisfy his soul. Worshipping anything other than Us leaves one feeling empty in the end."

"So," David asked, "why is Gary here now?"

"This is his favorite place in the world. Gary flies out here by himself five or six times a year. He calls Vegas his happy place. His marriage has become stagnant, he and his sons are no longer close, and he is disliked by most of his employees. His wife refuses to accompany him on these getaways. He really comes here to escape. As long as he is spending money at these tables, every casino employee on this floor makes him feel loved. The love is fake, of course, and Gary knows it. But at this point in his life, he truly believes that this is the only love he can get."

"Does he want to change?"

"Yes, but he fools himself into believing that he doesn't know where to begin."

"I know where he can turn," stated David. "He needs to turn to his Bible! He needs to return to his Maker."

"Exactly! And Gary knows that."

"Will he do it?"

"Yes...eventually." Jesus looked at the floor, then turned to David and said, "But many times with someone like Gary, they must lose much before they return to Our unconditional love. We call it hard grace. Pride, shame, and guilt are hard obstacles to face, especially for a human. And it's even more difficult when that human is a proud man. Right now, this unhappy and emotionally unhealthy Gary is only a shell of his former self. When he turned to the money and turned away from Us, he also turned away from himself. Each year he grows to be a little more miserable than the year before.

"Men and money," Jesus shook his head as he said this. "Men and money—understanding how to manage money is an extremely important human challenge. Most men, and women, get very emotional when a pastor preaches on the topic of money and tithing. Most people, especially those that are wealthy according to the world's standards, actually believe that the pastor is overstepping his bounds when he preaches to them about money. What the majority of people don't understand is that the tithe is just another very necessary form of obedience. Believe me, David, the Trinity is not in need of man's money. Money only serves its purpose on Earth, it has no value in heaven.

"Obedience is required with so many aspects of a Christian's walk— in allotting time to read the scriptures, in parents providing for their children, in regular church attendance, in serving towards God's work on Earth, in honoring your spouse, and in tithing. People don't seem to get up in arms when the pastor instructs them to provide for their children and raise them in a Godly home. They don't seem to get hot under the collar when the pastor urges them to spend time each day reading their Bibles. No, David, when it comes to money—everything changes. The sensitivity level escalates to the red zone.

"Here is my question to mankind that needs to be included in your letter: Where does the tithe go? What purpose does it serve?"

"That seems to be quite a simple question," stated David.

"I know, but sometimes simplicity can be very powerful." Jesus affirmed. "So, David, what's the answer?"

"I assume that the tithe supports the church. It pays for the church property and building, the utility bills, the weekly programs, the workers' salaries, bus ministries, choir uniforms, church media, and on, and on…. And, oh yeah, the charities, other churches, and missions that the church supports."

"Excellent summary."

"And?"

"Well, David, if this is truly what the tithe is used to support, then where is the problem? Why do people resent the pastor asking for the tithe? God doesn't need the tithe. Mankind's fellow human beings are the ones who benefit from the tithe. God wants man to tithe to show his compassion for his fellow human beings while demonstrating his obedience to his Creator. By giving of his own money, he shares with them the money that God has blessed him with.

Most non-tithers don't see the money that is in their bank accounts as a blessing from God. They see the money as theirs: earned by them, hoarded by them, and, more often than not, loved by them. Their position on how they spend the money is often stated like this, 'It's my money and I'll spend it how I choose. Even if that means wasting it.'

"Look at Gary. Believe Me—he was so happy and blessed back when he loved to give to his church. He was close to his children and his marriage was wonderful. His soul was at peace and his employees felt honored and appreciated. He walked in an obedient relationship with the Trinity. Now, his life has become the complete opposite of that earlier bliss.

"Remarkable, David, since the day Gary stopped giving, the amount of money in the Father's bank account hasn't changed a penny! The

Father doesn't need Gary's money, the Father has no use for an earthly bank account, or any type of bank account for that matter! Now that Gary has hoarded his money, he is truly unhappy. So, it appears that hoarding of the money has hurt Gary, not helped him. So, in the process of not tithing and being stingy with his money, Gary has shortchanged himself, his church, his pastor, his own family, and his employees—but not God. God doesn't need Gary to tithe. Gary needs Gary to tithe. In turn, We will bless him and use his obedience to transform his heart and life. He will come to have Our heart and Our priorities and he will be a blessing to all those around him."

Jesus looked at Gary then announced to David, "Gary will tithe to this casino to the tune of $250,000 tonight. And he calls this his happy place."

As David surveyed the players at the table, Gary was one of the only players that wasn't cheering Woody on with every roll. Gary was losing. He wasn't worshiping like the rest. Then David thought, "I bet he is a great worshiper when he's winning."

Jesus placed his hand on David's shoulder and the two vanished. In an instant, they were back at the camp. It was still early morning.

"So is it strictly a guy thing?" was David's question. "Do the women of my day sometimes choose inappropriate objects to worship?"

"They most certainly do," Jesus affirmed. "Okay, one more quick trip. I'll show you men and women in full worship mode together."

No sooner had Jesus finished the last sentence than the two companions were on the sidelines of a soccer game. David was able to determine that it was a boys soccer game somewhere in America. The kids looked to be about thirteen to fourteen years old. Parents were scattered up and down the opposing sidelines. The game was tied at two goals each and time was running out.

David and Jesus were standing at one end of the field, very near the goal. They watched as a forward dribbled the ball with expert agility directly toward the goal. He had worked his way around the last defending fullback and was headed toward the goalie. David thought, "This could be the game winning goal."

Jesus touched David's arm and pointed to each sideline. Any parent who had been previously watching from a seated position was now standing. Several of the parents were actually running along the sideline, in-step with the forward who was advancing toward the goal. The parents on the sideline of the team in possession of the ball were screaming at the top of their lungs and pointing, very energetically, toward the goal, screaming, "goal, score the goal." The parents on the opposing sideline were yelling at their fullbacks to hustle and steal the ball away from the potential scorer.

As David took in the energy of the scene, he realized how several of the parents had worked themselves up into an emotional frenzy. They acted as though their very lives were dependent upon the outcome of this soccer game. A game that would be forgotten by everyone in attendance within the next week or so. What a pitiful predicament.

"I see the worship here as well, Jesus," David said. "It feels different than the prior two situations, though. It feels fierce."

"It is fierce. These parents are too intense to see how foolish they look. They embarrass their children and their coaches every time one of them gets to running and screaming like some out-of-control four year old. More often than not, things are said that hurt feelings. They are either throwing ugly words at their own children or at their opponents. Sometimes the confrontation escalates to involve parents against parents or parents against the coach. It's so sad. No, not sad—it's pathetic."

Jesus then turned to David and pointed to a woman on the opposing sideline. "You see the lady in the orange jersey, number thirty-three?"

"Sure do."

"That is her son on the field, orange jersey, number thirty-three. He was the last defender that the forward just passed on his way to score."

"Score? When?" David asked.

"Now." As Jesus spoke, the forward kicked the ball with great force, rocketing the ball into the top, left corner of the net.

David smiled—spending time with Jesus was never boring!

"On the drive home, Mrs. Number Thirty-three is going to verbally attack her son for allowing the opposing team's forward to score the winning goal. She is going to unleash on him with her extraordinary command of profanity. Once she feels vindicated, she'll inform him that he is grounded for two weeks. During this whole ordeal, the son will be hoping that she doesn't get out the 'big belt' when they arrive at home."

Jesus then expanded the discussion, "This mother makes her son take one hundred shots on goal each evening before dark. She bought a soccer goal for their backyard and she plays goalie during the mandated one hundred shot exercise. Her dream is for her son to work his way up to the position of forward on his team. 'I don't want you to settle for the lowly position of fullback,' is her quote that her son has grown to loathe. So, she forces him to practice each and every evening to strive to become what she wants for him. The boy has grown to despise soccer, but even worse than that, he has grown to despise his mother.

"David, do you know the number of evenings she has required her son to read a chapter from the Bible? Do you know the number of evenings she has led her son to talk to Us in prayer as he turns in for the night? The answer is zero, none, not one! She claims to be a Christian and a great mom. I see no genuineness with either of her claims."

Jesus looked at David and asked, "So, do you see how the women of your day can worship and get very emotional in public regarding an inappropriate thing? I love sports, and I know they serve a very healthy purpose. But this type of parental behavior produces just the opposite effect—it is extremely unhealthy. You do see, though, how the worship is evident everywhere. This soccer mom worships the idea of her son becoming a great soccer player, but it's for her own selfish and childish desires, not his."

Following that last statement the two men were instantly transported back to their camp. Jesus asked David, "Will you be able to express in your letter how the men, and the women, of your time are really good at worship?"

"It will not be a problem. Your examples were perfect."

"Please urge them to direct their well-honed expertise in worshiping toward their Creator. We created man. We wired him to worship Us! He can still enjoy his professional sports and other healthy entertainment. He just needs to be correct on the number one worship priority."

Jesus turned and walked briskly from the camp.

"Wow!" David proclaimed to himself. He wondered if Jesus knew about his recent trip to Vegas and the time and money he spent at the craps table. Then he said to himself, "Let it go. Jesus knows all; therefore, He is fully aware of it. At least you weren't worshipping the game and you only lost a small amount of money."

David spent the remainder of the day by himself, writing in his journal, but also doing a lot of walking and reflecting. He was impressed by his lesson on worship. He concluded that, "Jesus was right. Men are wired to worship—and they are really good at it. They are experts as a matter of fact. Yet, when their wives and girlfriends drag them into church, they seem to forget all their worshipping skills."

David thought about the depth of the lesson on worship. "How ignorant we humans are," he deduced. "We will worship grown men on the football field as they engage in a physical battle to outdo each other, and for what? We will worship a game of chance that involves an opportunity to win money. We will worship the dream of our children winning a game against other children in structured physical competition."

Then he drew the miserable, yet honest, conclusion, "But we will not worship our God. We will not worship our Creator. Our Creator who has given us these very lives we are allowed to experience. The Trinity who loves us beyond compare. The Trinity who expects us to worship Them! Which makes perfect sense, especially given all that They have done for us."

The day ended with David dozing off in his tent, struggling with the visions of the men wearing their plastic dog noses replaying in his mind with the background chanting of, "Here we go, Brownies, here we go. Woof! Woof!"

CHAPTER 11

THE FATHER'S PERFECT WILL

It is the morning of his thirty-ninth day in the wilderness as David wakes up to the sound of Nathan singing by the campfire. It's an upbeat tune and, even though Nathan is singing in a language unrecognizable to David, he immediately likes it. As he emerges from his tent, the young American sees Nathan not only singing but dancing around the campfire very energetically. Upon further inspection, David stands in amazement. Nathan is also sporting his newly acquired Ray-Bans and is singing to a somewhat disinterested audience—the donkeys.

"My, oh my!" David exclaims, "We are in one fantastic mood this morning aren't we?"

David's angel friend nods, without missing a beat, and says, "I am headed back to heaven very soon, my friend, and I am so excited. I need God to recharge my batteries and I am so ready for some singing and some love!"

David smiled and said, "I am headed back home tomorrow and I am so ready to see my wife, share my letter with her, and sleep in my own bed. Then the real fun will begin with a publishing company, the media, and Christian churches all over the world."

As Nathan continued to sing, David noticed that every time he hit a high note—he floated about twelve inches off the ground. Based on Nathan's intensity, David concluded that Stubby had no idea he was defying gravity every time he hit a tenor note.

As the two were enjoying each other, Jesus surfaced from His tent. Jesus laughed as He fully took in Nathan's jubilant performance. Once things calmed down, David looked at Jesus and realized how much he was going to miss all three of his new friends, but especially Jesus.

As he continued to gaze at Jesus, he realized how weak He looked today as compared to the first night he had met Him. Jesus had faint black circles under his eyes. He was pale and He had probably had lost ten to fifteen pounds. The fasting had definitely taken a toll on His body.

David had grown so fond of Jesus' determination with the fasting that he chose to eat his meals when Jesus was either outside the camp or in His tent. David really admired Jesus' commitment to the fasting—he could see the importance of this undertaking in Jesus' eyes. It seemed with each passing day, Jesus became more connected to the endless spiritual power of the Father.

Jesus walked up to David and smiled. When David looked into His eyes, he saw energy. It seemed as though His eyes were dancing with joy while His body seemed to be completely exhausted. Jesus spoke softly and said, "The Holy Spirit is dancing in My heart. My daily prayer times have energized My soul. I am ready for tomorrow's test."

David felt so blessed and at the same time so insignificant. He was literally standing in the presence of God, a God so loving that He was willing to suffer a cruel death to secure for those whom He loved, the opportunity to spend eternity in relationship with Him.

David announced, "I have finished my letter! I added a tremendous amount of content over the last few days and was up late last night, writing the closing remarks. The letter is complete and ready for my people. I'm not so sure, however, that my people are ready for this letter. But I am sure of one thing: this letter will *rattle* the people of my generation. It is bold! Nathan and I are going to make a trip over to Hercules today to ensure that everything is in order for my return trip tomorrow. Do You want to look over my letter and ensure that I have covered all the necessary items?"

Jesus replied, "The Holy Spirit was writing with you, David. I know every word in the letter. It is a wonderful piece of work. The Father and I couldn't be more pleased with your achievement. Its purpose, to rattle the men of your generation, will indeed be accomplished. Thousands of souls who enter heaven will thank you, David, for motivating them to read the Bible, evaluate their priorities, and seek guidance from the Holy Spirit."

This moment, to David, was so surreal. The completion of the letter was, in his opinion, the most remarkable feat of his life. Sure, he had accomplished some techno-magic at NASA over the last six years, but nothing like his letter. The letter was a game-changer. Jesus had said that it would affect "thousands." David reflected on his feelings regarding the letter realizing how he had changed over the last several weeks. He didn't feel a sense of pride—he felt a sense of victory. He will strike a major blow to the enemy. A blow to Satan and his band of demons.

David Hart had experienced a significant transition during his five-plus weeks here. He had grown from a creature focused on materialism and luxury to one focused on other people and spirituality. The old David would have laughed in the new David's face if the latter had told the former, "The most significant feat in my life involves motivating men to get in touch with Jesus and secure their places in heaven." The new David now understood that the Earth was primarily a place of materialism, thanks to man's glaringly obvious sin nature, and it was all temporary. The things that were important, for all eternity, were the things of God.

As Nathan and David approached Hercules, David realized that he had forgotten to ask Jesus about the return trip. David had assumed he would board Hercules and God the Father would return him to the cradle of Catapult. He also assumed that he would be returned on August 16, 2015 at 3:31 a.m. More than assume that, he needed that.

He did not want to even entertain the thought of him not returning to NASA during the wee hours of that momentous Sunday morning. If time had actually elapsed back home since he had left, and if he couldn't return to that morning, things were gonna be ugly. Him gone, Stuart incensed, Angela alone, and Jesse freaking-out…. That was an ugly picture. He chuckled to himself. God is a God of wisdom—surely David's assumptions coincided with God's plans.

When they reached their destination, the two companions removed the NASA tarp and David released Hercules' vacuum hatch. He and the angel climbed into the capsule. David closed the hatch, fired-up the power, flipped on the instrument panel, and began his system checks. Nathan gleamed with excitement as he watched David in his role as NASA pilot. Nathan reached into his tunic, extracted his Ray-Bans, and slid them on.

The first time that the computer's female voice spoke to the pilot, it startled Nathan. David's little sidekick, however, quickly recovered his coolness. The whole process took about an hour. During that entire time, David kept wondering why he was going through the motions.

Jesus had already informed him that he had not traveled through time because of Hercules' design and the launch of Catapult but only because God the Father had placed him here. Jesus had gone on to state that man would never overcome the chains of time on the human side of heaven. (David could not even begin to fathom how he was going to share that little fact with Jesse, 'Mr. Time Travel' himself.) Nevertheless, he completed the checks and Hercules was "all systems go."

Periodically as David was conducting the system checks, he would get a good glimpse of Nathan. "He would be the perfect mini-me for Arnold Schwarzenegger in the original *Terminator* movie," David snickered to himself.

"This puppy is ready for action!" David announced to Nathan, "All systems are go." Much to David's surprise, when he turned and looked at his little buddy, Nathan looked somber. It was as if the angel's entire demeanor had changed. He didn't look like the dwarf *Happy* but David couldn't recall one of *Snow White's* little friends that went by the name of *Gloomy*. Nathan was definitely looking more like a *Gloomy* than a *Happy*. "What's wrong?" David inquired.

"Oh, nothing," Nathan replied, "even though I am excited to go back to heaven, I now realize our time here is drawing to an end. It will be hard to tell you and Jesus goodbye, even though I know it is only a temporary goodbye." Nathan couldn't tell David the real reason for his sudden sadness.

The two climbed out of Hercules and Nathan watched as David secured the vacuum hatch. After covering the capsule with the tarp, the two started walking back to camp. In an instant, Nathan gasped and stood still in fear. David immediately looked for the cause of Nathan's fear and saw directly at Nathan's side, in the shade of a large cactus, a desert cobra that was coiled, hissing, and ready to strike.

The two companions had apparently startled the snake, just as the snake had startled them. "Don't move," David whispered. David slowly reached into his backpack and retrieved his hand gun. "On the count of three," David murmured to Nathan, "you step to the side and I'm gonna pop our little friend. One, two, three...."

Nathan stepped back; David stepped forward and raised the hand gun. A shot rang out into the calm desert setting. It was loud—the gun could be heard for miles. David, however, had missed his mark by a few inches. As he went to squeeze off the second shot, the cobra lunged from its coiled position. But unlike David, the cobra hit its mark. The cobra dug its fangs into the underside of David's right wrist, striking the radial artery. David dropped to his knees, shucked the snake, picked up the gun with his left hand, and shot the cobra twice. Even though he was now using his left hand, one of the bullets actually removed the majority of the snakes head. The cobra was dead. Nathan was in a panic. He had never seen a hand gun much less heard the loud report of a shot being fired.

David turned to the angel as he was digging through his backpack and said, "Okay, the snake is dead. I am going to isolate this wound with a makeshift tourniquet. I need you to go and get the first-aid kit from the capsule. It is in the same pilot's console as the picture of Angela." David was in pain and Nathan was slowly calming himself down.

Nathan sprang up into the air and quickly soared over to Hercules. As he struggled to remove the tarp and open the hatch, Nathan uttered under his breath to God, "Why did this have to happen?" But Nathan knew it was the perfect way, because it was God's way. Not that God had caused the snake to strike David, but that God had *allowed* the snake to strike David. Nathan floated back to the scene with the first aid kit. About twenty minutes had elapsed since the cobra's attack.

As Nathan checked on David, he found him unconscious. Nathan was frazzled; he didn't know the first thing about administering first aid for a snake bite. "This wasn't an angel thing," he muttered. Nathan dragged David's limp body under the shade of that large cactus. Now David was lying motionless directly beside his dead, motionless attacker.

Precious time was passing; it had now been over half an hour since the cobra's venom was injected into David's bloodstream. Nathan knew he needed to hurry and find Jesus. He wanted to help even though he already knew the final outcome. As he turned to run, he ran into Jesus as He walked up to the scene. Nathan didn't need to relay to Jesus what had happened… Jesus already knew.

Jesus took off His cloth belt and made a makeshift pillow. He knelt, lifted David's head, and placed it on the cloth. "David," Jesus said sympathetically, "please wake up." David opened his eyes. He was very weak, yet he managed a smile for Jesus. "David, the bite of the desert cobra is fatal. This may sound a little strange to you right now, but in a very short time, you will be in Paradise." As Jesus spoke, tears streamed from His eyes and He was having difficulty producing the words. Here He was, God in the flesh, experiencing the mortal, vulnerable aspect of human life on Earth.

Jesus went on, "This incident is horrific for you and very painful for Me. It is part of the suffering that we talked about. This incident, however, fits into My Father's perfect plan and the purpose for your life. As you know, David, because of your choice, you will live eternally in heaven. And as you will come to know, your *Letter to the Nations* will serve its purpose. The letter will make it to its intended destination, to the nations of your generation. I love you David and I will see you soon. The pain and suffering of this world is about to end for you. When you pass, it will be much like your trip when you initially came here in Hercules. You will become completely unconscious. Then when you awake…you will be in Paradise." David closed his eyes and within minutes the young

American was dead.

Jesus, now on both knees, stared into the lifeless face of His young disciple. His heart grew heavy and He cried. Marcus walked up on the scene. Nathan and Marcus knelt down beside Jesus and they cried as well.

After a long while, Jesus and Nathan got up and returned to camp while Marcus remained with the body. Jesus searched in David's tent and found his journal with the *Letter to the Nations* while Nathan retrieved a clean white sheet and rounded up one of the donkeys. They then returned to Marcus.

Jesus retrieved David's backpack and returned the gun to the pack along with the journal. Nathan and Marcus waited there, next to the towering cactus, while Jesus made a quick trip to the NASA ship.

He opened the hatch and climbed into the pilot's seat. Jesus removed the journal from the backpack and grabbed a pen from the pilot's console. He reflected for a moment, then thoughtfully jotted something in David's journal. Jesus then stood, placed David's backpack and the journal on the pilot's seat, and climbed out of the only time machine that would ever actually travel through time.

He closed the vacuum hatch and placed the brown tarp over the vessel. But He turned the tarp over so that the NASA emblem faced the vessel, not the outside. The color of the tarp blended-in quite nicely with the surrounding sand and rock. "That should keep you nicely concealed for a few thousand years," Jesus whispered under his breath.

Jesus returned and joined the angels. The three of them carefully lifted and placed David's body across the back of the donkey. They slowly led the donkey to a small, remote cave just outside of their camp. They caringly wrapped David's body in the white sheet and placed it in the cave there in the Desert of Judea in the year 27 AD. No one spoke. Jesus prayed over the body, speaking to His Father in His native Aramaic.

Jesus wondered if He should have shared with David that David himself was a descendant of one of the twelve tribes of Israel—Israel, the very nation of God. And not just any of the twelve tribes—David Hart was a descendant of the tribe of Judah. This is the very tribe that

Jesus was a descendant of. David Hart, just like Jesus, was a direct descendant of King David himself. Jesus and David Hart were relatives! This family connection was an important aspect of the Trinity's decision to choose David for this mission. Jesus thought to Himself, "He will know soon enough." With that, the three returned to camp.

Jesus continued on to His place of prayer in final preparation for the following day. His last day in the desert was upon Him and it would be one of the most demanding days of His human life. Nathan and Marcus began packing the non-essential items in the camp for Jesus' return to Galilee.

The angels couldn't wait to return to heaven and give David a great big hug. "Hey," Nathan thought, "Maybe I can teach him one of my favorite songs!"

CHAPTER 12
THE VICTORY

On the morning of the fortieth day, Nathan crawled out of his tent at dawn. He was full of emotion—the previous day had been so difficult. He was excited to be heading back to heaven, but he was worried for Jesus. He had noticed as the days had passed how weak Jesus had grown. Then, adding to the exhaustion was the emotional tragedy of David's death yesterday. Now today, Jesus was facing the temptations of Satan, 'the required tests.' Nathan crawled out of his tent and ventured to Jesus' favorite place of prayer.

Jesus had told Nathan and Marcus that He would be praying through the night. Nathan approached Jesus carrying a large wineskin filled with water. When Jesus looked up and acknowledged Nathan, the angel offered Him the water and said, "Good morning Jesus, it appears that the fortieth day has arrived."

"It has indeed," Jesus responded. As Nathan watched Jesus drink the water he reflected on this adventure in the wilderness. He was so thankful to have been picked by Jesus to accompany Him here. Nathan had watched as Jesus managed the days as a human.

Nathan had noticed that when Jesus hurt Himself resulting in a cut or scratch, He bled. At night when it was time for sleep, Jesus was tired and needed the sleep. On many an occasion he had heard the growling of Jesus' hungry, empty stomach. Nathan had also noticed how Jesus became tired following long walks.

Yes, he witnessed firsthand as his Creator dealt with the day-to-day challenges of being human, of utilizing a created body. It had taken

Nathan quite some time to become accustomed to this human Jesus. He had lived in heaven with Jesus for many thousands of years, and there, Jesus was God. He was part of the Holy Trinity, He was revered and worshiped. Nathan had tried on several occasions, but to no avail, to understand the magnitude of love required for the Creator to humble Himself to the point of living as the created. Since this facet of Jesus' choice was incomprehensible to him, Nathan never ventured to understand Jesus' choice to be killed for His creation, for mankind.

Nathan hoped that the exhaustion, hunger, and needs of the flesh were going to prove to be no match for Jesus' strong will on this important day. As Nathan was reflecting on all this, his former, fellow angel who had been cast out from heaven appeared out of thin air. There he stood in all his God-given beauty—Satan himself. He stood over six feet tall, a muscular and handsome figure. He had long, jet black hair pulled back into a pony tail allowing full view of the chiseled features of his face. His eyes were shaped like those of a cat—the iris, also jet black. He was wearing a long, black silk tunic with a bright red belt. His mannerisms were quick and proud, like those of a cat. When noticed from a distance, one would instantly conclude that he was haughty and conceited.

He approached Jesus with a patronizing smile on his face and spoke, "Your Father has turned His back on You today, Son. I have come to satisfy Your every desire. I know that You are starving and weak. First Jesus, You and I, will see to it that You eat. Once we fill Your stomach and You begin to feel better, I will show You kingdoms of the world over which You can begin to reign on this very day. Why live among these lowly men as an equal when You can join me and immediately get the recognition You deserve? You must admit, it is a much better choice!"

Jesus was sickened by Satan's face as He looked upon him and recounted their history. In the eyes of the Devil, Jesus saw hatred, evil, and death. Satan was a big disappointment to Him. When the Trinity had created Lucifer he was the most important of angels. The Trinity had blessed him with great wisdom and perfect beauty. After Satan revolted against his Creator, Jesus referred to him as the father of lies.

And here he was, the father of lies, lying to his Creator on this very day.

Jesus looked straight into the eyes of His greatest enemy and quietly said, "I was expecting you." With that, Satan smiled his pretentious smile, snapped his fingers, and the two disappeared. Nathan was left alone in an eerie morning quiet. The angel closed his eyes and prayed to the Father.

After praying for a significant amount of time, Nathan turned his attention to picking flowers there at the oasis. It had become quite a somber day and Nathan's heart was heavy. When he felt that he had a respectable amount of flowers gathered, the angel floated into the air and headed to David's tomb.

Even though Nathan knew that David's soul was in heaven, he felt a strong desire to pay his last respects to his human friend. Nathan had grown to love the human David. The angel laid the bouquet of flowers at the entrance to the cave and then looked toward heaven and said, "I see why You cherish men like You do—the good ones are priceless."

The angel stood and reflected on his knowledge of David's situation and God's will. *The Letter to the Nations* needed to be written and the Trinity had chosen David to be the author. David was the right choice, a very bright young man and a descendant of King David. If the Father had delivered David back home, present day, after he had written the letter, the result would have been a catastrophe. David on military trial for government theft, a world not believing his story, and NASA, his employer, denying all of David's claims regarding time travel….

Since the Father had brought David to 27 AD to write the letter with Jesus' necessary influence, David was stuck. Expecting David, a product of the twenty-first century, to stay and fit into this ancient world would have been futile. The perfect answer was allowing him to go to heaven at the end of the forty days. After all, he had secured his salvation and accepted Jesus as his personal Savior.

Jesus was absent for the entire day. The tests of Satan occurred exactly as they would be outlined in the New Testament Gospel of Matthew. Later that evening, as Nathan and Marcus were preparing a meal for Jesus, they spoke little. They knew that mankind's future hung in the balance. Then, in the twinkling of an eye, Jesus appeared in front of His tent. Satan's shadow was there and then it was gone.

Jesus looked at His two angelic friends and smiled from ear to ear. "My ministry will continue as planned. Satan was unable to sway Me and My Father is pleased." With that the angels smiled, knowing that Jesus had not succumbed to the empty promises or selfish challenges of Satan.

Nathan tentatively asked, "How, King Jesus? The human body is so weak. The last forty days have taken their toll."

Jesus clenched His fists, reflected on the day, and said, "I fought him with heart-felt scriptures of My Father's truth. All Satan's promises and power melt in the presence of Truth. Fighting evil with scripture is like fighting it with a great sword. My weapon proved to be so much greater than My foe's. Spiritual warfare is so much more demanding and significant than physical warfare. On the one hand, eternal life is at stake. On the other hand, human life on Earth is at stake—huge difference."

"Now, let's eat," Jesus proclaimed "or more specifically, I'll eat." Jesus shared the experiences of the day with His two buddies as He ate His first meal in over a month.

After the meal, Jesus once again visited His place of prayer. Within an hour, He had returned and was ready for bed. The following morning, Marcus and Nathan finished packing up and accompanied Jesus and the donkeys back to Galilee.

The three of them walked for several hours, then stopped a mile or so short of the home where Mary, Jesus' mother, had been visiting. Nathan and Marcus each gave Jesus a warm embrace and said their goodbyes. Jesus thanked them for all the help. The two angels then sprang upward and soared into the afternoon sky. Within minutes, they had vanished from sight.

As Jesus was tying up the donkeys outside the Galilean home, Mary came outside to greet Him. Both spoke in their native Aramaic.

"Hello, my Son. I have missed You dearly." She ran over and hugged Him to the point where Jesus didn't think she was going to let go.

Mary was in her late forties. She had long, dark hair and a pretty face. Her demeanor was pleasant, but solemn. Her wisdom was obvious to those who knew her. She often would smile and say, "How could I raise the very Son of God without ensuring that every step I took was the right one?" Her purpose, to raise Jesus, was a daunting task but obviously one that she had performed successfully. Jesus had not fully appreciated it before He stepped down from heaven, but the human Jesus, Mary's son Jesus, needed Mary's motherly love. Her love was something He would cherish for eternity.

"Were You able to complete the work that You said You must do?" she asked of her Son.

Jesus reflected on the last forty days and confidently answered, "Yes. Yes, mother I did. The most significant day was the last."

"Well Son," she continued, "I hope the prior thirty-nine days yielded some benefit."

"Oh…," He said as He reflected on the special days with the angels, and more importantly with His disciple, David, "they did. Somehow I managed to keep Myself busy." Jesus cracked a big grin as He looked into His mother's eyes.

"Well," she said, "come inside. You look miserable. I want to feed You, draw You a warm bath, and then let You get some sleep."

Her Son replied, "I love you, Mother, and am so thankful for you. After I get some rest, I need to be on My way. I have much work to do. I need to begin assembling My disciples for My ministry."

Mary gave Jesus a mother's smile of loving fondness and said, "I know You do my Son. I know You do."

CHAPTER 13

DISCOVERY IN THE DESERT

Angela, along with David's parents, held his memorial service on Tuesday, September 22nd. David had disappeared on the prior August 16th and all hope was gone. The service was held in a small chapel on NASA Parkway only a few miles down the road from the NASA facility. The young couple did not attend a church regularly so David's parents searched for and found an online pastor to conduct the ceremony.

There was a large turnout of family, friends, and co-workers for this somber occasion. Angela's parents were in attendance, of course. Their home was also in the Clear Lake area and within ten miles of Angela and David's. The small chapel only held two hundred people and when the services began at 10 a.m., the place was packed. Jackie was there with her husband and Mikey.

There wasn't enough room around the altar to place all the flower arrangements that had been delivered so several had been placed outside at the front entrance. Numerous pictures of David were placed on two front tables on either side of the altar. A slideshow of family photos chronicling David's short life was playing on a flat screen television in the foyer. Angela was keenly aware of David's love for the Rolling Stones, so the slideshow was created with a few of David's favorite Stones' songs playing in the background.

After David's parents and Angela had personally welcomed the bulk of attendees to the service, the three of them became transfixed on the slideshow. Without sharing even one word between them, all three knew that the slideshow seemed to make David come to life. It was so refreshing to view all the now very-memorable photos but it was even more refreshing to experience the feeling of David alive.

The somber crowd slowly filtered into the main room and filled all the pews in the chapel. Angela was so relieved that John Stuart had not come. She had worried that his presence would have been such a distraction for her and the family. The true intent of the service would have been diminished with the unsettling tension. She and David's father had already experienced yet another ugly face-to-face with Stuart just one week prior to the service.

When David was assigned to Project 13-03, he was required to join the US military. The project, after all, was a classified military undertaking. Now, David's devastated family was holding a memorial service to celebrate his short life and go through the motions of laying him to rest.

"They couldn't actually lay David to rest," was pointed out by Angela multiple times, "because Mr. Stuart and NASA lost her husband's body!"

Angela along with David's father, Jonathan, had gone to Stuart to request a full military funeral. David had been lost while conducting a military mission, on military turf, and operating classified military equipment.

Stuart, acting in the only manner he knew how, literally laughed the two out of his office. He peered directly into Angela's grieving eyes and asked, "Have you already forgotten about the charges I have pressed against your husband? He is charged with breach of protocol and theft of military property. Have you forgotten the investment that the government made in the Hercules capsule? Well, let me remind you, Honey— $200 million. Now good day to you both!"

Stuart never made eye contact with David's father and essentially ignored his presence. Mr. Hart came extremely close to punching Stuart square in the face on that day but restrained himself: he knew better. He and Angela left NASA feeling completely defeated and humiliated.

If Stuart had shown up at the chapel for the memorial service, Angela felt confident that Jonathan Hart would have tried with every ounce of his being to toss Stuart out the door and onto his face in the parking lot.

Now with all the guests seated in the main room of the chapel, the pastor slowly walked to the foyer and waited for Angela and David's parents to finish viewing the slideshow. After waiting for more than five minutes, the pastor felt it necessary to instruct the three to take their seats. He then reached over and flipped the television off. He followed the trio back into the main room and waited for them to get seated.

The pastor then walked up to the podium at the altar and asked all those in attendance to stand as he began the service. After recognizing the family and sharing a few kind words about David, he led the opening prayer. He then asked the group to once again be seated.

David's father stood up and walked towards the altar. Jonathan Hart was fifty-eight years old and in perfect health. He had worked for Exxon in Houston as an accountant for thirty-two years and retired on his fifty-fifth birthday. He was a family man completely devoted to his wife and only child.

Some of his fondest memories of David involved the annual science projects that the two of them relished. These occurred from the time his son was in the second grade up through the eighth grade. David would come up with some of the craziest ideas and then the two would take the ideas and dive into the projects. The projects were fun but the father cherished the quality time spent with his son more than any of the products produced by the annual undertakings themselves.

Jonathan Hart walked up to the podium, opened his speaking notes, and addressed the grieving crowd. He recalled how David had always wanted to be a scientist and how his favorite cartoon character while growing up was *Poindexter*, the child professor on *Felix the Cat*. He shared his memories of the annual science projects that he had conducted with his son, "the child professor."

Mr. Hart talked about how David was always tearing into toys, old appliances, and anything mechanical to "see how it worked". And sometimes he was able to put the contraptions back together. He actually laughed out loud as he described the time when David, then eleven years old, had completely disassembled an electric can opener. Once he felt like he understood how the internals made the device work, David put it back together. He then approached his father with a long face explaining that the contraption wouldn't work anymore as he shamefully handed over the can opener and three left-over parts.

Jonathan stepped through David's short life, touching on his days at Texas A&M, his successes at NASA, his marriage, and his beautiful wife. When his father returned to his seat, there wasn't a dry eye in the house.

Following David's father, the online pastor officiated the remainder of the service. He read a few scriptures and spoke kindly of David, even though the two had never met. He shed a tear and said that, based on several conversations that he had had with those attending, he knew that David was a good man. He went on to say that he felt assured that David was in a better place, rejoicing in heaven with God and His angels.

If David had actually been there, he would have been the first to pull the pastor to the side and object.

"Good men don't necessarily go to heaven," David would have said. "I know it sounds so appropriate at a funeral to envision that our deceased, our beloved, is in heaven—but really, Pastor, it is so wrong. You need to tell this gathering how important it is for them to search for and learn the truth!

You need to persuade every individual to read the Bible and get to know their God, their Jesus. Then, Pastor, only profess their presence in heaven if you know they chose Jesus, that they chose the only One to save them!"

But…, David wasn't there and the service continued as per the program.

The pastor led a closing prayer and the service was over. Angela stood at the exit and thanked everyone as they slowly filed out the door. Jackie and her family were the last in the line. The two friends shared a long hug, then looked into each other's eyes. No words were spoken but the message was clear: "I love you Angela Hart and I know that words cannot begin to express my extreme sorrow for you in this time of tragedy in your life." With that, Jackie slowly walked toward the parking lot with her husband and son following close behind.

After Jackie's family had left, Angela returned to her seat, front and center in the chapel. Her father slowly approached and asked, "Honey, what are you doing? Let's head home. Your mother and I plan to return in the morning to clean the place up and gather all the belongings."

Darren Banks was a big man. He stood six feet, four inches tall and weighed-in at 250 pounds. Regardless of his size, however, he had a very gentle demeanor. His wife and closest friends had given him the nickname Teddy Bear. He was actually more emotionally in-tune with Angela than his wife. Darren Banks was a strong Christian man, devoted to his church and Jesus Christ. He had struggled with comforting Angela from the time this nightmare had begun. He was in so much pain that it was hard for him to be her rock. But he knew she needed to lean on someone and he knew that he was that someone.

"I cannot let this be over. Daddy!" she announced, "My David is not here! He disappeared and I have no proof of his whereabouts. I know he is probably…probably…you know, gone. How can that be, Daddy? He is twenty-eight years old, he is in perfect health, and the last time I saw him he was as alive as ever!"

She dried her tears and regained her composure. She then turned to her father and asked in a very hopeless tone, "Why, Daddy?"

Darren Banks' eyes were overflowing with tears as he looked at his distraught daughter and said, "Honey, people say that things happen for a reason. I suggest that we ask God to show us a reason for our loss. Maybe the future will bring us answers that we are not aware of today."

Her father's words did not soothe Angela's brokenness. How could God bring her answers? God had never talked to her before. What could possibly happen in the future that would allow her to understand the reason for her loss? Why would a good God let something like this happen to her? And more importantly, why would He let such a wonderful man as David simply disappear from the face of the Earth?

The family members slowly found their way to their cars and headed home.

Now that Angela had held the memorial service, she was overflowing with nervous energy. Three days had gone by since the service and she needed a project, something to focus on and keep her mind occupied. It was the morning of September 25th and tomorrow would mark six weeks that David had been gone from her life. She was contemplating her return to work but she needed a few more weeks to recover. She did, however, need something to take her mind off the loss of her husband—or, as she liked to refer to it, the presumed loss of her husband.

She poured herself a cup of coffee and flipped on CNN and stood in amazement at what she saw on Headline News. There, splattered across the screen on national television, was a picture of her wonderful husband in his NASA uniform. The news anchor seemed to be flustered and was trying to piece together the news from his foreign correspondent in Israel.

Angela listened as the anchor spoke, "Our correspondent in Israel is indicating that a goat farmer in the Israeli Judean Desert happened upon some type of a large rocket ship. As many of you know, CNN brought you breaking news yesterday of an earthquake in the Middle East along the Dead Sea fault. As first reported, the magnitude of that quake was pegged at 6.4 on the Richter scale, quite large for this specific region of the world based on recorded activity over the last one hundred years.

"Much to the surprise of many seismic experts, even though it registered at 6.4 on the Richter scale, the quake caused very minor damage and there were no deaths reported. The key saving grace for the limited destruction is the fact that the majority of the affected area is desert. Seismologists now believe that the shifting caused by this quake along the Dead Sea strike-slip fault caused this rocket ship to become exposed. The ship appears to be well preserved because of the arid desert climate and the fact that it was buried beneath sand dunes. There appears to be no damage to the rocket from the movement of the quake itself.

"The discovery was initially made last night. Israeli officials, or more specifically the Israel Antiquities Authority, mobilized an expert archeological dig crew immediately and, after several hours of on-site inspection, are now holding a press conference.

"It appears that the supposed spacecraft has been identified as NASA's. NASA authorities were contacted late last night. There is one very perplexing issue that the archeologists are struggling with: they have dated the spacecraft and its contents to be from the time window of 10 BC to 50 AD This of course would be literally impossible if it is truly a NASA capsule."

The anchor continued, "This odd news comes on the heels of NASA's other big story that surfaced only last month. That, of course, was when the agency reported that an employee was missing following an unauthorized experiment at their Clear Lake City, Texas facility. The FBI later declared that David Hart, pictured here in this NASA photo, was the NASA employee in question. And furthermore, the FBI had fully investigated his disappearance and had officially ruled him to be missing and presumed dead.

"CNN will continue to keep you informed as we hear more on this breaking news." Angela looked at the clock on the family room wall; it was 9:15 a.m. She contacted her and David's parents as well as Jackie so they could tune-in, then she stayed glued to the TV for the next several hours.

At 9:45 a.m. NASA held its first news conference related to the Israeli announcement. Standing "front and center" was none other than John Stuart himself, in full USAF uniform, no less.

Mr. Stuart began speaking, "NASA personnel have reviewed an enormous volume of photos and other information forwarded to us from the Israeli archeological crew and CIA personnel on-scene. We have verified from the markings on the capsule and other key identifiers that it is indeed NASA property. Furthermore, we have confirmed that the name of the ship is Hercules and that it is impossible for the ship to be two-thousand years old. We designed and built this state-of-the-art vessel over the last two years."

Angela could hardly breathe. "David is alive, David is alive, David is alive," she kept repeating. She had remembered Jesse and Stuart referring to a Hercules capsule multiple times on that horrible day when David had disappeared. Hercules was the "government hardware" that Stuart had accused David of hijacking. This was David's capsule!

Angela was overcome with confusion. How did the capsule travel to and land in Israel? How did it go unnoticed by military surveillance all over the world? What's more—where was David?

Stuart continued, "NASA will continue to keep you abreast of additional information as we investigate further. Thank you."

The CNN blurbs continued for the next several hours with no substantive new information. The network did air numerous shorts from its archives about the possible existence of UFOs and potential historical visits by space aliens. They also interviewed seismic experts about the history of earthquakes in the region dating all the way back to the huge earthquake on the day of Jesus Christ's crucifixion. Then…, the second NASA news conference—once again Stuart was front and center. It was 1:15 p.m.

"NASA has received further information to confirm that this is definitely our Hercules capsule. We have no reason to believe any of the carbon-dating work done by the on-site archeologists. It is our belief that this capsule was stolen from our Houston-area facility and transported to the Middle East last month and we have facts to support that position.

"This vessel was not developed for any type of space travel. The FBI and CIA have become fully engaged in this matter. Initial speculation is that this was an act of terrorism and early discovery of the capsule has probably circumvented any use of it by the terrorists responsible. The terrorists had apparently tried to conceal the capsule temporarily by burying it. NASA will continue to keep you abreast of additional information as we investigate further with the other agencies. Thank you."

Angela was so shaken by this second news conference that she would have no recollection of charging to her car and bee-lining to Stuart's office. Once there, she waited impatiently for three hours while Stuart was preoccupied with Washington DC, Tel Aviv, and his people there at NASA. Angela read the nameplate on Stuart's executive assistant's desk, Juanita Ruiz. She watched as Ms. Ruiz skillfully handled all the incoming calls, high-level visitors, and other traffic wishing to have time with her boss. It was obvious that Juanita understood Stuart and managed the affairs of the office to his liking.

At 5:15 p.m. Angela calmly approached Juanita's desk and informed her that, if Stuart couldn't break away to speak with her, she would be calling the Houston Chronicle. "Juanita," Angela asked, "is the public aware of the connection between the disappearance of David Hart and the discovery of the Hercules capsule in Israel yesterday?"

Angela got her wish—Stuart summoned her into his office within the hour. "Angela, I do not know how to begin to share this with you. From every piece of information that we can glean, David traveled through time in our Hercules capsule. It appears that he landed in the Judean Desert about two-thousand years ago. The contents of the capsule have been very well preserved since the capsule has a vacuum hatch and was apparently buried under sand dunes for a majority of the time. The Israeli authorities have recovered David's NASA ID, iPhone, and hand gun. Additionally they have recovered a photo of you. Everything is a positive ID, except...well, everything is two-thousand years old! We have CIA intel on the ground at the site confirming all this. There are no terrorists and the capsule was not physically transported from Houston to Israel after being stolen."

"What about…," she blurted out but Stuart cut her off.

"There is absolutely no sign of David."

Angela quickly interjected, "So maybe David didn't go on the journey, maybe just the capsule went."

"Well," Stuart continued, "we have positive confirmation that he was there. In addition to all the other things recovered, his journal was also found. It appears that he wrote in it for a period of thirty-five to forty days after he arrived. We have confirmed his hand writing as well as his DNA on several pages in the journal."

"Angela, the content of the journal is, well, it is quite unusual," Stuart continued. "David explains in the journal, that when he landed in the Judean Desert, it was the year 27 AD. He also wrote that he had met up with three men, with whom he spent his time."

"That isn't 'quite unusual,'" Angela retorted.

"No," Stuart replied, "but this is! David claimed that the three men were Jesus Christ and two angels named Nathan and Marcus!" Stuart couldn't contain himself and a laugh snuck out of him before he could suppress it.

Angela sunk into the oversized chair across from Stuart's desk. "Could this crap get any worse?" she whispered. Her thoughts continued, "My husband disappears and is presumed dead. This NASA jerk files ridiculous charges against him for breach of protocol and theft of government property. Jesse's half-billion-dollar project gets shut down with all blame placed on David. And now, with this journal, he is the laughing stock of all NASA, along with the FBI and CIA uppity-ups."

Well, it could get worse.

Stuart added as he composed himself and pretended that he did indeed care. "Angela, please know that NASA, the federal government, and myself are very sorry for your loss. At least you can now put some closure to David's disappearance. And we now know that he did travel through time, even though he wasn't able to make the return trip. This project that he had worked on so diligently did result in the achievement of time travel. This is something that you—and eventually the rest of your family, can be very proud of.

"Now, back to business—Angela, you will not be able to share the specific details of this with anyone. It is more classified now than ever before because we know we accomplished time travel and a foreign government has become involved. No entity beyond those already involved should have any reason to tie the disappearance of your husband to the discovery in Israel. That is how this circumstance will remain."

As Angela was driving home, she kept sarcastically repeating under her breath, "And that is how this circumstance will remain…And that is how this circumstance will remain…."

After dinner, Angela flipped on the TV again. Before she had time to change the channel, CNN was announcing an upcoming live interview with a disgruntled NASA employee who wanted to share some relevant information related to the discovery in the Israeli desert. It was 8:15 p.m. and the interview was scheduled for 9:00 p.m. Angela surfed the channels for the next forty-five minutes, killing time until 9:00.

At 9:00 she flipped back to CNN to catch the live interview. When the CNN anchor, Anderson Cooper, announced his guest's name, Angela's mouth dropped wide open. It was Jesse Black!

Anderson explained that Jesse had worked for NASA for twenty-eight years and was recently fired following the disappearance of David Hart. Anderson turned to his guest and asked, "So, Mr. Black, were you given a reason for being terminated?"

Jesse answered, "Yes. John Stuart blamed me for the disappearance of David Hart and Hercules on August 16th." As Angela took in a screen full of Jesse; she thought he looked tired, or hung over, or maybe both.

"What does the disappearance of David Hart have to do with the Hercules capsule that was discovered in Israel?" Anderson asked.

"I was in charge of the Hercules project and David reported to me—he was my Chief Technical Director. Our project was classified. We had designed and built Hercules over the last two years for the sole purpose of time travel. David, an extremely intelligent physicist, became impatient with the slow pace at which the project was moving over the last several months, so he apparently decided to take Hercules for a test drive," Jesse laughed as he finished that statement.

"What do you mean by time travel?" Anderson asked with some reluctance.

"Just that...time travel. You program the capsule to journey to a specific time and place and then you go there. This project was my baby and, based on the information released from Israel today, it worked! According to the flight computer data that I retrieved on the day that David disappeared, he had intended to visit Rome in 44 BC. Looks like he ended-up in Israel around the time of Christ instead. Oh well, can't be perfect. BUT, the damn thing worked! I still can't figure out why David didn't return from his journey." Jesse's chest was puffed-up and he was really enjoying his moment of fame.

"So," Anderson continued, "you actually believe that David Hart traveled back to the time of Christ in this Hercules capsule and became stranded there. And then, by coincidence, the world discovers the capsule only a few weeks after his disappearance—even though the capsule has essentially been lying in that very spot for two-thousand years."

"Exactly," Jesse proclaimed. "Aren't the archeological experts dating the vessel and its contents at two-thousand years? Think about it.... Would it be possible to actually steal a seventeen ton vessel from NASA, cart it across the US, across the ocean, and into the Middle East without being discovered by a single soul? To complicate things even further, the destination is Israel. I'm not so sure that a group of terrorists could sneak a pocket-sized bomb into Israel, much less something the size of an airplane. And then to top it all off, do it within a period of four to six weeks. Of course Hercules traveled through time—there is no other logical explanation."

Jesse continued, "And regarding the coincidence of the timing related to discovery of the vessel, maybe the world should be focused on the contents of the vessel. Maybe God, or whatever higher power you believe in, wanted us to discover the vessel at this time. What exactly is the CIA and Israel potentially 'hiding' that has yet to be revealed to the rest of us?"

Anderson interrupted, "I have been told by my producer that it is time for a commercial break. We'll be right back."

Angela jumped off the sofa pumping her fist and screaming, "Take that, Mr. John Stuart! I guess that is not 'how this circumstance will remain'."

When the show resumed, Anderson Cooper was on-screen, but alone. He explained that something had suddenly come up and Jesse Black was summoned to a higher-level, more urgent meeting. Anderson promised to continue the interview as soon as possible and then spent the rest of the hour recounting what Jesse had already shared. This news was crazy-big and Anderson loved the fact that it had occurred during his show.

CHAPTER 14
THE TWIST

The following morning, Angela headed to Starbucks for a Café Latte and a newspaper. Jesse Black's outrageous claims from the previous night were major headlines. She had called Jesse's cell phone several times last night and once again this morning—no answer. She wanted to dig through the paper and see if any additional information had surfaced since last night. As she sat at Starbuck's sipping her Latte and closely studying the newspaper, her cell phone rang. She glanced at the caller ID and read, international call, "Hello," she answered with the assumption that the caller had dialed the wrong number.

"Hello. My name is Efraim Rabin and I am trying to contact Mrs. Angela Hart," the man announced as Angela picked up a hint of a foreign accent in his speech.

"This is Angela Hart," she replied with some reluctance.

"Mrs. Hart, I am the director of the Israeli Mossad, Israel's Intelligence Agency. The Mossad is, in some ways, similar to the US's CIA. I office at our headquarters here in the Tel Aviv area. I am in the midst of a very unusual investigation and unfortunately it involves the disappearance of your husband, David. Do you have a few moments to talk?"

"Yes, please go on," she urged. Just the mention of David's name caused Angela to perk up instantly.

Efraim continued, "Based on all the evidence I have reviewed, Mrs. Hart, I believe that you should consider yourself to be in grave danger. You have intimate knowledge of classified intelligence that goes beyond what most authorities in your country would consider, what is the word..., acceptable. I am positive that you are currently considered by the CIA to be an unacceptable risk—that is, as long as you are alive. And I must let you know that my agents in the US have informed me of the unfortunate disappearance of Jesse Black."

"What do you mean by the 'disappearance' of Jesse Black?" was Angela's response. This phone conversation was getting more intense by the minute.

Efraim replied, "Yes, apparently the higher-level meeting that Mr. Black was called to last night, during his interview on CNN, was his last. In the complicated world of international intelligence, one would say that Mr. Black was, well, taken out. He apparently not only knew too much, he seemed way too eager to share it with the rest of the world. Now, thanks to the CIA, Mr. Black won't be involved in any more surprise interviews. I understand that he was single and had no children. I doubt if the public will ever hear of his convenient disappearance."

Angela immediately became very uncomfortable. "I can sort-of believe that," rolled out of her mouth. Her heart rate was increasing and she was beginning to sweat a little.

"Now back to you, Mrs. Hart. I know you must have numerous unanswered questions related to your husband's disappearance," Efraim went on. "If you agree, I will have one of our Houston-based agents meet you at your home within the hour. The agent can escort you to Hobby Airport and we can fly you to Tel Aviv this afternoon on one of our Mossad jets. You can see everything firsthand, here in Israel."

After a few more brief exchanges, Angela agreed to travel to Israel. Mr. Rabin seemed like a very genuine individual who truly wanted to help Angela. Angela did feel "completely uninformed" and Stuart had belittled her, showing no sympathy for her in the midst of all this tragedy. As Angela had mulled over the options in her mind, she thought "How can I say no? There is so much mystery involved in these crazy events associated with David's disappearance. I need to learn more and here is a source willing to share some coveted information." Angela honestly admitted to herself that she had become quite desperate.

Efraim explained that the Mossad escort agent would have proper identification and he gave her the agent's full name and a brief description of his appearance. Mr. Rabin's people had already arranged for Angela to stay at the Sheraton Hotel in Tel Aviv. Efraim promised to promptly contact her upon her arrival at the Sheraton.

"Please, Mrs. Hart, for your own safety, do not let anyone know about your travel plans, especially John Stuart and other US government personnel, until after you have arrived here in Israel, if then," Efraim advised. "Furthermore, now that Jesse Black has told the world about the connection between the discovery of Hercules and the disappearance of your husband, your phone will be ringing continuously. Every reporter worth their salt will want to get that first interview with the wife of the missing NASA time traveler. I would suggest that you make our current conversation your last phone conversation until you are safely in Tel Aviv."

Angela followed Efraim's advice regarding no more phone calls, less one. She called Jackie and let her know her plans but with one condition: that Jackie tell no one. Jackie immediately became worried and strongly advised Angela to wait and learn more about the whole situation before jumping on a plane to Tel Aviv. "This Efraim character seems way too mysterious to me!" Jackie concluded. "You don't know him from Adam and you have only met over the phone."

Angela listened to her friend's advice and then replied, "Jackie, your points are all valid but I must go. I owe this to David and, well, to myself. I wish there was more time to consider the options but, for all I know, the US government would like to expedite my convenient disappearance! I guess what I am saying is—I don't feel like I have any time!"

"Okay! But promise me that you will take your cell."

"My cell won't work overseas. I will share one more small detail with you. I will be staying at the Sheraton in downtown Tel Aviv. But please only call in an emergency. I don't want to get you mixed-up in this deadly CIA business!"

"Deal!" And with that, Jackie wished her friend, turned international fugitive, good luck.

The following day, Angela found herself at Mossad headquarters in Israel across the desk from Director Efraim Rabin. It had been a whirl-wind twenty-four hours and Angela was ready for some answers. The Mossad headquarters were quite unusual: they were underground and outside the city. Angela had to be blindfolded for the majority of the limo trip from the Sheraton. Her blindfold was not removed until the vehicle was underground.

Angela entered the headquarters and was immediately in awe. It was like a complete underground city in itself. Everything was so clean and so modern. As she was escorted to Mr. Rabin's office, however, she slowly became irritated. She and her escort were required to pass through three different levels of security to get to the "inner core", as the Mossad referred to it. The last security station was the most thorough and Angela was actually required to undress and be strip-searched by a female officer.

Angela was truly relieved when she finally reached Efraim's office. Efraim Rabin appeared to be in his mid-forties. He had a thin build with dark hair and eyes. He had a very professional appearance and was dressed to the nines. His office was pristine, about twice the size of any office Angela ever had, with a desk that appeared to be made of solid mahogany. His vocabulary was extensive and his command of the English language was impressive. He spoke with a slight accent that Angela found quite appealing.

Efraim explained that the CIA was twisting his arm to perform a cover-up. He thought they had some good reasons for this; however, he was torn. He and the Americans had confirmed that David Hart had traveled through time. This fact, in itself, was quite overwhelming. Efraim shared the intense conversations he had had with the CIA and how they were very concerned with how much of the puzzle Angela was keenly aware of. The only other person who had given them this type of heartburn was Jesse Black and that circumstance had been resolved.

"Now back to the discovery in the desert," Efraim continued talking. "Actually accomplishing time travel in itself is overwhelming. Then to take the issue from overwhelming to miraculous, add the finding of David's journal."

Efraim shared with Angela that he was a Jewish Christian and had read the entire journal prior to Angela's arrival. Additionally, he wanted Angela to read it as soon as possible.

Angela blushed and reluctantly whispered, "I understand that the content of the journal is a bit unusual."

Efraim went on to point out that not just the journal but the capsule and all of its contents were currently possessions of the Mossad. All this hardware was discovered on Israeli soil and is, at present, the sole property of Israel. The Mossad, as an international courtesy, could hand over all the items to the CIA...or not. Efraim declared that the CIA pushed around most international intelligence agencies—but they did not push around the Mossad.

Efraim continued, "I can assure you that a terrorist organization, or any entity for that manner, did not steal and transport this vessel from Texas to the Israeli desert. The logistics and secrecy of such an operation would be impossible, given the size of the vessel and the locations involved. I'm sure you are aware of Israel's precarious location, surrounded by Islamic nations in all directions.

"The Israeli military conducts constant and redundant surveillance of our borders in order to protect our people from our hostile neighbors. Our military would have identified any secretive group mobilizing heavy equipment on our soil. Additionally, the carbon-dating and DNA tests have not only been re-done and verified by our Mossad lab here in Tel Aviv but also by one of the CIA's labs in Europe."

Efraim had concluded that the evidence was abundant and irrefutable. The iPhone and hand gun serial numbers were exact matches to the original owner—David Hart. The photo of Angela was also a positive ID. All these items were two-thousand years old as well. Odd since the iPhone and hand gun were both manufactured in the year 2014.... Experts had also noted an excessive amount of rust buildup on the exterior of the capsule. The vast array of batteries within the capsule were all shot and the computer would not boot-up.

"We have a dilemma here, Mrs. Hart," Efraim stated. "I believe that every word written in your husband's journal is the truth. I have been a student of the Holy Bible for many years, and the doctrine in his journal is biblically accurate. As a Jew, I initially sought to study the Bible in order to convince myself that Jesus was not the Son of God—not deity. Fortunately for me, the Bible transformed me from an unbeliever to a firm believer in Jesus Christ, the Messiah. After studying the Bible, my life was changed forever.

"I am forced to keep my Christian faith secretive while serving as Director of the Mossad. Jewish Christians face many roadblocks in our country, but we still love Israel."

Angela spoke in disbelief, "Doctrine? Holy Bible? David?"

Efraim responded, "Yes. Your husband explains in his writing that prior to this event he was not a 'Bible guy' so I understand why this all sounds so foreign to you."

"Incidentally, David's history, prior to this writing, is what makes it so spectacular. The knowledge and faith that is demonstrated in this journal would take a man several years to study, grasp, and believe. Yet, on the day that David arrived in the Israeli desert, he knew nothing in-depth of Jesus, the Bible, creation, or the nature of God. Then within forty days he created this masterpiece," Efraim exclaimed as he reached in his desk drawer and held up the journal, clenching it in his raised right hand.

"I am convinced that your husband was supernaturally transformed by God during those forty days in the wilderness, Mrs. Hart. Before we talk anymore though, I would suggest that you return to the hotel and spend the next day or so reading this journal. We cannot make any final decisions until you have read it. And since the CIA is breathing down my neck, I would suggest that time is of the essence. I will have an agent stationed at your door during your complete stay at the hotel. The Mossad has gone to great lengths to ensure that the CIA does not know that you are in Tel Aviv but we must take every precaution.

"I also need to ask an immediate favor of you, Mrs. Hart. Please do not mention to a solitary person that I am a Christian. This information would quickly lead to the loss of my job and possible extradition from the country, or worse. This little secret of ours is very volatile. It must remain unspoken."

Angela promised silence on the matter. "Believe me, Efraim, I am so overwhelmed with information overload, I cannot assure you that I will even remember your secret!"

"Okay. Prior to sending you back to your hotel, I have one more thing on our agenda for today. This will help you to get your bearings, so to speak, while reading David's work."

"I'm wondering how you expect to accomplish such a feat," Angela remarked.

"Oh, it will be quite easy in fact. You will savor this little trip we are about to take for many years. And I do hope that you appreciate it because I am doing it against the wishes of all my top advisors!"

"Now you have really aroused my curiosity!"

Efraim stood and walked over to the far wall of his office. He pointed to a red pushpin that had been inserted in the middle of some type of unusual photo. "This is the location of Hercules," he announced.

After hearing the word, Hercules, Angela quickly stood up and walked to Efraim's side.

Efraim explained, "This is a satellite photo of the region where Hercules was discovered. This particular photo was taken at 7:00 a.m. this morning. My people are hoping to pin point some of the key landmarks that David mentions in his journal. Now granted, things change over time, especially in the desert with all the shifting sand. But, based on estimated walking distances and using the exact location of Hercules as our reference point, we hope to determine the location of the camp. The camp where David spent his time with Jesus and the angels."

"I can barely make out the ship on this photo."

"Yes, this photo covers quite a large area and, relative to the size of the area, the ship is not that large. Now, back to landmarks...we also hope to locate a certain oasis mentioned several times in David's writings. This will all make more sense to you after you have read the journal."

"Great. This is getting more interesting by the moment!"

"So, let's head to the helipad."

"Helipad?"

"Yes. We are going to do a flyover."

"A flyover?"

"I want you to see, first-hand, the discovery site. I want you to see Hercules. Just the outward appearance alone will convince you that the capsule has been lying in the desert for many, many years. You will also begin to appreciate the environmental conditions of the place where David spent his time with Jesus. We cannot land, however, and spend any time at the physical site. The place is swarming with people and, in particular, swarming with CIA agents. All of whom have your mug shot."

"Let's go, Efraim! Oh, and before we go I just want to say I cannot get over your obvious kindness. It is a much needed boost for me after experiencing so much negativity from the Americans."

Once the Mossad chopper was in the air and on its way, Angela removed her blindfold. It would only take half an hour to reach the site. As they approached the outskirts of the wilderness, Angela surveyed the scenery of the vast landscape before them and concluded—the only phrase that seemed to apply was ruggedly beautiful. Efraim had referred to the wilderness as the Judean Desert. He had also pointed out, once it came into full-view, that the large body of water to the east was the Dead Sea.

As she admired the beauty before them, Angela saw mountains, vast expanses of sand dunes, areas of vegetation complete with flowing streams, and so much more. The terrain was varied, which made this wilderness seem so unusual to Angela. The one thing that didn't surprise the American was the scarcity of people. Other then periodically coming across a goat farmer with his herd, Angela saw no other people.

The chopper pilot had radioed ahead and informed the site-captain that Mr. Rabin had wanted to perform another flyover. The people on-site had taken cover in several mobile housing units to avoid the sand storm that the chopper would cause. Every time that Efraim or any of the other VIP's requested a flyover, it irked the Antiquities Authority's archeologists and other staff on site. Their top priority was to investigate the scene without disturbing anything. These flyovers were just an annoyance and they never left the location undisturbed.

As they approached the site, the pilot slowly brought the aircraft to within three hundred feet of the ground and Hercules. Efraim then motioned for him to circle the ship three times. As they slowly circled Hercules, David's plight became all too real for Angela. Seeing the physical, very tangible presence of Hercules, here in the Judean Desert, literally a world away from Houston, was quite a convincing scene.

When Angela looked upon the capsule, she immediately recognized the faded NASA insignia and the name HERCULES in dull blue letters covering a significant amount of the length of the craft. The presence of rust in various places along the length of the craft combined with the obvious fading of the paint on the shell, caused Angela to conclude that Hercules had been here for years. She couldn't jump to the conclusion that it had been thousands of years but she knew it was much, much longer than six weeks.

While she gazed at the ship, it was easy for her to imagine David arriving here and experiencing his great adventure. Actually traveling through time and then encountering the most important man in history. Then spending his time getting to know Jesus as he experienced the rugged beauty of his destination.

"Angela!" Efraim had to shout to be heard over the noise of the chopper's twin engines. "Do you see all the portable housing? Between the Israeli Antiquities Authority, Israeli government officials, the Mossad, the CIA, and site security, there are over 150 people on location." Angela nodded as she looked upon several grey portable buildings strategically placed around the location. She was also amazed at the magnitude of the sand storm the chopper had instantly created.

Efraim asked the pilot to ascend and head over to a patch of trees that Efraim pointed at. Once over the trees, as they hovered, Efraim shouted, "This is one of three possible campsite locations. We are using subtle descriptors in David's writing in an attempt to pinpoint which of the three options was the one where the group's camp had been. You see the small brook that passes through the trees on the north end? That is a feature we are keying on."

"Okay," Efraim motioned to the pilot. The pilot quickly banked the chopper hard right and headed back to Mossad headquarters. Once there, Angela and Efraim headed to his office, she retrieved her purse and the journal; then he bid her farewell until the following day.

Angela's mind was reeling during the limo ride back to the hotel. She had flipped through the journal back in Efraim's office before boarding the limo and being blindfolded again. She had easily recognized David's handwriting. On almost every page she saw references to Jesus, to God, and to the Bible. "What was this all about?" she wondered. "Did time travel warp David's mind? Did he transform into some type of holy-roller? What kind of decision did Efraim think needed to be made?"

One firm conclusion that Angela had arrived at was this: Efraim was a kind and caring man. Even though he was the director of a very secretive and mysterious organization, she was convinced that he could be trusted.

Shortly after Angela had left his office, Efraim's assistant informed him that Joshua had just called and was holding on line one. Joshua Baumann was Efraim's best friend. They had met at an underground Christian bookstore in Tel Aviv some ten years ago. Joshua was several years younger than Efraim but Efraim loved to engage him in detailed discussions involving Christian doctrine. Joshua had been working for the Israel Antiquities Authority since he graduated from the Hebrew University of Jerusalem.

Efraim picked up his phone, activated the voice scrambling mechanism, and punched the button for line one. They conversed in their native Hebrew. "Hey, Josh, what's the latest?" The two friends had been constantly communicating since the discovery in the desert.

"I was going to ask you that!" responded Josh. "Did your people successfully translate the note on the last page of the journal?"

"They did! The message is brief, just like we knew it would be, but the signature is gonna knock your socks off! It does so much for the cause. But rather than discuss it over the phone, we'll talk about it this weekend. Rest assured that it's more good news!"

"Great! Well I need to go."

"Okay. I know it must be crazy out there on site," and the two men ended the call.

Efraim and Josh were ecstatic about the discovery of the NASA vessel, the truths in David's letter, and all the carbon-dating proof. This discovery was shaking the very foundation of the Jewish premise that Jesus was not the Messiah. The irony of the entire circumstance was that the highly respected Antiquities Authority was the very agency rendering all the expert opinions and tests verifying that all the discovered items were two-thousand years old. Israel, the Jewish nation, was in the midst of a discovery so big that it could have a profound impact on the traditional religious foundation of the country. And the discovery was found right on Israel's very soil and was being investigated by some of Israel's most brilliant minds!

If the country were to accept the authenticity of the carbon-dating and the fact that David did indeed spend time in the desert with Jesus, how could Israel not accept Jesus as the Messiah? If Jesus was not deity, how could one explain the trips that He took with David to the year 2015? If Jesus was not deity, how could one explain His grasp of modern physics and mathematics back in the year 27 AD? How could Jesus know, in the first century, David's birth date, future wife, and parents if he wasn't truly God in the flesh?

Efraim was so elated with the way that the whole matter was unfolding that he actually envisioned a changed Israel in the immediate future. "What a miracle that would be...! Maybe this discovery is the very means by which God will reconcile His Nation, Israel, and His Son, Jesus!" Efraim hoped.

CHAPTER 15
THE DISCIPLE'S JOURNAL

After getting some much needed sleep, Angela showered, freshened-up, and ordered breakfast delivered to her room. She had slept twelve hours the previous night. Once she possessed the journal, she found peace in knowing that there was more to learn about David's disappearance. She felt like she had a little piece of David with her. She had slept soundly and with no help from her sleeping pills.

As she looked at the journal lying on the table across the room, Angela felt the presence of David. This journal was about to give her some intimate time with her husband. She was somewhat hesitant to start reading because she feared that, when she had finished, the intimacy would end. This journal was a gift and she planned to experience David as she read.

Her breakfast arrived and the Mossad agent posted at her door allowed room service to enter her room with the food. The agent followed closely behind, observing every move. He frisked the waiter, raised the hanging tablecloth, and checked under the food cart. He then allowed the man to set up Angela's breakfast. The agent had the server exit the room first, then followed.

When she had finished her breakfast, Angela settled into the big, cozy chair in her hotel room and dove into the journal. It was 9:00 a.m. As Angela read, she became as surprised as Stuart. David did explain that he had arrived in the year 27 AD and spent this time with Jesus Christ and two of His angels. After reading the first four or five pages, Angela stopped and thumbed through the entire book.

It appeared that David had written brief summaries of each day's happenings in about the first third of the journal, much like a diary. Then the remainder of the journal was a letter—a Letter from David Hart, a disciple of Jesus Christ, to the Nations of the World. "How unusual!" she mumbled. She immediately resumed reading.

When Angela finished the first portion, the diary section, of David's writings, she stopped and reflected on all that she had read. All the references to Jesus, God, and the Bible were overwhelming but one thing stood out more than all of that. David's last entry indicated that he was preparing to return, to the present, on the following day. "What happened? What happened during those last twenty-four hours?" she questioned as she looked upward towards the heavens. "If God had taken David from the cradle of Catapult and placed him with Jesus in 27 AD, then why couldn't God return him to the cradle when his mission was complete?"

She phoned downstairs and ordered lunch to be delivered to her room as well. All the excitement associated with reading David's work had suppressed her appetite. She ordered light: a chicken salad sandwich with a cup of potato soup. Her stomach was somewhat unsettled. She hoped it was due to the adrenalin rush and not an indication that her body was rejecting the foreign hotel's food or water.

She returned to her task and now began reading the letter. It was unlike the diary portion. Instead, David used a different writing style for the letter—it was written with a sense of urgency. The spiritual knowledge and wisdom that emanated from the work was quite impressive. It was obvious that Jesus truly did bless David with immediate knowledge of the Bible just as he had indicated in a previous portion of the diary. Angela was able to quickly pick up on the theme of David's letter, his God-given theme. "Wake up, world! God is unsettled and wants us to know that many of us are hopeless because we don't know Jesus. Jesus is the only way to heaven! You must study your Bibles and learn the truth of God and apply it to your life!"

As Angela finished the last page, she struggled with a brief note written at the bottom. It appeared to be written in a foreign language and was definitely not David's handwriting. She made a mental note to ask Efraim about it when they reconvened to discuss the journal.

Now that Angela had finished reading the letter, she returned to the piece about David giving his life to Jesus. She read through it again very slowly. She sat and pondered this significant moment in David's life. Somehow, even though she didn't understand all that she had read, she knew that David was okay. This eternal spiritual life seemed very real to David as he wrote and she hoped that, with time, it would become real for her. She had decided that the Bible would be her priority once she returned home. David's journal had definitely convinced her of that. She also knew that her decision to focus on the Bible would please her father.

Angela's father was a devoted Christian man. He had hoped to see Angela follow in his footsteps as she grew up and became an adult. Angela's mother, however, was very outspoken against most things religious. She had been raised in an overly strict Baptist home and had promised herself at an early age that she would not raise her children in such a demanding, uncomfortable environment. As Angela matured, she found it much easier to "stay at home with Mom" rather than tag along to church with Dad. This adventure of David's was about to drastically change Angela's stance on church and religion.

The caring and friendly nature of Jesus was easy to grasp from David's writing. Jesus' passion for mankind radiated from the letter. One surprising fact that David had taught Angela with his writing was the supernatural intelligence of Jesus. He was the most intelligent man who would ever exist on the face of the Earth! Angela really enjoyed reading about the relationship that David had developed with Nathan, the little angel. Angela could feel David's commitment to the letter as she read it. She could sense David's drive to fulfill this purpose, the writing of the letter that Jesus had relayed to him.

As Angela flipped the journal closed and went to lay it on the hotel room desk, she noticed a blue piece of paper inside the leather cover opposite the last page. She raised the inside flap of the cover and removed a blue envelope. Jotted on the outside of the envelope was one word:

Angela.

Angela tore into the envelope and quickly read the note from her husband.

Dear Angela,

If, for some reason, Hercules makes the return trip home, but I do not, I hope this note finds its way to you. First, I love you with all my heart and apologize for my decision to make this journey. I have spent forty days in the desert with Jesus and I can assure you that He is God in the flesh. My "Letter to the Nations" is my most prized accomplishment and it must be published.

Angela, it is imperative that you read my letter for yourself and take action. Please read, and work to understand, the Bible, from cover to cover. The Spirit of God will change you forever! The Spirit will lovingly guide you. I am forever changed! If you are reading this, it is safe to assume that I have perished so…. I can't wait to see you in heaven!

I love you, I love Jesus!
David

Angela stared at the letter as tears rolled down her cheeks. She sat still for a while reflecting on her days with David. They were so few but they were so powerful.

"I hope," she whispered, "that I will somehow learn more about what happened to you, David Hart, after those forty days in the desert were over. You were not in the capsule when it was discovered so where are you? I know that you would want me to move forward with the journal and my personal growth. And yes, I will do that. But, David, I do know that as I move forward there will not be another love in my life that will ever compare to the love we shared. I know it was taken from us on this side of heaven but believe me, I do plan to catch up when we are back together again. Somehow…, someway…."

Angela eventually picked up the phone in her room and called

Efraim. "Hello, this is Efraim Rabin," Efraim said in English as he answered his cell phone, knowing that the call had come from the Sheraton Hotel.

"Hi Efraim, this is Angela Hart. I have finished reading the journal. I think I understand it well enough for us to talk."

"Great," Efraim replied. "How about discussing this over a nice dinner?"

"Sounds great!"

"Can I pick you up at 7:00 p.m.?" Efraim asked.

"You bet," answered Angela. Angela looked at her watch; it was a few minutes past 6:00 p.m.

Efraim took Angela to a classy restaurant in downtown Tel Aviv that served authentic Mediterranean style food. After the meal, they began discussing the topic at hand over a couple of espressos. Efraim had requested a secluded table on the second floor of the restaurant. By the time they had finished their meal, there was no one else within hearing distance of their table.

Efraim spent a few minutes jotting down some notes on a paper napkin. He then slid the napkin across to Angela and said, "I believe these truths to be things that David was completely unaware of on the day he disappeared. These truths he writes about in his journal."

Angela looked at the napkin and slowly read:
- Jesus' native tongue was Aramaic
- Jesus did spend forty days in the Judean wilderness
- Angels did attend to Jesus at that time
- Satan was a fallen angel cast out from heaven
- The Trinity is a true biblical concept
- The Bible teaches that salvation is a gift from Jesus
- Paul's writings in the New Testament are in the form of letters
- The resurrected Jesus was witnessed by hundreds of people

"The best explanation for the depth of David's knowledge displayed in this journal is the very story that he recounts," Ephraim proclaimed. "He was with Jesus in the desert. Jesus did bless him with the knowledge of the complete Bible." When Angela looked up, Efraim added, "Based on DNA evidence and carbon-dating, the journal was indeed written by your husband in the year 27 AD."

As Angela stared at the napkin, she suddenly remembered the odd note jotted on the bottom of the last page of David's letter. "Efraim, when you read David's letter, did you notice the unusual note at the bottom of the last page? It appeared to be written in a foreign language and seemed to end with some type of a signature."

Efraim's demeanor changed instantly. It was as though Angela had flipped on some secret switch within the depths of Efraim's soul. Angela could tell that he was recalling the short note as his eyes slowly filled with tears of joy. He looked at Angela and began to speak but stopped. Efraim actually lost his composure for a moment. Angela thought to herself, "Where is Mr. Calm, Cool, and Collected? Is this the same man I met yesterday?"

Efraim spoke softly, "Yes, I did notice the note and signature when I read the letter. I know several languages but did not recognize that specific one. I also know from my research that David had not learned any foreign languages during his prior training in school or at NASA. Our handwriting and language specialists have spent a great deal of time analyzing this note. It is the Aramaic language, the very language that Jesus spoke."

"Well, what does it say and who wrote it? Do you believe that David may have learned the Aramaic language while he was being taught by Jesus? How do you…"

"David didn't write the note on that last page, Angela," Efraim interrupted. "It is not his handwriting and the hidden meaning in the signature definitely points to one specific person. I believe it was written by Jesus Christ Himself!" Angela noticed that Efraim's hands were trembling.

"What was Jesus' message?"

"It was short and sweet." Efraim steadied his hands and reached for another napkin. He took a deep breath and wrote a short sentence on the napkin. He gazed at the words for a moment as if he were trying to envision the moment when Jesus had actually penned them on that last page back in 27 AD. Angela had deduced that the true emotion Efraim was experiencing was excitement—adrenalin pumping excitement.

Once again, he slid the napkin across to Angela.

Angela slowly read the sentence and immediately looked at Efraim asking, "And then He added His signature following this note?"

"No...the signature is there. At the end of the note."

"Where?"

Angela looked at Efraim's reproduction of the note and was nothing but puzzled. She kept looking for the name—Jesus Christ:

I fully endorse this written work of My beloved disciple, David Hart.
I Am

"I don't get it, Efraim," was Angela's frank response.

"It is only a matter of time, Angela, and you will grow to look upon this note, especially this signature, as sacred—just like I do now! Do you realize that, up until the discovery of David's journal, the world has never seen one historical document with Jesus' authenticated written words? In the Old Testament, God gave Himself the name 'I Am'. The Israelites often referred to God as 'I Am' and they all cherished this term.

"When Jesus performed his ministry on Earth, He often referred to Himself as the Son of God or the Son of Man. On one specific occasion recorded in the New Testament Jesus actually told the Pharisees that His name was, I Am. In the Gospel of John, chapter 8 and verse 58, Jesus states, while on the temple grounds. 'I tell you the truth, before Abraham was born, I Am!'

"This, of course, upset the Pharisees to no end, since they did not believe that Jesus was the Messiah, the Son of God. When Jesus called

Himself I Am, the Israelites that were present actually wanted to stone Jesus, to kill Him, but He was able to escape. Using this very bold signature in the journal is Jesus' way of letting those educated in God's word know that He truly did endorse David's letter. This unique signature is only special, of course, to those of us who believe in the deity of Jesus—since He is in-fact using the signature to validate His deity.

"All this evidence only points to one conclusion, Angela…. Your husband spent forty days in the desert with Jesus, God in the flesh. The journal is authentic and the letter is intended for the 'Nations of the World'. Angela, have you done the math? The capsule was discovered in the desert exactly forty days after your husband, and the capsule, disappeared from NASA's facility!"

Angela sat in silence and stared into Efraim's eyes. "I…I don't know what to say. I feel the same as you—that the journal is authentic and David intended for it to be made public. You had said that we needed to make a decision. What did you mean by that?" Angela inquired.

Efraim looked at her and continued, "Angela I have prayed almost non-stop since I read David's work. I have discussed it at length with my wife. I know the right decision to make but it's a difficult one."

"What?" Angela asked somewhat impatiently.

"The *Letter to the Nations* must be published," Efraim replied without the slightest of hesitation. "The world needs to hear what Jesus has said. It is a specific document intended for the people of the world today. I believe that your husband lost his life in the process of bringing this message to us. We must not fail him or, more importantly, fail God. The message is destined to be shared."

"So, you believe that David has passed?" Angela slowly asked. She realized, as she asked the question, that she seemed to be coming to terms with the passing of her husband.

"Yes," Efraim then expounded, "I think that he has suffered his physical death but you and I have read the promise of Jesus in his journal, that David lives forever in heaven. I believe that David is in heaven right now."

"All that is very strange to me," Angela replied uncomfortably.

"You'll grow to understand as you study the Bible," was Efraim's response.

"Even though this may be very uncomfortable for you to hear, I need to share something else with you," Efraim continued, "I have concluded that David perished in the desert at the end of the forty days. He had become such a devout follower of Jesus that, if he had lived on, he would have been Jesus' first disciple during His ministry. We both know that there is no mention in the Bible of a disciple named David, and, initially, there were only twelve disciples, not thirteen.

"Or, more precisely, there were thirteen initial disciples of Jesus; but the world has yet to be introduced to the thirteenth! Only one human during Jesus' time ever knew this thirteenth disciple, and that was Jesus Himself. The thirteenth disciple was not intended to be revealed until this time in history."

Efraim then encouraged Angela to move forward with publishing the letter. In Efraim's mind, the letter truly belonged to Angela since her deceased spouse had written it. Efraim explained that he had a close, Christian friend in the UK that owned a small publishing company.

His friend had already promised Efraim that he would print as many books over the next several days as what his little company could generate. They would then sell the book online via Amazon.com as well as to local bookstores. He felt that they could move somewhere around five hundred copies into the hands of the public within seven to ten days. Then, once the book was made public, Angela could approach a much larger publisher to ensure that the publication went worldwide.

"Just one little problem, Efraim," Angela reeled out with some sarcasm. "What about the CIA?"

Efraim then explained the beauty of his plan. "You are going to steal the journal from me! Then, you are going to disappear. The next time you surface, about ten days from now, will be at a book signing for your husband's new book in London. By this time, a few hundred books will have been sold via Amazon.com and a few hundred more will be in London bookstores. The CIA and the Mossad will, of course, have no choice but to leave you and the book alone. Because, thanks to the release of the book, all the information that the CIA wants suppressed will be common knowledge to the public."

Efraim went on, "In the meantime, I will turn over everything still in my possession to the CIA. They will get Hercules and all its other contents along with a copy of the journal. I will, with great anger, convey to the CIA and my fellow Mossad brethren how you had promised to return the journal to me following your initial reading but instead you vanished into thin air. The CIA and the Mossad will be searching for you all over the globe. You, however, will be comfortably tucked away in a quaint little section of downtown London, with the publisher, as David's book is being printed and bound.

"I will give you a day to get settled in London before I set all of this in motion," he assured her.

"The whole CIA cover-up, as I see it, is a useless exercise anyway," Efraim added. "You and I have both read and are now aware that Jesus told David that man would never travel through time without God's help, of course. So the US military, wanting to conceal their time travel technology from the rest of the world, is ridiculous. They possess and have already read a copy of the journal. The journal clearly points out that the man-made technology of time travel will never occur. Yet they are convinced that the technology did work."

Efraim raised an eyebrow and concluded, "So, as a Christian, I look at your government, a government initially founded on sound Biblical principles and an outspoken belief in God, now giving no credence to the fact that God, not a man-made machine, caused this time travel to occur! What an ironic, but sad, circumstance. I guess it's just a sign of the times and another strong reason for the need of David's letter. The most powerful nation in the world, the United States of America, has lost its true God-focused identity."

The two continued to discuss the details of Efraim's ingenious plan at the pub on the first floor of the Sheraton. Angela bid Efraim farewell at 1:30 a.m. promising to mail him one of the first published copies of David's work.

CHAPTER 16

THE LETTER TO THE NATIONS

Angela met the young Mossad agent in the hotel lobby at 9:00 a.m. the following morning. Just as Efraim had promised, the female agent was wearing a royal blue dress accompanied with white heels and a bright red purse. She carried a black leather attaché case and was standing near the women's restroom. The agent handed Angela the small attaché, gave her a thin smile, then left without uttering a word.

Angela entered the restroom, locked herself in a stall, and opened the attaché. It contained a commercial airline ticket to London, a counterfeit United States passport for one Angie King, along with several pieces of identification and credit cards belonging to Angie King, and the business card of Efraim's friend in London. And, oh yeah, Efraim had included five hundred quid of British currency. The classified documentation from both the CIA and Mossad labs on the authenticity of—the journal, David's DNA, iPhone, hand gun, and photo was included in a manila envelope. Angela exited the hotel and climbed into a taxi. "Airport please," she said to the driver.

Angela was experiencing an adrenalin high. She was bubbling over with emotion. As she stared into the eyes of the Israeli taxi driver in the rearview mirror, she began to take a mental inventory of those emotions. She was scared—she had essentially agreed to make herself an international fugitive. Now she was on the lam. Excitement was definitely an emotion that was driving her. The excitement of publishing her husband's book, a document written two thousand years ago, a message from Jesus Christ Himself. Then, at the other end of the spectrum, was the grief.

The pain associated with the overwhelming loss of her young husband, her best friend. Every time the grief surfaced, Angela felt the nausea well up in the depths of her being.

Her thoughts were interrupted, "We will be at the airport in ten minutes," the taxi driver mumbled with a strong Israeli accent.

"British Airways please," Angela responded.

As the taxi approached the terminal at Ben Gurion International Airport, Angela was surprised to see a significant amount of armed security officials at the main entrance. The entering vehicles formed into four separate lines. A group of armed guards was assigned to each line, and the guards only allowed the vehicles to pass one at a time. It became obvious that these guards would randomly choose a vehicle for more in-depth inspection and questioning of the occupants.

The taxi driver chose a line and worked his way forward. When their turn came, the armed guard motioned to Angela's taxi and the driver inched forward. He rolled down his window and greeted the guard in what Angela assumed to be Hebrew. The two spoke for a moment then the driver turned to Angela and asked for her passport. She quickly produced the document and handed it to the driver. The guard inspected the passport, returned it, and the driver gave the document back to Angela. The guard smiled, the driver rolled up his window, and they were on their way.

"Whew," Angela sighed under her breath, "I'm glad that went so smoothly." She then reminded herself that she was in Israel, a country with a well-known reputation for extensive security. "They had to have it—they were basically nestled in the midst of several hostile neighboring countries," she thought. This thought, of course, only caused her to become more nervous. "You're not on that plane yet. Keep your cool and steady your nerves!"

When they arrived at the passenger drop-off area of the terminal, the driver helped Angela with her luggage. As she reached into her purse for cash, it suddenly dawned on the traveling American that she possessed no Israeli currency, she had not one new shekel. Efraim had taken care of her every need since she had arrived—she had no need for cash. As she approached the driver to explain, she was staring helplessly into her purse.

"No payment necessary, Mrs. Hart," came from the drivers mouth before Angela ever uttered a word. She immediately noticed that the driver's pronounced Israeli accent had completely disappeared. "Mr. Rabin said to wish you well and to urge you to stay on high alert. Many men and women in our business are harsh and cruel." The taxi driver flashed his Mossad credentials for Angela to see, disappeared into the taxi, and was gone.

Angela was pleased to know that Efraim was taking such good care of her. But, at the same time, she began to look at everyone around her with suspicion. Just how many agents were hidden in the crowd posing as commoners, and by which country were they employed? She reminded herself to be extra cautious each time she interacted with anyone.

Satan had called an urgent meeting of his European contingent of demons. The king of evil was extremely frustrated. He was so proud of his success with John Stuart and the CIA. NASA and the US government were so focused on their own agendas that they had not even considered giving the very truth of this whole event any serious thought. They had not once entertained the idea that one of their best and brightest men may have actually been completely honest—honest about his heavenly companions in the desert, honest about his spiritual awakening, and honest about his *Letter to the Nations*. Satan knew that the US authorities would never attempt to publish the letter; they were too enamored with the extraordinary potential of time travel and their own selfish plans.

Satan was delighted with the egotism, closed-mindedness, and spiritual apathy demonstrated by the Americans. North America was becoming one of his easiest territories of dominance.

Now the Devil had a problem to deal with, one that caught him by complete surprise, coming from the most unusual of sources—a Jew!

Efraim Rabin, a Jew who happened to be an idiotic believer. Once Lucifer realized that this believer had studied the Bible and become a self-convert, he resented him all the more.

Efraim Rabin was intelligent. Efraim Rabin was wise. Even the Devil knew that Jesus was authentic. The more open-minded humans always seemed to figure out the truth. Now, because of Efraim Rabin, Satan had work to do. Efraim had convinced the young American widow to take a risk and publish the ridiculous book.

Satan's powerful group assembled in an abandoned warehouse on London's south side. The majority of the fiends were able to be present on short notice and numbered about two hundred. Even though the creatures were of the spirit world, the room reeked of evil. The stench was powerful and smelled of death, like the stink of a dead animal. Most of the demons' appearances were repulsive but a few were extremely handsome, like their master. It was an unusual scene because none of the spirits were seated or standing—every one of them was floating halfway between the floor and the ceiling.

Satan called the meeting to order as he floated toward the ceiling of the warehouse. He was front and center of course. "I have a critical need for some human intervention. One David Hart, a disciple of Jesus Christ Himself, no less, has written a book that enrages me! If it gets published and into the hands of some of your loyal subjects, it will enrage each of you as well.

"It represents all that we are against and, if it is successfully delivered to a certain publisher in London, it will eventually lead to thousands of souls being stolen from our kingdom. This must not happen!" Satan took a deep breath while all the demons looked on in silence, anxiously awaiting the master's request.

"The dead Mr. Hart's young widow is currently traveling to London," the Devil continued. "She will arrive here at 2:00 p.m. this afternoon, on a flight from Tel Aviv, with the stupid book. We must not allow her to enter London and go into hiding, but instead she must be sent back to Israel to be intercepted by the CIA and Mossad. They will then be able to confiscate the book and it will never be published, ending the sly scheming of the Mossad's traitorous director, Efraim Rabin."

Satan looked upon his hideous audience of followers and inquired with a loud and demanding tone, "How will we accomplish this?"

The warehouse was instantly filled with the rumble of demonic voices as the constituents brainstormed on their master's request. They all knew that the one, or ones, who came up with the solution would stand to be rewarded handsomely. Then one of the demons, Cyclops, began to hurriedly drift through the air toward Satan, his eye crazy with excitement. He moved quickly, hoping to be the first to suggest an idea.

It was an unsightly moment as Cyclops soared through the crowd. He was elevated about six feet above the floor of the warehouse just like all the other attendees. As he navigated through the group, he bumped into several of his comrades as he hurried along. He had lost full sight in his left eye in a sword fight with a holy angel during the fourth century. This made it difficult for him to maneuver through the horde.

"I have the answer, master. I have the answer!" flew out of his mouth as Cyclops finally arrived at the front of the warehouse and timidly drifted upward toward the high ceiling and his master. "I have a human subject under my control and he works at the London Heathrow Airport. His name is Paul Newbury and he is employed by the UK Immigration Services. He is a sorry excuse for a human being and one of my easiest acquisitions.

"He is scheduled to work this afternoon. I will cause him to deny this devious Mrs. Hart entry into Britain, and he will ensure that she is on the first plane destined for her forced return Tel Aviv later this afternoon." A wide grin surfaced on Cyclops hideous face as he peered at his master with his one good eye, hoping for an indication of approval.

"Do it!" commanded Satan. "Do it. And if you are successful, you will be rewarded with a pack of demons under your command. Well done, Cyclops! I will be more than happy to join you in this undertaking."

Satan and Cyclops disappeared. Then all the demons disappeared. The warehouse was once again abandoned. Cyclops was in Paul Newbury's head in an instant. "The name is Angie King", Cyclops whispered, "she must not gain entry. She is coming from Tel Aviv and to Tel Aviv she must return!"

Angela's flight was right on time; it landed at Heathrow at 2:10 p.m. Angela was nervous but determined. She was not very conniving, so presenting fake identification made her very uncomfortable. She retrieved her luggage and stood in line at Immigration Services.

A tall, handsome man, who appeared to be an airport employee, approached Angela in the long line and asked her to please form a new line as another agent was now "open for business." The man had long, jet black hair pulled back in a pony tail to allow full view of the chiseled features of his handsome face. He wore a black silk suit with a bright red tie. Angela couldn't help but notice his long, well-manicured fingernails, "How unusual," she thought. His smile seemed artificial to Angela, almost patronizing in a way.

Angela followed him and was now first in a new line for processing. She turned to thank the man for moving her to the front of a new line but he was gone. It was as if he had vanished into thin air. "What is that awful odor?" Angela whispered to herself as she waited to be called. The processing agent was getting settled into his booth as Angela read his nameplate, Paul Newbury. Mr. Newbury called out in a mousy voice, "Next in line please."

As Angela stepped forward to be processed, another Immigration agent approached her and gently took her by the arm. "Please come with me," he said to Angela as he motioned to Paul Newbury to continue with the next person in line. Angela followed the little fellow to a side office. "We randomly pull people from line for a more thorough processing in private," he explained. "I apologize but you are my next passenger to process."

This is exactly what Angela had feared. The last thing she needed was a thorough peppering of questions regarding the "life and times" of Angie King. Her heart began to race as they entered his office. The agent walked around his desk and asked Angela to be seated across from him. He was only about five feet tall. Angela read his nametag, Nathan. Nathan looked at Angela and gave her a big, welcoming smile. Angela couldn't help but return the smile, even if she was extremely nervous. With some effort, the tiny agent managed to climb into and get settled in his chair.

"I need to see your airline ticket, your passport, and one other form of identification," the agent stated. Angela already had the items in her hand and quickly laid them on his desk. After a swift examination of the documents, the agent stamped Angie King's passport, returned her documents, and said, "Welcome to London, Mrs. King. I hope you enjoy your stay. Please be careful."

He escorted Angela to his office door and bid her farewell. Angela thought to herself, "And you call that a more thorough processing? That was about as easy as it gets!" As Angela headed toward the exit, the little agent called out from his office, "Mrs. King, Mrs. King!"

"What now?" Angela thought. She was almost home-free. What kind of problem had been discovered?

He quickly walked up to Angela and said, "These must have fallen out of your purse." He handed her a pair of sunglasses and disappeared back inside his office. Angela released a huge sigh of relief and exited the Immigration Services area as quickly as possible.

As Angela continued walking and calming herself down, she looked curiously at the glasses. They were not hers, but they looked vaguely familiar. Then it hit her—she was stunned. She stopped abruptly in the middle of the bustling airport crowd and closed her eyes. She was overwhelmed with emotion. She then looked on the inside surface of the Ray-Bans and steadied her shaking hands to read the real owner's name engraved there, David Hart! She didn't know whether to laugh or cry, so she did a little of both.

As she regained her composure, everything began to gel. Angela had read in David's journal where he had given Nathan, the angel, his Ray-Bans. That was Nathan! "He was really cute!" she thought, "no wonder he and David had become such good friends."

"I wonder what he is doing here?" Angela mumbled to herself. "What a wonderful gift…. Just another piece of tangible evidence validating David's writings." Those sunglasses would be forever treasured by Angela. She felt so blessed to have been graced by the presence of a true angel.

Malcolm Headley met Angela near the main exit of Heathrow's International Terminal. He was holding up a quaint sign that read Angie King. They exchanged pleasantries and the two were off. There was work to do. Upon arrival at his office, Malcolm introduced Angela to his small staff and showed her an upstairs apartment nestled above his publishing shop. "This is where you will be staying for the next couple of weeks," Malcolm said. "I know it's somewhat small but it's clean. I have stocked the refrigerator and pantry with food. The bed has clean sheets and there are plenty of towels in the bathroom."

Malcolm only lived a few blocks from his shop and told Angela that he would be spending most of the daylight hours at the shop for this project. "So," he concluded, "no need for you to feel alone." Efraim had explained to Malcolm how Angela needed to be hidden, and asked Malcolm to be wary of any strangers, especially ones in suits.

Malcolm appeared to be in his sixties, he had a full head of gray hair and a jolly face. Just a few minutes into her stay with Malcolm, it became obvious to Angela that he was "all business." He had a ruddy complexion and somewhat of an unhealthy appearance. Angela deduced that he continued to work at his age, instead of retiring, because he truly loved what he did. He proudly showed her a small booklet listing all the books and publications that had first been published by him. Many had gone on to larger, more elaborate publishing houses. Malcolm attributed this to his keen eye for recognizing fresh talent. He had never desired to increase the size of his shop or expand his business. He liked a small business where he could have complete control over every finished product.

Malcolm told Angela that Efraim had explained to him the main purpose of David's letter. That Jesus, through David's work, wanted the world to read the Bible. He wanted them to read the complete Bible, from cover to cover. He extended his sincere condolences to Angela for the loss of her husband. Then he stated, "Efraim is right. This letter needs to be published and distributed as soon as possible. I have been a Christian for over thirty years and David's letter has already caused me to change my ways! And I have yet to even read it."

"Change your ways?" Angela inquired. "I thought you just said that you became a Christian quite a few years back."

"I did," affirmed Malcolm, "but I have never read the entire Bible, cover to cover. I am very pleased to say that I have now begun this undertaking and I am already in the middle of the book of Exodus." Malcolm seemed so proud to be able to share his new project with the wife of the author who had inspired him.

Angela reflected on the hurried decision she had made when she took Efraim's original advice and flew to Tel Aviv—the decision had proved to be a good one. Both Efraim and Malcolm had become great allies in furthering David's purpose—to get his *Letter to the Nations* in the hands of its intended audience. People all over the world needed to embrace their Bibles. Angela's confidence was growing; she was beginning to envision a real future for herself.

She would be the champion for David's letter and its call for Bible education as the avenue to get to know the living God of this very Bible. It weighed heavy on her heart to actually imagine such a thing—a future without David, but her heart told her that it was the proper thing to do.

As Angela became securely tucked away in this quaint little section of London, the rest of the world was hungry for more news. Jesse Black, the fired NASA scientist, had vanished after dropping a bombshell of a story on the world. Now, just a few days later, the media was camped-out at the homes of Jesse Black and Angela Hart, just south of Houston.

Mrs. Hart, the wife of the missing NASA time traveler, appeared to have vanished as well. Following Jesse Black, she was the next most obvious person capable of providing some of the missing pieces to this most unusual of circumstances. The media had given up on wrangling any meaningful information from the authorities.

The authorities from NASA, the CIA, and FBI refused to comment on Mr. Black's outlandish statements. John Stuart had surfaced to release a statement indicating that the government was pursuing all available avenues to find both Jesse Black and Angela Hart. He felt confident that, once they were found, all this mess could be sorted out and things could return to normal. The world needed no more foolish talk about time travel and secretive cover-ups.

In order to have some kind of an update to report to the world on the NASA time travel mystery—all the major news networks had to be creative—so they focused on the possibility of an international cover-up. Since the reporters had absolutely no new information, they were forced to speculate. They needed to air something—this was the hottest story spanning the globe at the moment!

So speculate is exactly what the media did. And, oh, were they good at it! What did NASA and the US government have to hide? Why was Israel being so forthright with information? Was there some political tension between Israel and the US? If the young time traveler was missing and presumed dead, why was his body not discovered inside the NASA capsule? This, of course, caused all the authorities involved more heart-burn.

Back in London, once Angela felt settled in her new surroundings, she knew that she needed to secure the original journal in a safe and secret place. She also knew that Malcolm would need to be involved since he was specifically asked by Efraim to keep her hidden. Angela shared her desire to tuck away the journal with Malcolm. He agreed and the two came up with a simple plan to achieve the desired outcome. Early one morning, Malcolm drove Angela about ten blocks from the shop to a nearby bank. He parked on the street and waited in his car while Angela quickly entered the building.

Angela wasted no time in renting a safety deposit box at this London branch of the Deutsche Bank. The box was rented under the name of Angie King and, in it, Angela placed David's original journal. She also included in the box the documents of the carbon dating, the DNA testing, and other items provided by Efraim. With the items safely secured in the box, Angela slid the key into her purse and headed for the bank's exit. While walking through the lobby, Angela noticed Malcolm walking directly toward her at a very brisk pace.

"I thought that you planned to wait in the car," Angela whispered as Malcolm intercepted her in the middle of the lobby.

"That was the plan. But I saw two suits, complete with dark overcoats and sunglasses, enter the bank about five minutes after you so I became concerned. They both had dark skin and I immediately concluded that they could potentially be Israeli, you know—Mossad. Efraim has been very successful in teaching me one important aspect regarding the Mossad—they are great at what they do! So I hurried and moved the car to the bank's adjoining parking garage, to give us some cover, and quickly came inside. Thankfully, it turned out to be a false alarm. When I entered the lobby from the garage I caught a quick glimpse of the two as they exited through the bank's front doors. I guess I was just being too cautious."

"Thank goodness it was only a false alarm. If something had happened, Efraim would have our heads. Especially if they had successfully confiscated the documents and, most importantly, the original journal. Malcolm, at this stage of the game, I'm not sure there is such a thing as being too cautious!"

"Correction," said Malcolm, "on the—Efraim would have our heads thing…, Efraim would have my head, that is, if the Mossad didn't get it first. He gave me specific instructions to keep you hidden. Now, let's get out of here."

"You read my mind, Malcolm."

The pair abruptly turned and headed for the exit to the parking garage. Within minutes they were back at Malcolm's shop. As they walked in, closed, and locked the front door; Angela breathed a deep sigh of relief.

Other than Malcolm, Angela shared the location of this safety deposit box with no one. Furthermore, she did not share the number of the box with Malcolm and did not indicate to him the name under which she had rented the box. If something did happen to Angela, she felt comfortable that once Malcolm told Efraim about the bank and the safety deposit box, Efraim and his skilled Mossad would find the goods in a matter of hours.

Just as Efraim had predicted, Malcolm's little business was ready to print the first batch of books in four days. While his shop was busily preparing David's book, Malcolm had already secured deals with ten bookstores in London, each taking an initial twenty-five books.

The book went public on Amazon.com nine days after Angela's arrival in London. On day eleven, Angela was signing copies of the book at Blackwell's Bookshop in Downtown London. It was a surreal moment for Angela as she sat at a beautiful oak desk in the center of the bookstore with the small stack of David's books on the floor beside her. The customers all spoke proper English with what Angela considered to be delightful British accents.

When Angela had signed the last book, she quickly became disappointed. Even though she wasn't one who enjoyed "public appearances," this book signing turned out to be more fun than she could have imagined. She had beamed with confidence each time a customer had personally asked her to sign their new copy of David's book.

All two hundred copies on the Amazon website sold out in three days. The bookstores and the website had indicated that the book was moving quickly and wanted to order more. The *Letter to the Nations* was becoming a hit!

The limited readership was enjoying the content and loved the fact that the original journal was authenticated with David's handwriting and DNA, along with carbon-dating back to the time that Jesus walked on the face on the Earth. The Hercules capsule was some two-thousand years old, yet it had been built by NASA over the prior two years! Jesus Christ Himself had actually endorsed the letter. Furthermore, the original journal was in a safe place. Malcolm had included these key facts in the book's Preface.

The world, especially the Christian community, was a-buzz with all the unanswered questions. Was the book really authentic? Had man really accomplished time travel like Jesse Black had claimed? Why was NASA calling the whole thing a hoax—was there a cover-up? Why would carbon-dating classify something as "ancient" when it was relatively "brand new"? Where was this physicist-turned-author, David Hart? Based on Bible doctrine, was the *Letter to the Nations* accurate? All of these intriguing questions just added to the excitement and the wave of hopeful buyers for the book.

The media was in a frenzy. Now that Angela Hart had surfaced in London, all the networks were competing to be the first to make contact with her. Yet any attempt to communicate with Mrs. Hart became an exercise in futility. The small publishing house in London that had released her book had closed their doors for a two week hiatus. She was not registered with any hotel in or around London, and she was definitely not answering her cell phone.

The CIA and Mossad authorities were both embarrassed and furious. How did two of the most respected intelligence agencies in the world get outsmarted by a common American and an old Brit? Several key agents assigned to track down Angela in each organization had been summoned to their respective headquarters for interrogation. The director of the CIA, along with John Stuart, were called to a special meeting with the President of the United States. This was an ugly day. What a humiliating turn of events for the US government. "We look like a bunch of amateurs to the world today!" were the President's words. "You will find the incompetent bozos responsible for allowing this book to be published, and they will be reprimanded!"

Efraim Rabin had not waited to be summoned by the Prime Minister of Israel but had taken it upon himself to go directly to the Prime Minister as soon as the news broke. Efraim assured the Prime Minister that no one in his organization was more enraged than Efraim himself. Efraim promised to dig into the mishap immediately and report back within seven days. He would get to the bottom of this and proper action would be taken against those who failed their assignments.

CHAPTER 17

ANGELA'S TRANSFORMATION

Angela returned home to Houston the following week with a completely new outlook on life. She planned to spend a whole lot of time studying the Bible. She had a keen desire to get to know this Jesus that her husband had met and adored. This Jesus that her husband called God in the flesh. This Jesus that was the only way to get to heaven.

Unbeknownst to all the top brass at the Mossad, save one Efraim Rabin, Mrs. Hart was flown into Houston's Hobby Airport on a Mossad private jet. As far as airport personnel were concerned, the only civilian passenger on that flight was Ms. Angie King. Efraim had an agent escort Angela home via a limousine and literally protect her from the obnoxious media mob that had reassembled at her home when David's book went public.

The Houston-based Mossad agent had called ahead to ask the Clear Lake City police to ensure that the escort vehicle could access the driveway at Angela's home and enter the garage. When the limo turned onto Angela's street, the mob came into full view. The limo driver counted fourteen media vans in all. People were rushing from everywhere and jockeying for a position that would potentially allow them access to Angela at the rear windows of the limo.

Taking the advice of the agent sitting in the back with her, Angela laid across the seat and hid. The limo pulled into the garage but the vehicle was too long to allow the driver to close the garage door behind it. The driver approached the two policemen on the front lawn and asked for their help in removing the mob that had rushed into the garage and engulfed the vehicle. Mrs. Hart was extremely exhausted and did not wish to speak to any reporters at this time.

The policemen quickly restored order and Angela was able to ease into her home. As she exited the limo and slipped into the house, the mob of reporters, now amassed on the driveway at the garage entrance, must have snapped over one hundred pictures in a matter of seconds. Angela was completely flustered. The young American, turned instant celebrity, released a statement later that day indicating that she had reached an agreement with the FOX network and would recount her story on *Fox and Friends*.

"Until the story airs," Angela stated, "there will be no interviews." It took about two days but the relentless reporting crews all eventually withdrew from her home.

Stuart's executive assistant, Ms. Ruiz, had left Angela multiple messages on her home phone wanting to schedule a meeting with Angela, at her convenience, of course. Angela never planned to meet with or talk to Stuart again.

Angela had a God moment on the day she got home. While she was unpacking and returning all her belongings to their proper place, a note fell out of her counterfeit passport. She opened it and read:

> *Dear Angela,*
> *Your question about what happened during David's last twenty-four hours in the desert—it was a desert cobra that struck David. Its bite was fatal. We gave David a beautiful burial. Jesus Himself conducted the ceremony. Rest assured that David lives on!*
> *With Love,*
> *Nathan*

The note was typewritten and plain. As Angela reflected not only on the sobering message of the note but its origin—she solved the puzzle. Nathan had slipped the note in her passport at the airport in London.

She recalled that, while she was reading David's journal in Tel Aviv for the very first time, she had asked God what had happened to David during those last twenty-four hours in the desert prior to his planned return. This was God's answer. Now she no longer needed to wonder about the truth—God had given her the truth. Efraim's speculation regarding David's death was correct—he did perish there in the desert as his forty days with Jesus came to an end. Angela felt at peace with the knowledge. Not necessarily pleased but at peace. She truly was a widow.

On more than one occasion since Angela had learned where and when her husband had traveled, she had dreamt that David had married a beautiful Israeli woman back in the first century AD. Not only was the woman beautiful but she made David very happy and they were blessed with several healthy children. The couple lived long, happy lives and cherished each other.

Just the thought of such a thing actually occurring turned Angela's stomach. David was *her* husband, they were still married. Now, thanks to Nathan's note, Angela knew that nothing like that ever occurred.

Following her interview with *Fox and Friends*, Angela was an emotional wreck. She was a novice at this type of thing and the interviewers were seasoned professionals. The anchor dragged the interview in the direction he wanted and Angela reluctantly followed.

Angela had set out to focus on David's letter and the urgent message that the world needed to hear. The world—and FOX was keenly aware of this—wanted to know about time travel. The FOX anchor wanted to ensure that the focus of the interview was on time travel and nothing else.

Angela may have been a novice regarding television interviews but she was nobody's fool. She knew that she needed to tip-toe around the whole time travel issue so as not to stir-up the FBI or CIA. She stuck to the facts that Malcolm had included in the preface of the book.

During the course of the interview, the world heard that David had indeed disappeared on August 16th, that he was assigned to NASA's

Hercules project and, based on Jesse Black's prior statement, it was that very capsule that was recently found in the Israeli desert. They also learned that Angela was in possession of her husband's original journal, the journal had been carbon-dated to be two-thousand years old, the handwriting in the journal was a perfect match to David's, and David's DNA was confirmed to exist on several pages within the journal.

As to the content of the journal, every time Angela tried to steer the interview in this direction, the anchor would pull her along a different path. Angela was able to end the interview with an emphatic plea to the public to buy the book and read David's letter. She shared that the letter had changed her life and God wanted the world to read the letter and experience wonderful changes in their lives.

Angela had decided—no more interviews unless they were hosted by Christian-based networks. She felt that her best public appearance had occurred on TBN's *Praise the Lord* show, which was aired less than a week after the one on FOX. TBN was more than happy to allow Angela full liberty with her statements and pleas. The network backed the letter and urged their loyal viewers to heed Angela's advice and read her husband's work.

Since Angela had informed all media that her interviews would be limited and few, the major networks were forced to air clips from the Christian-based networks—because that was all that was available. They had to show something! The time travel story and the resulting divinely inspired book was the hottest story of the decade.

From the time of David's disappearance until her return home from London, Angela knew that she had been ignoring her health. Depression had taken its toll on her, both emotionally and physically. She had lost more than ten pounds and was still experiencing an unhealthy lack of appetite. The weary woman had grown sick of viewing the black circles under her eyes every time she looked in the mirror.

She contacted their family doctor and made an appointment for a complete physical. The receptionist at the doctor's office was fully aware of Angela's new celebrity-like status. She worked Angela into a time slot for the following day that had opened up from a cancellation.

Angela's doctor, Darla Moore, did a complete work-up on her patient. She also worked with Angela to schedule appointments with her gynecologist and a Christian psychologist. Dr. Moore had insisted on a psychologist and Angela had insisted on a Christian. Dr. Moore forwarded blood and urine samples to the lab for 24-hour turnaround. She checked all Angela's vitals and gave her a thorough exam, including an EKG.

As Angela sat alone in the examination room after two hours of poking and prodding, Dr. Moore re-entered the room. The doctor was young, 36 years old and Angela felt very comfortable with her. Dr. Moore was very sympathetic regarding Angela's loss and felt the psychologist visits would aid tremendously.

"Angela," Dr. Moore began with a smile, "I am so pleased that you chose to address your health issues sooner rather than later. What an ordeal you have experienced! I believe that, with time, we'll get you back to the healthy condition you were in before this whole stressful mishap occurred. I am very pleased to say that all of your vitals are normal, as well as your EKG. We'll get the results of the blood and urine analyses from the lab tomorrow."

"Great!" Angela replied. Even though, she didn't feel that great.

The doctor continued, "Angela, I have reviewed all the notes from your earlier discussion with my assistant regarding your health. And one thing sticks out like a sore thumb. My assistant immediately picked up on it and her hunch turned out to be correct. We confirmed it with a quick test on a small portion from one of your blood samples."

"Thank goodness," Angela proclaimed. Then she thought to herself, "I can get some meds, treat the problem, and get to feeling better." She was guessing that she probably had an iron deficiency in her blood or something simple along those lines.

Dr. Moore continued as though she had not even heard Angela's last statement, "Angela, I think under normal circumstances this would have been as obvious to you as it was to us. Unfortunately, you have been under such tremendous stress that the thought probably never entered your mind."

"Oh, no!" Angela thought, "I cannot tolerate any more bad news. If she is about to inform me of a diagnosis of some type of cancer or some strange Israeli blood disorder, I will absolutely scream! I am at the end of my rope! Please, Doc, I am desperate for good news!" Dr. Moore couldn't help but notice the look of dread on Angela's face.

In an effort to calm her unsettled patient, the doctor reached over and held Angela's hand. She looked into Angela's eyes and smiled reassuringly. "Angela, you shared with my assistant that you have been experiencing nausea, especially in the morning. You also informed her of the fact that you missed your last period. Angela—you are pregnant!"

Angela's mouth dropped wide open. "Pregnant!" she repeated. "Pregnant. I am pregnant." Angela sat and reflected on that new truth for a good minute or so. She looked at Dr. Moore and agreed, "Yes, it did all make sense. The symptoms fit the diagnosis, now confirmed with a blood test."

Angela stood up and began to dance with the Doctor. "Wow!" exclaimed Dr. Moore. "Looks like you're beginning to deal with that depression thing head-on."

"Dr. Moore," declared Angela, "I am carrying David's baby! This is truly a gift from God! I have got to go! I need to go see my parents and call David's parents as well. Jackie will be simply ecstatic. Good call, Doc, on scheduling the visit with the gynecologist. I'll definitely need to get in to see her as soon as possible."

As Angela left the doctor's office, she skipped and sang all the way to her car. While driving to her parents' house, she reflected on her prior fears of David finding and marrying a beautiful Israeli woman back in the first century. Now not only did she know that would never happen— she was actually carrying their baby!

Angela pondered on potential baby names as she drove. She was literally beaming with exuberance. After going through a mental inventory of a dozen or so names for a baby girl, Angela concluded that she didn't like any of them. Naming a girl would be somewhat of a challenge.

As her mind focused on the prospect of naming a son, she immediately grinned and announced to herself, "Yes, yes, I know the perfect name for a boy!"

Once Angela came down from her pregnancy high, she needed to address another important aspect of her life. Now that she had seen her doctor and spent the needed time to focus on her health, Jackie was next on the agenda. Angela felt so guilty. It seemed like forever since she had last talked to her good friend. "As a matter of fact," she thought, "I haven't talked to Jackie since the day I flew to Tel Aviv."

Angela called and invited Jackie to her house for a home-baked meal and some much needed sharing time. Angela apologized repeatedly during the course of the phone conversation for not having kept in better contact with Jackie but Jackie assured her that she understood. "Angela, girlfriend, you have waded through an obstacle course of challenging issues over the last several weeks—no apology required! I have learned quite a bit from your interviews on national television. I can't wait to hear all about it!"

Angela prepared one of the few specialties she had learned to cook during her short marriage, King Ranch Chicken. She and Jackie enjoyed the meal but enjoyed each other's company much more. After dinner, Angela downloaded to Jackie summaries of all the events of her life from the time she arrived in Israel up to her return back home.

After a few hours of recounting her action-packed adventures, Angela had worked her way to the point of sharing the details of her recent doctor visit. Angela relayed to Jackie, moment by moment, the complete happenings of her wonderful time at the office of Dr. Moore. Then she excitedly told her, "I am pregnant with David's child. I have been blessed with the most precious of gifts from my husband. God is good."

"I hope it's a boy!"

"You know, for some reason I seem to already know that it's a boy. Isn't that odd?"

"Not odd, honey. It's a mother's intuition."

"You know what, I think you are right. It must be a mother's intuition. I kind of like the ring to that new title of mine, mother."

"I think it fits you well."

"Okay, Jackie, I need to tell you about the contents of David's journal and letter. This will all make more sense to you after you read his *Letter to the Nations* but I must share this with you now. Jackie, David traveled through time. He really did! He met Jesus face-to-face. And not only did they meet, they became close friends. Jesus even declared David to be one of his beloved disciples!"

"That's…," Jackie stammered, "that's unbelievable."

"I know. That's what makes it so wonderful. This book is not just another book for the bookshelf. This book is a miracle. A miracle delivered to us by God with David's help. The proof related to David spending time with Jesus in the wilderness is staggering. I have the original journal itself, complete with Jesus' signature, along with carbon-dating documents, David's personal handgun and iPhone, and on, and on…."

"Why won't NASA acknowledge any of this?"

"Because—they are more interested in furthering their secretive time travel technology than admitting to the truth. They are convinced that countries all over the world will become obsessed with stealing their technology if those countries learn that time travel had indeed occurred with Hercules and that NASA had developed the scientific technology to make it happen."

"What about David? Where is David? Have you given up all hope of ever finding him alive?"

Angela stopped and took a deep breath. "I don't know how to share this with you without sounding completely insane. There were two angels caring for Jesus and David back during his visit. Anyway, one of the angels, Nathan, wrote me a short note. I'll explain to you how I got the note some other time. Anyway, in his note, Nathan told me that David was struck by a cobra at the end of his forty days in the desert. The bite was fatal."

"I cannot believe how nonchalantly you just shared that with me.

Your husband died, Angela. That is a big deal!"

Angela took another deep breath and said, "Jackie, you know me better than anyone else in my life except for maybe my parents. You saw David and me together all the time. You know how much I truly love him."

"I definitely do."

"I have shed thousands of tears in mourning the loss of David. And I am sure I will shed thousands more. But I am becoming more and more at peace with the loss of my wonderful husband as time goes by. I now know that David's journey through time was God's will. I also know that, if David had returned from his trip, Mr. John Stuart and the US military would have him locked up in some federal prison awaiting a court marshal trial. They have all the proof to ensure a guilty verdict and put him away for years. Our future would be wrecked and David would be labeled a traitor against his country."

"But why did he need to die?"

"I don't believe that he needed to die. He very well could have lived on following his forty days in the desert. He could have become another member of the world of 27 AD. Now this may sound somewhat selfish but, even if he had lived on, I would still not have ever seen him again. At least not on this side of heaven."

"Okay, I can see how your feelings have evolved over time regarding the loss of David. Man, what a crazy string of events. Enough of the death discussion already. And your whole holy-roller talk makes me a little uncomfortable as well."

"Oh, Jackie, don't be so silly. With time, you'll be talking just like this. Here is another mesmerizing fact that will cause your gray matter to ache. Think about the whole concept of time travel. Since God did transport David to 27 AD, David did truly experience genuine time travel. While there, Jesus told David that mankind will never accomplish this feat of building a true time travel machine. So, unless God intervenes again, David will be the only human to have ever accomplished this deed. Now—here is where it gets weird! David's death occurred two thousand years before his birth!"

"Crazy!"

"Yes, it is crazy. We are so fortunate that God will never allow man-made time travel to occur. Just think about the convoluted mess that men would throw the world into if they were ever successful with traveling through time on a regular basis.

"My comfort—no, wait; I'm not sure that comfort is the best word to use. My peace with David's death is caused by my newfound belief that only his body died from the fatal bite of the desert cobra. I believe—no, I know, that he continues to live. His spirit is alive in heaven and we will be reunited when my physical body dies and my spirit goes to heaven. I just need to dig into the Bible and gain the knowledge and faith that David gained from Jesus. I am convinced that I need to seek the salvation that David received. That is specifically what he called it, salvation."

Angela then said, "Now back to the miracle book. We'll spend a lot more time discussing the proof after you read it. But believe me, since you know and love David, once you have read his letter, you will feel the power of the truth in his written words—proof or no proof."

Angela had kept a few books from the original set that Malcolm's little company had generated. She gave Jackie a personal copy, complete with Angela's autograph. "Now, Jackie, you must promise me that you will read this. That you will read it within the next two weeks. Time is of the essence. You need David's message. Once you have finished, we need to talk again."

"Okay, I promise."

Angela then pulled out a *Life Application Study Bible*, the NIV version and handed it to Jackie. "When you finish reading David's *Letter to the Nations* you are gonna need this. David is going to give you a long homework assignment. This will come in handy once you get to that point. I have purchased dozens of these study Bibles. I plan to give them all away, then buy and give away hundreds more!"

The two friends continued talking and sharing into the wee hours of the following morning. Angela was so pleased to have set aside some time to share with one of her favorite people. As Jackie drove home, she reflected on the information overload that she had just experienced. She hoped that, with some time and patience, she could get to the point where she felt like she could get her head wrapped around all the events and concepts that Angela had just shared.

In a twisted kind of way, Jackie realized that she was actually jealous of Angela. Over the last few weeks, Angela had traveled the world in private jets and helicopters, visited beautiful and historic foreign cities, rubbed elbows with VIPs, appeared on national television, and published a book. Wow!

Then Jackie reflected on the recent suffering in Angela's life. She had lost her husband in a tragic and unforeseen way. She and her husband had become NASA outcasts. Angela's very life, for a period of time, was at risk—thanks to the CIA. And now, even though she was blessed with David's baby, Angela would be raising that child as a single mother.

"This series of events experienced by Angela and David was bigger than life! It seems more like a dream than real life." Jackie mentally replayed all the adventures that Angela had shared with her and then wondered, "How much of this adventure is my husband going to even believe?"

When Angela had bid farewell to Malcolm Headley back in London, he had strongly recommended Random House Publishing for Angela to approach in taking David's book worldwide. Angela moved quickly and struck a deal with Random House on November 1, 2015. They would have the book distributed across the world in a matter of weeks. They were somewhat discouraged with the length of the book—numbering right at seventy-five pages—but the content was so powerful that the publisher was convinced it would sell.

Eight weeks later, David's book, thanks to the diligent work of Random House, went worldwide and was soon at the top of many bestseller lists. Angela was funneling a large percentage of the book royalties to distribute copies of the Bible all over the world, particularly in the United States. She was very aware that David believed that so many Americans, like him, had become so comfortable in their ignorance of the Bible and of God's amazing gift of salvation. The gift was "there for the asking" and it was time for the public to get *rattled* and reminded of this.

By March of 2016, several Christian churches across the globe were conducting Sunday Sermon Series based on David's letter. The majority of the Christian community had embraced the letter as authentic and realized the urgency of sharing it with each other and the rest of the world. Many modern-day great Christian leaders had announced publically that they fully endorsed David's letter and vouched for the authenticity of its biblical doctrine.

Angela was a full seven months pregnant carrying David's son. She had learned that it was a boy during her fourth month. She was in great physical health and had made great strides with her emotional health as well. The baby's due date was pegged for May 10th. Angela had sold their home and had also chosen to live with her parents until after the baby was born.

Additionally, Angela had started attending Clear Creek Community Church in Clear Lake. The church was non-denominational and, as the senior pastor liked to boast, Bible-focused. Clear Creek Community was actually stepping though David's Sunday Series when Angela began attending.

Now, on her fourth Sunday at her new church following the service, Angela went to a prayer room with one of the pastors. She knelt down and prayed with the pastor as tears streamed down her cheeks.

While this was occurring, Jesus approached David in heaven. "David," Jesus said, "I want to share something with you My friend." Jesus grasped David's hand, and as He did, the two instantly appeared in that prayer room with Angela and the pastor. They were there in spirit only and could not be seen or heard.

Then David overheard that beautiful voice from his past as Angela said, "Dear Jesus, I want You to be my Savior. I know that You died on the cross as the perfect sacrifice to allow me to have the gift of heaven and, more importantly, the gift of You in my life now! I believe in You and want You to come into my heart today and be the Lord of my life."

David smiled as the Holy Spirit filled his wife's heart and soul. He felt even more complete. But he was also surprised and had many unanswered questions. As a saint in heaven, David had been completely unaware of the happenings on Earth.

"Oh, and one more thing," Jesus declared. "The title of the sermon today, the one that touched your wife in such a special way, was David's Choice; it's from your book, your *Letter to the Nations*. It is the chapter recounting the time when you asked for the gift of salvation for yourself."

Jesus smiled and said, "Oh, and one last thing. Your book has already sold over two million copies and is an international bestseller!"

David was nothing but confused as questions rolled around in his mind. "How did my letter get from the Judean Desert in 27 AD to the world in 2016? Why is this church preaching from my book? What the heck is my wife doing in church?"

"I'll share all the details with you when we get back home," Jesus answered. "Much has occurred on Earth with their recent discovery of your book. Let Me assure you, however, it is all good news."

"Please wait!" David pleaded. "Now that she has finished praying, I just want to take one long look at her beautiful face before we leave." Angela raised her head and wiped the tears from her face. She looked at the pastor and smiled.

David stared into her eyes and his heart was filled with joy at the sight of her face. He turned to Jesus and said, "Okay, I'm ready. Now that her salvation is secure, I can't wait for her to join me back home."

"Wait?" Jesus questioned. "We don't wait in heaven, wait is a 'time thing', it's an Earth thing. Our home is timeless."

David laughed. "I know," he said. "It will be but a moment and she will be with us in heaven."

"Look, David," Jesus said as He pointed toward Angela. As she turned toward the door to leave the room, she revealed for her loving husband to see the profile of a woman in her seventh month of pregnancy.

David was without words. Tears were streaming down his cheeks. He was elated. He was beyond elated.

"She will deliver the baby in early May, David. It's a boy!" Jesus whispered. You will simply love the name she gives him.

And, in a twinkling of an eye, the two vanished from the room as quickly as they had appeared.

CHAPTER 18
THE PROOF

It was mid-July, 2016 in Clear Lake City and, as usual for this time of year, the summer heat reigned. Angela Hart was having a great year. She found this rather hard to believe realizing how difficult the second half of 2015 had been. But even 2015 had ended on a very positive note.

David's book was continuing to sell like hot cakes and Angela was living a changed life. She had become a Christian just a few months ago. Christ had changed Angela is so many ways. She was still Angela but she was just different. The Holy Spirit of God was alive and well in Angela's soul. She could literally feel her life change as she and the Holy Spirit did life together.

And then there was the God-given gift of her son! The new addition to Angela's life. David Nathan Hart was born on May 2, 2016. David Jr. had weighed-in at six pounds, twelve ounces and measured a healthy twenty inches in length. He was born with a head full of dark hair and had a small heart-shaped birthmark on the left side of his chest. He was now two months old and very healthy. Every time Angela looked at her son, she was comforted in knowing that he was a product of her and David's love. A very tangible, very wonderful product of their love.

Angela swore that their son had David's nose, a bit oversized, just like his daddy. The baby's feet were also the spitting image of his father's, toes that resembled Vienna sausages. As he would grow, Angela would later add that, just like his father, David Jr. was also one handsome guy. He was genuinely fifty-percent David Hart, and she could hug and kiss him every time she longed for her late husband.

Angela had transformed in so many ways. The old Angela seemed to always be busy, actually, too busy. Angela had wanted to pour herself into her job, quite often putting her job ahead of other priorities in her life—like her health for one. It would not be uncommon for her to miss one or two visits to the gym in a week if things were really hopping at work. Often the hustle and bustle would lead to eating a lot of fast food rather than healthy meals.

Oh yes, and the old Angela was always worrying. Worrying about her look—wanting her make-up and hair to always be perfect. It was also very important to keep up with the latest fashions in clothing. It would not be uncommon for her to spend two or three hundred dollars a month to keep her clothing up to standard. A lot of energy was also spent in worrying about the next raise or promotion for both her and David.

Back at home, the old Angela had much to worry about there as well. The yard needed to be maintained and manicured so as not to be outdone by the neighbors. Also, to maintain appropriate status among friends, the vehicle one drove needed to be no less than four years old. A new car every four years was a perceived necessity.

She and David, prior to his disappearance of course, had also antic-ipated the need to purchase a speed boat in the not-too-distant future for weekend entertainment. Amongst their closest friends, two of the couples already owned speed boats. The Clear Lake area was the perfect location for boating. One of them, however, needed to get that next raise so as to work the boat into the budget.

Today, reflecting back on the old Angela, the new Angela could do nothing but laugh. She had hit rock-bottom, the lowest point of her brokenness, last September. From that point, Angela began to transform into the new Angela. There were some key drivers behind the transfor-mation—David's book, the Bible, her beautiful baby, and her new walk with Jesus.

Angela had immersed herself in the study of the Bible over the last several months. In order to read it in a relatively short period of time, she had come up with a game-plan. She read the Bible scriptures for two hours each morning and then spent two hours each afternoon reviewing the detailed study guide that covered the material she had read that morning. She used her brand new *Life Application Study Bible*, the same version that she had previously given to Jackie. Angela completed reading and studying the entire Bible, from cover to cover, in four months.

On the day she finished the book of Revelation, the last book of the Bible, she had planned to have a celebration dinner with Jackie. But, when she finished during mid-afternoon, she called Jackie and cancelled. Angela stayed home and cried, off and on, from that afternoon until she went to bed. She cried tears of joy. She cried tears of pain. Sometimes she just cried.

The Bible became real to Angela that day. She was a different person. Not only did the Bible now make perfect sense, her life now made perfect sense.

As Angela became more and more familiar with her new User's Manual, she reorganized her life. She came to grips with the fact that she was not in control; she knew that God was in control. It was difficult, at first, to let go. But in no time she realized that she had never really been in control anyway—it was an exercise in futility. God had always been in control. The key was to acknowledge that fact. Once she was honest with herself and stopped playing the control game, she began to notice *it*.

It was subtle at first, but then it grew. Peace grew within her. She became at peace with her look. The hair, make-up, and clothes didn't need to be perfect; they just needed to be nice. She became at peace with her status. Her status with friends and neighbors transformed into a focus on cultivating true relationships rather than competing over yards, new cars, and other expensive toys.

Angela felt so free. She had handed over her prior obsessive worrying to God. After all, He was in control. She wasn't competing with her neighbors and friends. She no longer demanded of herself to have a perfect look whenever she ventured into public. She was calm and she was sleeping better than she had slept since elementary school.

The void within Angela's soul, that she had experienced with the loss of David, was now filled with Jesus—there was no longer any emptiness. She now realized that this void should have always been filled by Jesus. A spouse is not responsible for their mate's happiness; they should complement their mate's happiness. A human life is designed to revolve around Jesus, which is the only way for a soul to feel and truly be complete. Jesus fills the void, then He transforms you over time.

Angela had reflected on all the incorrect ways she had witnessed people trying to fill their soul's void, including the old Angela. People hopelessly attempt to fill the void with their spouse, money, sex, their job, drugs, their children, alcohol, and on and on and on.... Jesus is the only proper fit. This is clearly pointed out in the User's Manual.

Angela had also decided to leave her marketing job and pursue something more in line with the person she was becoming. This new person had founded the David Hart Bible Foundation. It was the goal of this new foundation to teach and educate people on the Holy Bible and, more importantly, meeting and living in relationship with the God of that Bible!

It is no great secret that even the youngest book in the Bible is almost two-thousand years old. Most people can't just read the Bible and immediately comprehend the messages conveyed. Study and insight is a huge part of the understanding. The message from Jesus was clear: the Bible's great history, truths, and teaching must not be lost with new generations. So this foundation planned to initially open Christian Bible Learning Centers in cities across the southern United States.

It was Angela's desire to eventually go worldwide, but she knew it would take time. She had already opened two in the Houston Area and was spending a great deal of her time getting those centers up and running. She was funding this new adventure with royalties from David's book. The book had sold over six million copies, as of June 30th, and was still classified as a bestseller. Angela planned to seek future funding, in addition to the book sales, from churches across the globe. She wanted to get a handful of the centers up and running to establish the roots for future growth.

Icon Productions had contacted Random House wanting to schedule a meeting later that month to discuss a motion picture. This production company was responsible for the 2004 film, *The Passion of the Christ*, which had proven to be an international blockbuster. The Icon executives envisioned a film based on David's book as a perfect sequel to the original Passion.

Angela's parents pitched-in to help out in many ways. The one way that her father enjoyed the most was no surprise—taking care of his handsome grandson. Without their help, Angela would not have been able to engage in all the projects that she felt driven to pursue. Angela was busy but it was a good busy. And more importantly she was truly content.

Amongst all the good occurring in Angela's life, she was also facing a potential battle. A large contingent had surfaced over the last six months denouncing David's book. The contingent was quite diverse, consisting of atheists, Jews, Buddhists, Muslims, Hindus, and more. And, oddly enough, there were a significant number of Christians in the group as well. The non-Christians felt that the book was a fraud and not truly an account of David's time in the wilderness with Jesus Himself. And they, no less, wanted to discredit all the references to Jesus' deity.

The Christians in the group also called the book a fraud. They didn't like some of the statements in the book that were attributed to Jesus—especially the position that people didn't obtain salvation by living good lives, providing for their families, and being responsible citizens. They felt that good people earned the right to go to heaven. They found this whole idea of salvation being a gift from Jesus, and Jesus alone, a bit too easy of a path to gain the eternal reward of heaven.

Many of the Christians were also in disagreement with the positions stating that infant baptism and/or the blessing of a holy leader were not avenues for salvation. Why couldn't a devout man of the cloth have the power to guaranty another soul salvation? "And you call yourselves Christians?" Angela thought to herself. "Just read your Bibles people! It's all there."

The media had also begun to weigh-in on the matter and felt that the book was politically incorrect. Why did Jesus emphasize that the only way to heaven was through Him? Didn't all the good people who belonged to religions that didn't necessarily believe in Jesus' deity deserve to go to heaven as well? And furthermore, why did one even need a religion to go to heaven? There were lots of good, unreligious people. The media had concluded that the book seemed, well, too closed-minded.

Regardless of their make-up, all the people supporting the contingent wanted Angela to render the proof. They wanted to see with their own eyes the original journal, the DNA tests, and the carbon dating on all the items recovered from the capsule. On numerous occasions both the Israeli Mossad and the CIA had refused to comment on the existence of any of these alleged documents that were described in the preface of David's book. NASA had taken possession of their stolen capsule and had no further comments either.

As the media began to side with the contingent moving against Angela, Satan was crazy with excitement. His most successful North American demon, Warlock, was the original author of the phrase "politically incorrect." It wasn't the phrase that was so powerful—it was the meaning behind it that packed the real punch. Satan played on a person's guilt to coax them into accepting things that were completely unacceptable. Politically incorrect was one of the best weapons in Satan's arsenal.

As Warlock had proved over the last couple of decades in the United States: when societies have progressed to a point of extreme wealth, power, and comfort, the outspoken minority forcibly pushes for over-acceptance. It becomes politically incorrect to not accept everyone's religious beliefs, sexual behavior, cultural traditions, moral shortcomings, work ethics, and so on. And even more incredible, these societies actually have a more conservative, Christian-leaning majority, who seem to sit back and watch while the reckless minority not only promotes but succeeds in instituting rotten change.

Satan's evil masterminds were predicting the fall of the United States as the world's dominant superpower by the year 2025. By that time, the United States would be working its way into unimportant mediocrity, a label that would be given to the US by the newly established super-powers. This unimportant mediocrity would be caused by excessive deflation of the dollar (primarily due to unmanageable debt), a whit-tled-down and weak military, an education system failing at all levels, increasingly corrupt politicians, and an apathetic people.

So, now with the media waving the politically incorrect banner against Angela, Satan believed that he still had a chance to squash the book. He hoped that she would naively come forward with the proof so that his well-equipped, deceitful followers could perform their black magic on it. They were prepared to do whatever it took to discredit the truth and deviously manipulate the public to a position of doubt. He knew that, if he could grow the seed of doubt, he would be well on his way to stopping this Bible movement before it ever truly got started.

"Doubt," Satan repeated to himself, "Another one of my most valuable weapons."

Angela and Random House had yet to come forward with a public response to the contingent's request. As she reflected on the circumstance, Angela drew a parallel between the people of the world in 2016 AD and the people of the world in 27 AD.

In 27 AD Jesus Christ walked on the face of the Earth teaching and performing miracles. He spoke the truth and had courageously become God in the flesh, the Creator becoming the created. He healed the blind, the crippled, and the lepers. Jesus raised people from the dead on more than one occasion. He turned water into wine, calmed a violent storm, and walked on water.

Yet He was rejected by His own people and killed on a cross, having committed no crime. Jesus, the greatest man that ever lived, was rejected by masses of unbelievers. Many of these unbelievers were respected Israeli religious leaders who witnessed Jesus' miracles for themselves.

Now in parallel to the public of Jesus' day was the public of Angela's day, Angela mentally went over the facts that were known by the public regarding David and his book:

- Her husband disappeared from NASA premises on August 16, 2015 along with NASA's seventeen-ton capsule, Hercules.
- Forty days later the capsule, Hercules, is discovered on the other side of the world.
- A former NASA employee whose team had designed the capsule described on worldwide television how this capsule had been built to travel through time.
- The discovery location of the capsule was the Israeli desert where Jesus had spent forty days of his life in the year 27 AD.
- A group of expert archeologists inspected the capsule and its belongings and carbon-dated everything to be two-thousand years old.
- NASA disclosed absolutely no details related to the classified project involving David Hart and Hercules (a cover-up?).
- No government entity—not one surveillance satellite—had spotted any conspicuous transport of a huge, bullet-shaped capsule being hauled across the Israeli desert within the last forty days.
- Angela Hart, David's wife, publishes his book that is biblically accurate and recounts how David had spent forty days with Jesus in the desert in this very spot two-thousand years ago.

Then she thought about the theme of the book. The theme: "Wake up, world! God is unsettled and wants us to know that many of us are hopeless because we don't know Jesus. Jesus is the only way to heaven! You must study your Bibles and learn the truth of God and apply it to your life!"

Angela smiled and looked towards heaven. "It is such an innocent book, yet so many people are angry, so many people are bound and determined to discredit it," she said out loud. "You would think I was trying to start some type of military revolution! My revolution is simple, READ YOUR BIBLE AND RESPOND TO GOD. The Bible is a tangible, real gift from your Creator. The Creator of mankind has given mankind the User's Manual. Use it!"

Angela then realized that coming forward with the original journal and documented proof of David's DNA along with carbon-dating would just lead to another round of questions. She knew that the CIA and Mossad would both reject the authenticity of any documents bearing their agencies names, especially any lab tests. There would be more questions about the accuracy of DNA tests, the reliability of carbon-dating, the accuracy of the serial numbers on the iPhone and gun, and on, and on and on…. It would never end. Unbelievers and naysayers would always have reasons to question the truth.

Angela intended to immerse herself in her purpose. She intended to grow the David Hart Bible Foundation and Learning Centers. She was not going to get distracted trying to prove the truth. The truth was obvious.

Angela reflected on her conversation with her father on the day of David's memorial service. Her father's wise statement about God eventually showing her the reason for the loss of David had turned out to be absolutely correct. Now that reason had become her purpose.

Angela went to her bedroom and opened the top drawer of her jewelry box. She pulled out the key to the Deutsche Bank safety deposit box. She climbed into her car and drove to a public pier that stretched out several hundred yards into Clear Lake itself.

She strolled with confidence out to the end of the pier, humming a tune as she walked. She separated the key from the key ring that bore the number of the safety deposit box. "People," she said, "It all boils down to faith. The goodhearted will seek and come to know the truth. As to the unrelenting unbelievers—well, if Jesus Himself couldn't prove it to you, neither can I!" She flung the key into the lake in one direction then turned and flung the key ring, complete with the box number label, into the lake in the other direction. She breathed a deep sigh of relief.

As she was driving home, Angela retrieved her cell phone from her purse and called Random House. When she got through to her account rep Angela declared, "I have made up my mind. I am ready to go public with my response regarding release of the proof."

CHAPTER 19

IT WILL SHAKE THE NATIONS

Much to Angela's surprise, her account rep quickly accepted her position regarding release of the proof. Angela wanted it to stay put and her rep, Laura Brinson, seemed to be fine with it. "One less thing for me to worry about," thought Angela.

"The last thing we need," Laura declared, "is to get caught up in a war with a horde of devoted unbelievers. I want us to focus on getting the book into the hands of the curious, the lost, and Christians who have drifted from their faith—the intended audience. The diehard unbelievers are just a distraction."

Laura had been working as an account rep for over fifteen years. She was a devout Christian and loved the fact that her employer assigned her exclusively to books in their "Religion & Spirituality" department. After her first read of David's book, Laura became an instant fan. Now that the book was available worldwide, it was quickly rising to the top of the all-time bestsellers for her department there at Random House.

"Angela, on another note, I am so glad you called," Laura continued, "I have this idea. I shared it with my department head yesterday and he fully supports it. I need to share it with you and I just ask that you consider it with an open mind."

Angela was so relieved that Random House wasn't going to push her to release the original journal and other items in the safety deposit box that she was happy to move on to another subject. "Sure—hit me with your idea," Angela responded.

"Okay," Laura replied as she prepared to give her pitch. She took a deep breath, aligned her thoughts, and explained her proposal to her client. "Angela, I feel so blessed to be your account rep for David's book. It truly is a masterpiece. Our marketing group currently projects that we will ultimately sell eight to ten million copies. Additionally, our research department has told us that the majority of buyers are active Christians. This is where my idea comes in; I would like to get the book into the hands of a larger populace, especially non-Christians."

"A larger populace?" Angela questioned. "How could we possibly do that?"

"Well, that is exactly what I asked our marketing group." Laura went on, "Unfortunately, Angela, they informed me that our company's bestsellers usually involve stories with action, adventure, and suspense. And this is not just at Random House; all major publishers experience this same trend. And even though David's *Letter to the Nations* is chocked full of sound spiritual doctrine, the majority of our customers would never venture to read it. Now, don't get me wrong, David's book is one of our department's all-time bestsellers. Our department, however, moves much fewer books than some of the more popular departments.

"So, here's the idea…. We add-in all the action, adventure, and suspense! You and David have lived the story; it just needs to be fully assimilated. From the time that David was assigned to Project 13-03 until today, you both experienced enough action, adventure, and suspense to fill a complete series of novels. To date, we have only published David's *Letter to the Nations*. You still have his daily diary account from the original journal detailing the events of his forty days in the desert.

"Additionally, you can recount the events that occurred with you and David leading up to his disappearance, as well as those that have occurred since. We will strategically incorporate David's *Letter to the Nations* within and amongst the story. We will not, however, alter any of the original content. Our marketing group believes that, if we do this successfully, the novel could sell in excess of another twenty million copies. And the buyers would be of a completely different demographic as compared to the buyers of the Letter."

The phone line was silent. Laura began to doubt Angela's support.

Maybe ten seconds passed but to Laura it seemed like an hour. Then the silence was broken.

"I LOVE IT!" Angela exclaimed. "We take a relatively short book, the *Letter to the Nations*, and turn it into a novel. And in the process, not only do we add to the truth with additional information but, in the end… we reach a much larger audience! This allows us to get this urgent message from Jesus into possibly millions of additional hands and hopefully into their hearts."

After returning home, to her parent's house, it must have taken Angela a full hour to calm down from all the excitement that Laura had aroused within her. As she reflected on this new undertaking, she pondered on a name for the bigger book. The book that could potentially do more for the cause than David's original publication.

She kept thinking about the comment in David's diary where he had written that Jesus had said the letter needed to *rattle* the men of his generation. She closed her eyes and prayed for some divine guidance and then waited for God's lead.

Within a few minutes, God placed on her heart a book from the Old Testament. It was the book of Haggai. She knew the word that she was looking for in the verse, and she knew that it wasn't rattle, but it was similar. She retrieved her Bible and found the book of Haggai; Angela quickly skimmed through Haggai's only two chapters. Her hands were trembling with anticipation. There it was!

Haggai, chapter 2, verses 6 and 7: "This is what the LORD Almighty says: 'In a little while I will once more shake the Heavens and the Earth, the sea and the dry land. I will shake all nations, and the desired of all nations will come, and I will fill this house with glory,' says the LORD Almighty."

Angela was thrilled. The key to the name of the expanded book was right there in the Bible.

The book that was just recently discovered on the other side of the world in the Israeli desert, in the year 2015. The book, whose primary content was written two-thousand years ago but was intended to *shake* the nations of modern day. The book, written by a disciple, who came from the very ranks of the people that the book was intended for.

Shake was the word, shake—it was very similar to rattle. God would use this book as a tool in His plans to once more "shake the nations!"

Angela was so overcome with enthusiasm that she had to call someone. She grabbed her cell phone from her purse and called Efraim Rabin. She called his cell because, if her math was right, it was 3:00 a.m. in Tel Aviv and he wouldn't be in the office.

A sleepy Efraim reluctantly answered the phone as he read "Angela Hart" on his caller ID.

"Hello, is this Angela?" Efraim inquired as he answered his phone in English.

"Yes!" Angela exclaimed. "I apologize for calling at such an odd hour, but I have got to share the name of the book with someone who can truly appreciate it, someone who really knows the Bible."

"Angela, maybe I am not fully awake, but David already named the book—it's the *Letter to the Nations,*" was Efraim's sleepy but sarcastic reply. "It's on the shelves of bookstores all over the world."

"No, no, no," Angela interjected. She then went on to explain the idea for expanding the book and the added benefit. She also noted that no content of the original *Letter to the Nations* would be altered during the process. Efraim agreed with the concept and understood the reasoning.

"So," Efraim continued, "Lay it on me. What's the name of the expanded book?"

Angela took a deep breath and then announced, "Discovery in the Desert, It Will Shake the Nations!"

"I love it Angela!" Efraim replied. "Now, Mrs. Hart, I bid you goodbye. I plan to return to the peaceful state whence you plucked me."

"Oh, Efraim, one more thing," Angela exclaimed. "I want to go there. I want to see it"

"What, Angela?" asked Efraim.

"I want to visit the Judean Desert and put my feet on the desert sand. I know we did the flyover in the helicopter but I want to see the site where Hercules was discovered in-depth," Angela replied. "I want to visit one of the oases in that desert and I want to swim in one of its streams. I want to camp there and sleep on the ground in a tent. I want to take a bath in a brambling brook. I want to hear the night sounds of the desert animals and the whistling wind. Heck, I may even want to be baptized in one of those wonderful streams."

"Well, Angela if you want to go, I want to be the one to take you. Here is some really good news—my people have nailed down the locations of the special places from David's writings. When we camp, we can actually use the same campsite as David, Jesus, and the angels. When we swim, we can swim in the stream where Jesus baptized David. If you would like, I can baptize you in that very stream."

"Are you serious? You guys were able to nail down the locations?"

"I would say that we are ninety-nine percent sure. Even though I'm sure that he didn't realize it at the time, David included just enough clues and identifiers in his writing to guide us."

"Fantastic! I have got to come and see for myself. I cherish the thought of retracing their footsteps, so to speak. And, Efraim, you know me, I'll want to come and visit sooner rather than later!"

"It would be our honor, Angela, to host you. My wife and I are the outdoorsy types so we have lots of camping gear. I'm sure that I will need to hire a professional guide for safety reasons but that's not a big deal. We should also plan the excursion for one of the months with milder weather. Call me during normal hours and we'll plan a trip!"

"Okay, I'll give you a buzz during normal hours." The two friends shared a laugh as they ended the call.

Angela could not wait to get started on adding in all the adventure of her and David's great story to the book. And more importantly, she was confident that Jesus' message would reach the required populace, the critical mass, to truly shake the nations.

Amongst all the excitement of writing the more encompassing book, Angela stopped to reflect on a question that arose in her mind. "Why did Jesus go to such great lengths to point us to our Bibles? Over the centuries we have grown so distant from the Bible, so distant from its message, so distant from our God."

The answer, she thought…"Love! Jesus loves us and He knows that we have lost all respect for God's word—for the Bible. David's purpose, and now Angela's purpose as well, was to reignite the appreciation for the truth. Because the word is powerful. When people spend time in the word, the Trinity changes them. The truth in the Bible, along with the presence of the Spirit in one's soul, transforms a person.

"Jesus has not walked on the face of the Earth for two-thousand years. When He did walk on this Earth as a human, He stepped down from heaven to show the world our Creator. To teach us the most important lessons of all time. And now, because of God's immeasurable love for us, He has used David Hart to once again give the world of the twenty-first century a genuine glimpse of the Savior, the Messiah, God's Son, Jesus Christ!"

While building the more expanded version of the letter into a full-blown novel, Angela had uncovered a hole in the concept. On the day of David's tragic death, his thirty-ninth day in the desert, the occurrences of that day were not documented. Additionally, there was no written record for the fortieth day. Angela wanted to include the specifics of that crucial day when David died, as well as the happenings of the following day in the novel.

Laura Brinson had urged Angela to set aside this trivial distraction. They had plenty of material to more than make-up for anything that they lacked regarding that relatively brief period of time. But Angela, now an author herself, would not accept Laura's position. She was driven and wanted to include everything.

"Your insistence on including those occurrences is hampered by one little problem, Angela," Laura sarcastically informed her new author.

"Yeah, what's that?"

"They occurred two-thousand years ago and we don't have any eyewitnesses still hanging around!" Laura shouted. She was joking, of course, and the two broke out in laughter. Even though they shared the amusement of the moment, both knew that Laura was absolutely correct.

Angela was working ten and twelve hour days in order to complete her new project as soon as possible. She wanted the new book to surface while David's original *Letter to the Nations* was still at the top of the bestseller lists. This would allow Random House to transfer the sales momentum from the letter to the novel. This was a simple marketing strategy and made perfect sense to Angela. She knew that she could not delay publication while hoping that the details of the missing time-window, days thirty-nine and forty in the desert, would just fall out of the sky.

God's need to get the novel into the hands of the intended audience was so much more important than Angela's quirky hang-up with the missing details. Late one night, as Angela crawled into bed, she decided to turn to the Trinity concerning her little dilemma. She had been reflecting on David's letter and the time where Jesus was teaching about how the Trinity truly wanted Their children to turn to Them, to transform an undertaking from good to great. To not settle for something less but to reach for the stars and get their Creator involved.

Angela closed her eyes and prayed to Jesus. "King Jesus, I love You. I have this project on my heart and I so want Your teachings shared with David to reach to the ends of the Earth. I feel confident that I have poured all my natural energy and ability into my writing and I now need You to add Your supernatural energy to the work. If it be Your will, King Jesus, I ask that You share with me the missing pieces. The things that are not included in David's journal that You want in the novel. I love You and I pray to You in Your holy and precious name, Amen."

Angela on this night, like so many other nights over the last several weeks, was dead tired. Within minutes she was fast asleep and, within the hour, she was in a very deep sleep. She drifted off into a wonderful dream.

In this dream, Angela's bed had transformed into a huge, fluffy cloud. She sat up in her cloud-bed and almost immediately heard a familiar voice calling her from a distance, "Angela, Angela, where are you, Angela?"

"Over here!" she shouted. "I am over here, can you see me?"

She looked in the direction of the calling voice, only now it sounded very close. "Angela? Are you there, Angela?"

"Yes, I am right here." She smiled with great enthusiasm as Angela watched Nathan soar over to her bed-cloud. She patted a spot right next to her on the bed and Nathan quickly took a seat. The two exchanged hugs as if they were old friends. Nathan was all smiles—so was Angela.

"I understand that you have a little request regarding supernatural abilities," Nathan announced with a hint of sarcasm as he stood up next to the bed.

"Yes! I do, I do indeed!"

Angela surveyed Nathan from head to toe. He looked exactly the same as the first time they had met, only he was dressed very differently. He was wearing a gleaming white tunic, tied at the waist with a golden belt. His facial features were the same, but his skin seemed to radiate as though he were actually glowing.

"I owe you an apology," Nathan confessed. "I was so short with you at Heathrow Airport. I just knew that any discussion regarding angels and such would have added to your nervousness and stress. At the time, things were so tense and Satan was trying to destroy our plans to get the letter published."

"Oh, so that's why you were there."

"Yes. It is hard for humans to appreciate the amount and severity of spiritual warfare. Satan was actually present at Heathrow that day and his evil demon Cyclops was there as well. It was their intent to have you denied entry into London and then flown back to Tel Aviv. The Devil has a powerful Mossad agent as one of his key constituents. That agent had already taken post at the Ben Gurion International Airport back in Tel Aviv and was anxiously awaiting your return so that he could confiscate David's journal. They failed, of course, because Jesus had instructed me to pluck you from the line in Immigration and usher you through before Satan and company could regroup.

"That was a significant day but now we have a new agenda." Nathan changed subjects, "I understand that you have requested knowledge of important events that are currently not documented in David's work."

"Nathan, I want the novel to be as complete as possible. But I only want to add things that Jesus deems significant."

"I know—Jesus filled me in on the details of your request before He sent me. Let's go…"

CHAPTER 20
NOW IT'S YOUR TURN

Nathan reached over and took Angela by the hand. The two soared through the air together and dropped down below the clouds. Angela was beaming as she savored the thrill of flight. It appeared to be mid-day and the sun was shining ever so brilliantly. As Angela began discerning objects on the ground thousands of feet below them, she also recognized the rugged beauty of the terrain. She had witnessed it once before from a Mossad helicopter. It was the Judean Desert! As they continued to descend, Nathan told Angela to prepare for landing.

Their bare feet came in contact with the sand, and even though it was during the heat of the day, for some unusual reason, the sand felt cool to the touch. The sun was blazing down on them so the sand should have been extremely hot. She was staring at her feet in amazement when Nathan noticed her distraction and explained, "We are here in spirit only. That's why we don't feel the heat. Furthermore, anyone that we see—they will not see us. Follow me. If you want to sense something like the heat of the sand, just focus on it. Things can be as real to you as you want them to be."

Angela followed as Nathan walked a few hundred feet through the sparkling carpet of smooth, peanut-butter brown sand. When he stopped, the pair looked up and saw a large, light brown tarp secured over a relatively large object. Angela immediately noticed the blue NASA insignia identifying the tarp. "Hercules must be hidden beneath that tarp," Angela announced to Nathan.

"You are indeed correct, Mrs. Hart. And we are in the year 27 AD."

"Oh, Thank you, Nathan! Thank you for this experience."

"I need to warn you, Angela. You are going to see David in a moment. But unfortunately he will not be able to see you. You will probably find it a little overwhelming but maybe seeing him will also please you."

"'Maybe seeing him will please me?' Nathan, you have no idea! It will absolutely stir the depths of my soul! I want to see him! I would love to see him!"

As Angela finished speaking, she heard someone approaching Hercules. She looked up and saw David and Nathan walking toward the ship. Angela's body began to tremble with excitement. She couldn't move as David and Nathan pulled the tarp from Hercules and climbed into the cockpit. As she stared at her husband, she felt emotions she hadn't felt in almost a year. She instantly connected with her feelings of love, attraction, and passion for David. Tears were streaming down Angela's face as she whispered a prayer of thanks to Jesus for this precious visit.

Angela then let out a snicker as she turned her attention to the get-up that David was wearing. He was outfitted with a brown dress-looking thing and sporting a dusty pair of leather sandals. He completed his look with disheveled hair and scruffy beard stubble. "I kind of like the beard stubble look," the young wife thought to herself.

Now that the tarp had been removed, Angela turned her attention to the capsule. She marveled at the sight of Hercules in all its brand new glory. It looked so out-of-place laying on the desert floor in the midst of the wilderness. An engineering marvel from the twenty-first century, stranded in the middle of nowhere in the year 27 AD. She noticed how Hercules was laying in some type of crevice—only about a third of the vessel was above ground level. Angela recalled how Hercules had appeared on the helicopter flyover with Efraim, "Wow!" she thought as she confirmed, "It had been laying here for two thousand years." Seeing it brand new made it easy for her to contrast the new look of the vessel to the ancient one.

The entire scene was surreal—and surreal for several reasons. One, it was quite difficult to comprehend two Nathans. One Nathan was sitting there inside the cockpit with David and the second Nathan was standing beside the ship with Angela. One Nathan was very tangible and seen by David, while the other was very invisible and seen only by Angela. Furthermore, adding to her euphoria, Angela relished the sight of David. She had forgotten just how handsome he really was. She hadn't seen him in months…man what a catch he was! Angela was truly elated.

Angela turned to Nathan and declared with a very excited voice, "I want to touch him. No, correction, I need to touch him."

Nathan smiled and nodded, "Go ahead. He will not feel your touch but you will be able to feel him. You can touch and feel his skin. Remember, the more you concentrate on the sense of touch, the more real it will become. Since he has closed the hatch, you will need to enter the capsule to be able to accomplish that."

"How? How can I actually open the hatch without disturbing them?"

"Don't worry about the hatch, silly, just ease right through the shell—remember, we are both in spirit form."

Angela was amazed. She slowly approached the exterior of the capsule and raised her right hand. She touched and felt the outside of the shell. She looked puzzled and turned to Nathan as he said, "Okay, Angela, here is the really cool part. You can feel the things you want to feel and pass through those that you don't. Just think and your spirit form responds accordingly. Touch what you want, pass through what you want. Once you get accustomed to this adjusted thought process, it is really quite easy."

Angela began to adore this experience more and more by the minute! She closed her eyes, focused on Nathan's instructions, and adapted to this new way of thinking. She gradually opened her eyes to see that her right hand was no longer in sight—it was literally inside the shell of Hercules while the rest of Angela was on the outside! At first glance, it looked as though she had no hand and was pressing the stump of a partial right arm against the shell of Hercules.

"Angela, slip your head inside first," instructed Nathan. "Then you can inspect the interior layout and enter the ship at a point that makes sense."

She cautiously leaned her head into and through the skin of the ship. Her heart was beating crazily within her chest. This new spirit-body was a rush!. She carefully opened her eyes with great anticipation and was immediately startled for a moment as she found herself face to face with a sunglasses-clad Nathan, engaged in full conversation with David. Once she got her bearings inside the capsule, Angela waved her hand in front of Nathan's face to ensure that she was invisible to him. She then surveyed the interior of the pilot's area and chose a spot where she could sit very close to her husband.

She then eased her head back to the outside. She was wide-eyed with excitement as she looked at Nathan and said, "I'm going to enter on the other side, Nathan, close to David." The spirit-Nathan accompanied her as they walked around to David's side of the ship.

Angela then glided very smoothly back inside the ship and took a makeshift seat next to her husband. She got comfortable, and listened to the pair's conversation. David was periodically explaining to Nathan the various steps he was taking in his systems checks. He was getting Hercules ready for the return flight.

"This is the day!" Angela whispered to herself as she placed this circumstance in perspective. "This is the day that my unsuspecting husband will meet his human demise. It's his last day on Earth." She closed her eyes, collected her overwhelming emotions, and re-focused on the moment at hand.

She continued to watch her husband's every movement with adoring eyes. There were several thoughts that she wanted to share openly with David but the situation didn't allow for any type of communication. So she chose to speak them, even though she knew he would not hear them. "Oh, how I miss you, David Hart! And, oh, how I love you, David Hart! David Nathan Hart, our son, looks just like you. The entire family misses you dearly. I am so very proud of your work here in the desert. The letter, well…, it is simply amazing. Your message led me to the Bible, and also to Jesus. Jesus saved my soul. I cannot wait to see you in heaven but, until then, your purpose has become my purpose. When I join you in heaven, I cannot wait to share with you all the details about the David

Hart Bible Foundation!"

Realizing that her time in the cockpit with David would quickly expire, Angela knew that she needed to touch him before he and Nathan finished their task and exited the capsule. She slowly raised a hand to David's cheek. She touched him and then quickly retreated, in fear that he had felt it. It became apparent that he didn't. So she touched him again. This was magical! She touched his hair, she touched his lips, she touched his chest. She was ecstatic. She knew she was in a dream state—so, she thought, "Angela, there is no need to pinch yourself. Take delight in this moment."

She tilted her head toward the inside shell of the cockpit, away from David, and eased the upper portion of her body back outside of the ship. It was an odd scene. Angela's head and shoulders were now protruding outside of Hercules while the rest of her remained on the inside. She turned to spirit-Nathan and asked, "Would it be possible for me to kiss him? I really, really need a kiss!"

Nathan shrugged his shoulders and answered, "Sure, why not? Just please don't get carried away and do anything, you know, weird."

Angela nodded in agreement, brought her head back into the cockpit, and turned to David. He was focused on his systems checks and not talking at the moment. She touched his lips with her hand, held his chin in that hand, leaned over, and gave her husband a kiss. Not a huge kiss but not a peck either. She pulled away, closed her eyes and thought to herself, "remember this—you will need to savor this kiss for several years."

After truly enjoying the rush from the kiss for quite a while, Angela then seemed to be distracted by her subconscious, "What...?" she murmured to herself. "What...is that familiar essence?" Then she knew, she recognized it...it was David's smell. Oh, how she had missed that smell! She slowly leaned her face up against his chest, brown dress and all, and took in a deep, slow breath. As Nathan had instructed her, Angela concentrated on her sense of smell. She held that breath for several seconds then slowly exhaled, her eyes closed the entire time. "Don't ever forget his smell, Angela," she instructed herself. She was in a state of euphoria. "I am literally high on David!" was her jubilant conclusion.

Much to her dismay, David had finished his preparation procedure and he and Nathan were climbing out of Hercules. Angela reluctantly joined her Nathan back on the outside of the ship as she realized that the intimacy with David was over. Nathan looked at Angela and, in a very businesslike manner, said, "Now comes the ugly part. The cobra is just over there." Nathan pointed in the direction of a large cactus just a few hundred feet from the ship. "If you would like, I could tell you what happens next, that is, if you don't wish to see it for yourself."

"I definitely do not want to witness the snake bite and his passing. I want my last memory of David to be that very kiss that we just shared. I want memories of his touch and his smell but most certainly not his death!"

"Good call! I was hoping you would say that." responded Nathan. He took Angela's hand and looked toward the sky. He then turned to Angela and asked "One last look?"

Angela nodded her head, turned, and looked at her husband as he and his Nathan placed the tarp over the capsule. She focused all of her energy on her sense of sight, hoping to burn a permanent picture of the husband she adored into her memory.

"Ready?" Nathan whispered.

"I'll never be ready—but I know I must." With that the duo ascended towards the heavens and began flying back to Angela's cloud-bed.

"Nathan," Angela inquired, "would it be possible for us to fly over the campsite and also Jesus' prayer place before we return? I plan to visit this area within a few months and I would truly cherish the opportunity to camp where you four had camped and to get baptized where David had been baptized."

Nathan closed his eyes for a moment and whispered to himself. He waited a moment longer and then nodded, "Jesus said it would be fine." Nathan steered the pair in another direction and within minutes they were over a large patch of trees.

Angela squinted her eyes and was able to make out images of donkeys, a small campfire, and tents within the trees. Then she thought, "I need to identify a landmark, something that I can recognize two-thousand years into the future, when I visit this place with Efraim. That way, we can be positive about the location of the authentic campsite." As she tried to choose an appropriate landmark, she became frustrated.

Nathan glanced at Angela with a warm smile and said, "Just remember this. The campsite is the first large gathering of trees due north of David's capsule."

"Thank you, Nathan."

Nathan then guided the two over a tiny oasis. He turned to Angela and spoke, "This is Jesus' prayer place. He baptized David right there in that stream. The oasis is two kilometers due east of the campsite."

Angela closed her eyes and made mental notes. "Campsite—due north of capsule. Oasis—two kilometers due east of campsite."

Nathan then directed their flight back in the direction of Angela's cloud. As they floated through the sky, Nathan informed Angela regarding the details of David's funeral. He shared with her that they had placed David's body across the back of a donkey, transported his body to a small cave, and laid him to rest after wrapping him in a clean white sheet. He also recalled the heart-felt prayer of Jesus at the burial site.

Nathan also enlightened Angela concerning David's bloodline. "David and Jesus are distant relatives," he shared. "They are both descendants from the tribe of Judah, direct descendants of King David himself!" Nathan then expressed to her the love that he had felt for the human David, his desert buddy. He ended his recap describing his visit to David's burial site on the day following the funeral. This, of course, was the fortieth day, the day that Jesus faced Satan.

Nathan explained that the trio had left the desert on the forty-first day—the angels headed back to heaven and Jesus returned to Galilee. Jesus had joined Mary, His mother, at the home of some family friends on the outskirts of Galilee. Following His test in the desert, the time had come for Jesus' three-year earthly ministry to begin.

Just as Nathan wound up his information relay, he and Angela arrived at her cloud and Nathan quietly said, "Well, Angela, I think this is where we say goodbye. I don't expect to see you face-to-face again until you join us in heaven. I am so happy that Jesus chose me to share these unknown things with you."

"Nathan, I know that this is a dream. But it seems so real, so tangible. Did we truly visit David, did I truly see him, or were all the images merely re-creations in my mind? Did I truly kiss David or did I imagine that I kissed my husband? I must know!"

"Angela," Nathan looked into her beautiful blue eyes and saw into the depths of her caring soul, "It was all real. We went there, it was 27 AD. You truly touched the lips of your husband. You did sit by him, you did stroke his hair, you did touch his cheek, you did kiss him, and you did savor his smell."

"Thank you, Nathan! Thank you so much! I am not exactly sure why, but that truth, that knowledge that we were really there, means the world to me!"

Nathan smiled, then gave her a serious look. "Angela, I wish I could take credit for this amazing trip but Jesus made it all happen. He is the One to truly thank. You know what the Bible says, I can do all things through Christ who strengthens me. Jesus truly is the authority over heaven and Earth!"

The pair exchanged a healthy hug and Angela climbed into her fluffy bed. Within minutes she was, once again, fast asleep.

That morning, Angela awoke refreshed and excited. She dashed to her computer and began typing ever so quickly but her mind would routinely outpace her fingers. She had to make herself slow down; she needed to get all the details of her dream properly documented. She didn't want to leave out even the smallest piece of information. To add to her morning commotion, her subconscious kept replaying the kiss in her mind, over and over and over again. It was so WONDERFUL!

If she had whispered it to herself once, she had whispered it to herself a thousand times, "Now that you have a fresh memory of David in your mind—do not forget how handsome he was! And remember, he was gorgeous on the inside as well!"

Later that day, after calming down somewhat…Angela then reflected on the deeper significance of her witnessing David's presence in the desert. The eternal significance, something that went beyond human attraction or human love. Everything became real to her on that visit. Any doubt that had previously existed was utterly gone. Angela became truly convicted that day to carry the torch of the truth, God's truth, for the rest of her life. It truly was her purpose.

Over the next several weeks, Angela, Laura Brinson, and Random House completed and published Discovery in the Desert, It Will Shake the Nations. They did their job. Come to think of it, several individuals did their job...Let's see, there was Jesus, the Holy Spirit, God the Father, Mary, Nathan, Marcus, David Hart, Angela Hart, Efraim Rabin, Malcolm Headley, Laura Brinson, TBN, and Random House.

Now you have been given God's Urgent Call. NOW IT IS YOUR TURN TO DO YOUR JOB. It starts with the Bible—the readily available introduction to the God who loves you so much!.

EPILOGUE

What about you? Now that you, yes you, have read the book. What about you?

Do you have a relationship with Jesus? Do you know if you are truly heaven-bound? Hopefully you are not using the cop-out of being in a comfortable place with God like David Hart was before his journey. Don't feel bad if you are—thousands of people are in that very spot. I spent decades of my life in that spot. The good news is that you can begin your journey today to get out of that place and move into the light.

If you do know that you need a change in your life, I recommend that you make the reading and study of the Bible your number one priority. Do any of the concepts in this book related to biblical doctrine surprise you? I challenge you to study your Bible and learn these truths for yourself. You need to start today. You should be able to read from cover to cover in a year, reading thirty minutes each day (the length of one meaningless TV sitcom). This, of course, would be ideal if done in conjunction with a study guide or with other believers so that you can better understand. Angela gave Jackie the *Life Application Study Bible*—I think that was a good choice. The two pastors that have impacted my Christian life the most, both recommend to use the NIV translation of the Bible.

I promise you that, once you have accomplished this undertaking, your life will be changed forever. Doesn't your Creator deserve your effort to get to know Him? Or more importantly, don't you relish the opportunity to spend eternity in heaven with your Creator?

Don't make the mistake that I, and so many other people, have made. Don't let decades of your life slip away before you meet the true God by reading the Bible completely. The knowledge and insight that you gain from God's word immediately affects you. As your increasing knowledge draws you closer to the Spirit, the more He will transform you. The truths will steer you, your decisions will benefit you. You don't want to wake-up at fifty and wish you had read it when you were in your twenties.

However, if you do consider yourself older, don't be discouraged. No. Get motivated instead. Get started today!

If you are like me, you probably have several questions related to key biblical issues presented in this book. If you want some quick, biblically sound, answers I recommend you turn to this web site:

www.gotquestions.org.

The site outlines its purpose and key contributors and is very user-friendly.

ACKNOWLEDGMENTS

It is with great appreciation and humility that I acknowledge the two pastors that have changed my life forever. I look forward to personally thanking each one in heaven for all their devotion to teaching the truth of the Bible. Prior to their combined teaching over a period of eight years, I was so biblically uneducated. I am still learning each and every day, but am so thankful for all the progress. I will be forever thankful for the teaching of Pastor Bruce Wesley and Pastor Bil Cornelius.

While in the process of writing this book, I believe that God led my sister, Laura, to place a copy of the manuscript in the hands of Marlene Kelly. Marlene immediately became a strong supporter of the project and, more importantly, a guide on scripture and biblical truths. From the time of her initial involvement up to the time of publishing, Marlene devoted herself to advising me on these truths. Thank you, Marlene, for your invaluable input and support.

Just as I thought my writing process was drawing to a close, Marlene Kelly's husband, Pat Kelly, entered the picture. Pat immediately became very interested in this book and my vision. Within a very short period of time, two weeks, Pat contributed significantly to the finished product. It was obvious that Pat was led by the Spirit. Thank you, Pat, for your unselfish and caring attitude in contributing to this book. Your input resulted in a more refined finished product.

AFTERWARD

I have been a Christian since my early teens and have spent hundreds of Sunday mornings in church services. The Bible is indeed the key book that has been used by all the Christian church leaders who have shared the Sunday sermons that have shaped my life. Now, at the young age of fifty, I have come to realize how the Bible has become so unappreciated by the World, and in particular the United States. I am 'guilty as charged' and now realize how I grew up without properly appreciating this wonderful gift from God.

I decided to read the Bible from cover to cover about two years ago. I knew that it would be a struggle, especially with books like Numbers and Song of Solomon. They seemed so odd. As I began to read, however, the books became more and more interesting. Needless to say, the commentary that I chose to use as my study guide made a huge difference. If it wasn't for my study guide, I probably would have quit reading shortly after I began. The commentary allowed me to comprehend in-depth, which of course, is very necessary when it comes to the Bible.

And now, having read the Bible from cover to cover, I know that I am closer to my Savior than ever. I now know Jesus, I know God the Father, and I know The Holy Spirit. The Bible gave this to me; it has changed me forever. This is the most tangible gift from our Creator that we can utilize today. Don't you expect the automaker that built your car to provide you with its Owner's Manual, allowing you to get the most out of your investment? Well, you were built by God, and He has provided you with your User's Manual, the Bible.

Having read the entire Bible, I now feel so much more complete in my faith. Up until this point in my life, I have always doubted so much about the Bible, especially miraculous events from the Old Testament. I must admit, I had my doubts about the great flood during Noah's time. I not only doubted a flood that covered the entire Earth, but a man and his family building an Ark to house every creature on Earth...come on. Have you ever doubted the fall of Jericho? The Israelites simply marching around the city seven times and the city walls collapsing, allowing the Israelites to wipe-out the people and burn the town to the ground—now that's a miracle!

The book of Jonah recounts how Jonah himself was thrown into the sea during a raging storm. Jonah's life was spared when he was swallowed by a great fish. He survived within the fish for three days and three nights, and then God commanded the fish to vomit Jonah onto dry land. King David, while he was still a young shepherd boy, shows up as Israel's great army is in a stand-off with the Philistines and Goliath. He challenges and kills Goliath with a rock and a sling.... I must admit, the Bible is definitely not a boring read.

From the first chapter of Genesis to the last chapter of Revelation, one must read the Bible, the entire work. When I completed this task, a true miracle happened in my life! I became a total believer. I now know that it is all true, every word. How does one say it, "It is God's honest truth." Have you ever wondered why the pastor always seems to be the most motivated person in the house during a Sunday sermon? It's because he has completed the task, he has read the complete Bible, he is a total believer.

Looking back on my prior doubts about many of the miraculous events in the Bible, especially in the Old Testament, I have coined a new phrase—'selective belief.' I truly believed in my heart for decades some select miracles in the Bible. I believed in creation, the virgin pregnancy of Mary, the resurrection of Jesus, among a few more. But I struggled with so many others as I mentioned in the previous paragraphs. Logically, how does this make any sense? God is God, why would some of the Bible's miracles be true while others were fairy tales?

Shortly after I completed my first round of reading the Bible, God gave me this book, *Discovery in the Desert*. When I decided to write it, the story flowed from my mind to the keyboard so smoothly and quickly that I knew the Spirit was leading me. I know that this book is pleasing to God and is a significant part of my purpose here on the human side of heaven.

It is my belief that I have honored all fundamental Bible doctrine in my writing. (I did exercise some literary liberty with the angels, I must admit.) Other than Jesus, all the characters in my story are fictional. The story itself is fiction as well. But the core reason for the book, in my opinion, is fact. We have shamefully drifted so far from our Creator that we need to be *rattled* by Him, today, so that we refocus on the Cross. The tool that can jar us out of complacency and silence is...the Bible.

I hope the adventures of David and Angela Hart in this book motivate you to read the Bible and become a total believer. David has been chosen by God to change you forever. I hope he is successful!

ABOUT THE AUTHOR

When he graduated with honors from Texas A&M University with a BS in Petroleum Engineering in 1983, Tom Thiele had no idea about the unique calling he would experience later in life. He and those closest to him had pictured him moving forward as an engineer with a knack for mathematics and physical science, which did happen. In 2010, however, Tom discovered his calling to write Christian Fiction. After reading the Bible from cover to cover for the first time in his life, God moved Tom to write and publish the intriguing story of David Hart and the *Discovery in the Desert*. This became the first book of the Discovery Series, published in 2011.

Today, Tom has enjoyed over thirty years of success in the oil and gas business and has been able to see many parts of the world. Tom is a native of Houston, Texas, where he lives with his wife, Juanita. They have six children who all live in the Houston area. Tom feels blessed to have had the opportunity to live in Indonesia for four years and to visit Thailand, Australia, New Zealand, Italy, Austria, Germany, Switzerland, Brazil, Argentina, Mexico, the Bahamas, and Canada.

While Tom is thankful for his success in the oil and gas industry, he will be the first to share that his true passion is writing Christian Fiction. Tom is driven to share the good news of Jesus Christ and tell of the amazing gift that He offers to those who choose to accept it. The moving testimonials and positive reviews associated with the first book have inspired him to continue writing. The second book in the Discovery Series, *Discovery of Eternity*, was published in 2013 to even greater acclaim.

Tom continues to move forward with this newfound passion with the launch of his author website, complete with blog. He believes that God will continue to bless him with Christian Fiction stories to share with the world, resulting in more books to come.

Tom would love to hear from you. He devotes time each day to interface with his readers. Visit his website and read the blog, add yourself to his mailing list, or order another one of his books.

Visit his website:
authortomthiele.com
Feel free to drop him an e-mail:
authortomthiele@gmail.com